I0738595

Love,
Dad

Scott W. Rasco

GRAPH
Publishing, L.L.C.

Love, Dad

by Scott W. Rasco

For more information contact:
GRAPH Publishing, LLC.
www.graphpublishing.com

Printed and Bound by:
Ingram Publisher Services

2018 Cover Art Designed by Scott Rasco

1

The steam radiated off the hood of the 1996 Mustang sitting with the passenger side tires up on the curb. Mark had slowly been driving around on the icy streets for over an hour trying to figure out where to go. He had no way to call anyone, so he was glad when he saw the pay phone downtown. His car slid to a stop right when it popped up on the curb.

Music blared loudly from inside his car, as Mark stood in the phone booth trying to contact one of his friends. It was probably the last payphone left in all of Oklahoma, since it seemed that everyone, except Mark, now carried cell phones. The payphone was in use only because it was located outside an eighty-year-old mom-and-pop pharmacy in the center of town. The people wanted to keep it in service to help maintain the old-fashioned feel of the community.

It seemed like the pharmacy had been there forever. It was still owned by the original family and passed down from generation to generation. In the 1950's and 1960's it contained a soda shop, where students would line up after school waiting for the soda jerk to serve their favorite flavored sodas or milkshakes. The dust-covered fountain station was still behind the counter to add a sense of nostalgia, but it hadn't been used in decades.

Mark loved to go inside with his mom. The store displays were covered with various sized mortars and pestles that pharmacists used throughout history to crush and combine medicines. There were also numerous bottles of all shapes and sizes. The labels were faded and peeling, but Mark always struggled to read them. When he was younger, he had imagined working in the pharmacy until he fell in love with writing. He never would have imagined where his life would have taken him. For now, he found himself looking in through the darkened windows while he called his friends to see who had an extra bed for him to crash on for the night.

As he listened to the monotone ring, he looked out at all the older buildings. Some were vacant, their windows necessarily boarded-up because some neighborhood kids had thrown rocks and busted them out. Others were storefronts that housed businesses trying to compete the with national chain discount and dollar stores in the area. Most people went to the mall for clothes or drove the two hours to Oklahoma City or Tulsa for a larger variety. In the part of the town where Mark lived, the buildings had been built in the early 20th century, with brick fronts and large plate-glass windows. They had been built before the great depression, when people believed that the economy would never fail them.

Then when the stock market crashed, many people left the smaller Oklahoma towns and moved to metropolitan areas in search of food and jobs. Most of them never came back to their original communities. A once-bustling section of town was now surviving only because of its faithful families, in their run-down homes and trailer houses. It would have all but dried up if it weren't for a branch of Northeastern Oklahoma State University located nearby.

After listening to five unanswered rings, he hung up the phone again and waited for his quarters to fall into the change slot so he could make another call. He was freezing. Running outside without a coat in the middle of December in Northern Oklahoma isn't the smartest thing to do. Although snow in this part of the state was common, Mark had rarely seen this much of it the night before Christmas. The weatherman had been right when he predicted a white Christmas this year.

Now, a mixture of sleet and snow was falling. Mark's Mustang still had ice on the roof and doors, but the windows were finally clear, and the warmth of the engine kept the hood from freezing back over. He could see the bright light blinking from his right turn signal. The lens was cracked from hitting a sign a few weeks before, and he hadn't taken time to fix it.

Tonight, there was no one on the streets. The Northeastern Oklahoma community just outside of Muskogee looked like a ghost town, except for a few houses with blinking Christmas lights, and the pharmacy's decorated Santa Claus dancing in the window. Families were probably in bed trying to squeeze in a few hours of sleep before being awakened to open their Christmas gifts.

After reinserting his quarters and dialing another number, Mark listened again to the ringing on the other end of the phone. He couldn't believe that his friend, Jason, hadn't picked up the phone when he had called his number. Mark thought if anyone had stayed in town, it would have been Jason. He knew that none of his other friends were around; they had all gone to visit family, so Mark was running out of options. If he couldn't find a place to stay for the night, he would end up sleeping in his car. He was determined not to go home, and he had no money for a hotel. The only other person he could think of was Shawn.

Shawn hadn't been around as much lately since he finished school and began working at the hospital. Mark hadn't seen him since the end of the last school year. He wasn't even sure if Shawn still lived in the same apartment, but there was no one else to try.

"Hello?!" The voice on the other end of the line sounded startled and confused.

"Shawn, did I wake you?" Mark knew that he had awakened Shawn, but he didn't know what else to say.

"Yeah, its 3:00 am! Who is this?"

"It's Mark Cooper. I need to know if you have a place I can stay for the night."

"Man, I'm sorry; I have to be at work at 6:30. I can't come and get you. I thought the bars closed at 1:00 am."

"No, it isn't like that. I just need a place to crash for the night. Can I drive over and sleep on your couch?"

"I guess," Shawn replied, "I'll leave the light on for you, just be really quiet when you come in."

Before Mark could say anything else, Shawn hung up. Mark hung up the phone on his end as well and looked back out at his car. As he breathed, he could see the fog that formed on the glass door of the phone booth. He opened the door and began to step out on the cold ground. All it would take was one wrong step, and he would slide out into the street. That would be just his luck.

Happily, he didn't slide down, and when he got back in the car it was warm on the inside. The air conditioner might not work to keep him cool during the summer, but the heater was in perfect condition. When Mark shut the door of the car, he sat for a moment listening to the song on the radio, "…Oh, tidings of Comfort and Joy." He thought to himself, *For us, this time of the year has never been filled with 'tidings of comfort and joy'.*

It had been many years since Mark had believed in anything. He had known the truth about Santa Claus from an early age. When he and his siblings had received presents, they were always things that their mom had gotten from the Goodwill store. Every year at Christmas time, Mark, his brother, and sister would get toys that were used instead of new. Some were faded and discolored with stickers peeling off. Mark's mom would use tape to reattach the decals and markers to adjust faded colors. Mark was never worried about having used things, but when friends would come to play, they would make fun of the toys. However, this was only one of the reasons Mark dreaded Christmas.

Mark looked at the houses as he drove by, headed to Shawn's apartment. Some had Christmas trees in their windows; others had lights and candles. He even passed a church that had a manger scene with Baby Jesus in front of it. All might be calm and bright everywhere else in town, but not in the Cooper house.

Mark noticed a stop light up ahead. It had just turned yellow. Normally, he took this to mean he should speed up, but with the ice on the road, he didn't think that was a good idea. A new silver Lexus pulled up beside him at the stop light. It was the first car he had seen on the road since he left his house.

A man and woman were sitting in the car. The couple were apparently having some problems navigating. The woman had a map out while the man was on his phone, apparently trying very hard to get directions. Mark could tell that the man was yelling at his companion, hands flailing in the air. The woman appeared to be yelling back.

Mark got very frustrated watching them. It seemed like the red light was taking forever to change, and the longer he sat there, the angrier he got. It reminded him of the events that had happened earlier that evening.

He could still hear his father's voice, "You're so stupid. You can't do anything right!"

Mark's face began turning red. He could feel his ears burning. His Irish nature always came out when he was angry. His face would turn about as red as his hair. He began breathing deeply trying to move passed his frustration. When Mark closed his eyes; he could see the argument all over again.

"I'm sorry; I can warm it up for you," Mark could hear his mother, Elizabeth's, voice.

"I don't want you to warm it up for me. When I get home, I expect my food to be on the table piping hot," Mark's father, Gorman Cooper, replied.

"But you just got home," Mark could hear the fear in his mother's voice.

Their fighting had awakened Mark from a deep sleep. It seemed like every night his father found something to be upset about. The food wasn't on the table when Gorman got home, the television remote wasn't on the recliner in the living room, or his cigarettes weren't lying on the dresser. For one reason or another Gorman always found excuses to yell at his wife.

Most of the time, the fight was induced by his father's love affair with Jack Daniels. It seemed that every night after he got off work, Gorman did nothing but drink beer and Jack Daniels. Gorman never had to look for a reason to go out with his friends. On holidays, birthdays, and sometimes just because it was a Tuesday, or a Thursday, or any day of the week, he would get off work at five and head straight to O'Donnell's Pub for a few drinks. It would be "last call" before he realized it was so late, and he would head home.

Gorman always expected his food to be hot, waiting on the table when he got there. No matter the time, Elizabeth diligently submitted to her husband's irrational demands. Tonight however, with the busyness of Christmas Eve, she had dosed off on the couch. That's where Gorman had found her.

Regrettably, Gorman didn't find his plate waiting on the table. He looked back into the living room and saw Elizabeth lying peacefully asleep. He could have easily fixed his own plate of food, warmed it up, and let her rest, but that wasn't his nature.

He went into the kitchen and popped the top on a fresh, ice-cold beer. He loved the taste of ice-cold beer; the almost stagnate flavor of fermented hops and barley. It soothed his mood and calmed his frustrations.

Crossing back to the front door Gorman stood there for a minute watching his patient, loving wife. A half smile came across his face as he took a sip. Then slowly he tipped his beer bottle and poured enough on her head to run down her face.

Elizabeth, startled by the cold brew, sat up quickly, looking around the room to find the origin of the spill.

"Now that you're awake, where is my food?" Gorman demanded.

Elizabeth, quickly wiping away the beer that was now running down the back of her neck, said, "Honey, I'm so sorry, I must have dozed off. I will have it ready in just a moment." She hurried to the kitchen to get his plate ready.

Gorman followed her to the kitchen, "This trash is ice cold."

"I'm sorry; I can warm it up for you." Elizabeth tried to keep her voice from quivering.

"I don't want you to warm it up for me. When I get home, I expect my food to be on the table, piping hot," Gorman replied.

"But you just got home, and we ate six hours ago. Just let me warm it up," Mark's mother begged as she quickly tried to put his food into the microwave.

This act of insubordination caused her husband to lash out in anger. Gorman snatched the plate from his wife and threw the whole plate into the trash. "I want supper, and I want it now."

"I'm sorry; I'll get started on your food," she said as she grabbed a frozen package of ground beef from the freezer.

Mark could hear the entire conversation from his room. Most nights he tried to stay out of situations like this. It would always turn out worse when he got involved. He could hear his mother rustling through the trash can to retrieve the plate, and his father scolding her for not waiting until his food was done before digging through the trash.

Mark couldn't understand why she didn't stand up for herself. At two in the morning he was demanding that she cook supper for a second time. Mark couldn't stand it any longer; he decided that he had to do something.

2

Quietly he got up from his bed and slipped on his pants. He didn't want to wake up his younger brother Benjamin who slept in the bed across the room. While passing through the door Mark picked up the deer rifle Ben had borrowed from his friend and hid it behind his back.

As he walked down the hallway, he could smell the food as it cooked on the stove. The smell exacerbated his anger. He couldn't believe that his mother was actually cooking for his dad this late. The sounds of his father's continued berating of Elizabeth caused Mark's anger to burn in his face. It was all a loud roar in his ears, until he heard the slap, and everything went silent.

Mark hated that sound. These arguments didn't always end in a physical assault, but far too often they did. Gorman would hit her across the face or in the back of the head. At other times he would drag her to the bedroom by her hair or kick her with his boots. Physical violence seemed to pleasure him.

Mark came down the hallway and into the kitchen. The kitchen had an adjoining wall to the living room. The door that opened to the living area was directly across from the front door. Along the adjoining wall was the hallway that led back to the bedrooms and bathroom. As Mark came through the hallway door, he saw his mother standing at the stove which stood just to his left on the wall it shared with the bathroom. She was rubbing the red handprint on her face. The cabinet door above the sink stood open. In the center of the kitchen was a small table. It was only big enough for four people, but there were times when they squeezed in more. On the other side, opposite the stove, a refrigerator stood beside a door that led to the garage.

"Leave her alone!" Mark yelled.

Gorman was seated at the head of the table near the sink facing the living room. He was still nursing his beer bottle and was now puffing on a cigarette. He was shocked that Mark had actually said something. "What are you going to do about it?" he chortled.

Mark pulled the gun from behind his back.

"Oh, you think you're going to be a real man? You won't shoot me," Gorman seethed.

"I said leave her alone," He replied slowly and with emphasis.

Gorman taunted, "And I said shoot me. You wuss, you don't even know how to hold that thing."

Elizabeth, recovering from the slap, realized what was happening, "Mark, please put that down. And go back to bed," she intervened. "Baby it's OK. I'm fine, I just opened that cabinet and hit myself in the face with the door. It really is OK."

Elizabeth looked pleadingly into his eyes. He hated it when she gave him that look. He wanted to protect her, save her, but when she looked at him that way, he couldn't help but give in. She took the gun from his hand and propped it up against the wall. She then took his arm and turned him towards his room. He feared disappointing her. Every day his dad hurt her, and so he didn't want to make matters worse. She followed him down the hall to keep him separated from his father.

Gorman, never taking a good fight sitting down, pursued him. Standing in the hallway door he called out, "Yeah baby, suck your momma's tit a little more and go back to bed. You'll never be a real man and do something for yourself. So, go back to bed, Mommy will come tuck you in and wipe your little tushy."

Mark spun around in anger, accidentally knocking his mother to the floor as she followed him down the hall. Before he realized what he was doing, Mark lunged forward swinging at his dad, punching him in his nose. Gorman fell back into the kitchen toward the table, holding his face. He stood in shock for a moment, as blood from his nose began seeping between his fingers. Mark turned and knelt beside his mother who had knocked a picture down from the wall as she fell. "Mom, I'm so sorry, I didn't mean to knock you down."

Elizabeth sat on the old tattered and stained carpet, trying to gather up the broken glass from the family picture that was now lying on the floor. Mark looked down at the picture of his family. They had been so happy back then, before the drinking took over. Mark picked the picture up off the floor. Quickly, Elizabeth snatched it from his hand. It was one of the few memories she had left of her happy little family.

"Mark, please go back to bed. I don't want you to hurt your dad," she begged.

"Hurt me? That boy couldn't hurt me. Come on, little boy," Gorman said as he continued to hold his nose. He had grabbed the dish rag from the sink and was using it to stop the bleeding. As he rinsed his hands in the cool water, Gorman noticed the kitchen knife that Elizabeth used to open the ground meat. He slowly picked it up, staring at the serrated edge, as the blood continued to drip from his nose into the running water. The drops of blood chased each other around the drain before continuing their way down to the sewer.

Mark helped Elizabeth off the floor and back into the kitchen and turned to find his father leaning back against the sink wielding the knife in his right-hand. Anger blazed in Gorman's eyes as he come around the other side of the table. Instinctively, Mark slid between the stove and the table in an attempt to get away. In the process he knocked the pan of cooking meat off the stove top, splashing grease and half- cooked ground meat on the floor.

Gorman chased Mark around the table stepping through his ruined dinner. He exclaimed, "Boy you just knocked my food over; your mother is going to have to start over again, and it's your fault."

"Please stop, Gorman, put the knife down," Elizabeth grabbed Gorman's arm pulling him back.

"He was the one that came in here with a deer rifle, so I'm calling his bluff." He pushed her away. Turning back to Mark he growled, "You want a piece of me? Come and get it. I'll give you what you want,"

Trying to get away from his father, Mark tripped over a chair and went sprawling.

"I got you now, and I'm gonna take you out," Gorman threatened.

There was no way that Mark was going to get away. He braced himself for the attack, closing his eyes and waiting for whatever would come next.

It didn't happen. He didn't feel anything, just heard what sounded like a melon getting hit with a hammer. He opened his eyes to see his father fall to the floor and his mother standing behind him with the hot frying pan. His father was out. The ground meat and grease were all over the floor, still sizzling and popping.

Elizabeth dropped the pan into the sink as she turned the water on to cool her burning hands. She acted instinctively, on auto pilot. Mark tried to help her. He could see the red whelps from the hot skillet already starting to form. If the handle hadn't been insulated, she would've burned her hand even worse.

She held her hand under the cold water. Her insides were torn apart. Gorman was her husband, and she loved him. She had never been without him. On the other hand, Mark was her son. Her maternal instinct had taken over, and she had done what she had to do to protect him.

Searching through the kitchen drawer for burn ointment, Mark pleaded, "Mom you have to get out of here; just wake up Ben and Jess. We can get packed quickly. I have some money, so we can find a hotel room."

"Mark, stop; you know he doesn't mean to get drunk. He won't even remember all this tomorrow morning. Just help me get him into bed, and tomorrow everything will be fine, as if nothing had ever happened."

"No, he is going to end up killing you. Let's go before anything else happens." As Mark pulled his mother's arm, she pulled away. "Then I'm leaving, I can't handle seeing you die because you aren't willing to save yourself."

Mark went back to his room to put on a pair of jeans and grabbed his shoes.

"Mark, please don't do this, just help me get him to bed." Elizabeth's plea was ignored as Mark came out of his room with his shoes and headed out the front door. Elizabeth felt the tears welling up in her eyes as she heard the Mustang's engine start and then speed out of the driveway, leaving ruts in the snow.

As Mark replayed the events of the fight in his head, he sat blankly staring at the signal light. He heard a honk from behind him, snapping him back to reality. Looking over, he noticed that the Lexus was gone. A man in an older Ford honked his horn again as he pulled around him.

Mark had no idea how long he had been sitting at the stop light. Slowly, he began to pull out into the intersection, still trying to get his bearings.

Mark continued to move through town at a snail's pace to avoid sliding on the ice. Larger flakes of snow were now falling, decreasing the visibility significantly. Mark didn't want to get up on the highway for fear of an accident but staying on the access road would take longer to get to the apartment complex where Shawn lived. Slowly, he pulled his car onto the freeway.

The traffic on the freeway was moving a little faster than it was on the roads in town, but not much. Several cars were sitting in the ditch along the way. De-icing trucks were spraying down the pavement in a last-ditch effort to prevent the roads from freezing, but it didn't seem to be working. The flashing lights of wreckers and police cars could be seen in the distance, but the few accidents that Mark saw didn't appear to be very serious.

Finally, he saw the exit he was looking for. There was a fast-food restaurant on the corner and a gas station next door. Both had their lights off, probably because of the holiday.

As Mark pulled into the apartment complex, he could feel the tires struggling to grip the road. The buildings were two stories tall and held four apartments on each side. There were about ten buildings in total. A cluster of mailboxes stood beside the office in the center of the apartment complex. An empty lonely looking swimming pool was located behind the office.

Mark noticed, to his chagrin, that every parking spot was taken. Most of the cars were covered with ice and snow, and it was obvious that they had been sitting where they were for at least several hours. As he made the circle and drove slowly past the front office a second time, he noticed that there was one small space right by the dumpster. It may not be a parking spot, but the trash truck wouldn't be making its rounds on Christmas morning. He carefully maneuvered his car between the dumpster and the curb.

Slowly, he opened the door and stretched his leg out. As he attempted to stand on it, he could feel the ice slightly give way beneath his weight. He steadied himself and tried again. Holding on to the door, he pulled himself from the car. After shutting the door, he used the car to steady his gait as he prepared to slowly make his way across the parking lot to the sidewalk.

He couldn't remember which apartment Shawn lived in. Carefully, he walked among the apartment buildings to see if he could find anything that would spark his memory. While the sidewalk was slick from the ice, the grass was frozen and covered with snow which gave way slightly when he walked on it. He realized quickly that walking on it would be safer than walking on the sidewalk. The frozen grass made a crunching noise beneath his feet.

The lights over the front doors of most apartments were turned off, so he couldn't see the numbers. His only hope was that the mailboxes beside the office would have tenants' names on them. Mark carefully walked to the mailboxes to check. Luckily, the last names of the tenants were listed on each box. His fingers traced the names before he found the name he was looking for.

"Number 326, S. Peterson," he read aloud to himself. "That should be him, Shawn Peterson."

He started the trek to the building with a big number 3 on the end of it. From the parking lot he could see that building. Three was past the pool towards the back of the units. The pool had obviously been emptied for the season, and the poolside chairs were covered in snow. As he looked back towards his car, he noticed his trail of footprints following him like an invisible friend.

As he arrived at building Three, he noticed that all the units had their front lights off except the one on the top left side. As he got closer, he could see that numbers of the units on the ground floor had a prefix of 31, so it stood to reason that the prefixes on the second floor would be 32. He looked at the long staircase that led to the upstairs apartments facing the office. It was covered in ice and snow. It had iron handrails, and the steps themselves were precast concrete with no face. Icicles were dangling beneath each step. They reminded Mark of jagged teeth, taunting him to attempt to make it to the top without falling.

Mark began climbing the stairs. There was enough ice on them to cause him to slip a little. He held tightly to the railings, which were frosted over, also. Slowly he made the ascent to the top. The temperature must have been dropping because the falling snow was much thicker, circling around the streetlights and falling to the ground. The icicles hanging from the eaves of the buildings looked like the plastic ones used for decoration.

Mark made it to the door without falling, and slowly opened it, hoping to avoid waking Shawn. The front door opened into a very short entryway. To the right of the exterior door was another one that opened to the first bedroom. If he remembered correctly, the first bedroom had its own bathroom. Moving from the entryway, the room opened into a living room. On the front wall of the living room was a glass sliding door that led on to the small balcony. Opposite the glass door Shawn had an L-shaped sofa against the wall that the living room shared with the kitchen. The couch faced an entertainment center with an older TV and DVD player.

Past the edge of the couch the room narrowed and made a slight corner into the attached dining area which shared a wall with the second bathroom. The dining room table was small, built for four people. It had only three high-backed chairs. Each chair was painted a different color. Hanging on the back wall that the dining room shared with the adjoining apartment there was a picture of a Native American on a horse looking over a large canyon. Underneath the picture was printed, "The End of the Trail."

The man in the print looked very tired, like he had travelled a long way and finally made it home. The exhaustion was evident on his face, and he looked like he wanted nothing more than to find a place to lay his head. Mark couldn't help but feel the same. He was consumed with loneliness and felt lost. He had no place to rest. Right now, he didn't even have a home.

Mark was thankful that Shawn had answered the phone when he had called. It had been a while since Mark had been in this apartment, but it wasn't the first time that he spent the night there. About a year before, a close friend of his, named Michael, was living in the extra bedroom. It was through his friendship with Michael that Mark had met Shawn for the first time.

Shawn and Michael had been hosting a coed party, and their friends were hanging out, drinking, and playing pong. Mark was very particular about his choice of drink. While his father enjoyed beer and whiskey, Mark's taste leaned toward Jose Cuervo Tequila. When he finished off a few shots of tequila he would lose his inhibitions and would talk to everyone around.

At that party, Mark had learned two things. First, never do chin ups on the shower curtain rod. Second, downing a whole bag of cheese puff chips after drinking several shots of tequila isn't the best idea. They didn't taste as good coming up as they had going down. Since that time, he couldn't even look at a cheese puffs without feeling nauseous. The next day following the party, he woke up hugging the toilet, with a pounding headache, and cheese crusted fingers. At least tonight Mark had a warm couch to sleep on instead of the bathroom floor.

Before Michael moved to Tokyo for a job, Mark would see Michael and Shawn at the clubs on the weekends. Shawn seemed nice but always looked out of place in the club scene. Mark, on the other hand loved it. The loud music and the flowing booze helped him escape from the thoughts of his home life.

Tonight, he wished that he were at a club. He wanted to forget all about what had happened between his parents. After a quick stop in the bathroom, Mark went back to the living room and noticed that Shawn had left a blanket on the back of the couch. Mark's exhaustion was catching up with him and as soon as Mark lay down on the couch, he fell into a fitful sleep.

Five-thirty came early. Mark felt like he had just dozed off when he heard the bedroom door open. Apparently, Shawn had forgotten to turn the clothes dryer on the night before, and so he was impatiently waiting for his scrubs to dry.

Mark and Shawn had several things in common. For instance, they were about the same age. Both were in their mid-twenties. While Mark was still in school, Shawn had finished his schooling and passed the exam to become a registered nurse and had begun working at the local hospital.

On the other hand, they had many differences. When it came to looks, they were opposites. Mark was thin and gangly with a ruddy complexion and covered with freckles. He had bright red hair, and he could get a sun burn just walking across campus. Shawn, on the other hand, had a rugged build with a chisel-cut chin and high cheek bones. With his dark hair and dark eyes, he could easily pass for a foreigner, but that notion would be dispelled the moment he opened his mouth and exposed his speech Oklahoman accent.

"Sleep well?" Shawn asked as he sat down in the recliner at the other end of the couch to put on his shoes.

"I guess as well as I could. Thanks for leaving the light on for me," Mark replied.

"It wasn't a problem," Shawn finished putting on his shoes, "You can feel free to sleep as long as you need to. I'll leave my number on the table. Just lock the door when you head out." He stood up and straightened his pants, before walking into the kitchen. A moment later he was back, pulling on his scrub top that still seemed to be a little damp. He then grabbed for a jacket that was hanging on a hook by the front door.

"Yeah, ok, I should be out of here pretty quickly. Tomorrow's…" Mark stopped and thought for a second then slowly said, "well *today* is, Christmas, and I'll have to be at home to open gifts with my kid brother and sister."

Shawn pulled a beanie onto his head and began to open the door. "Whatever, I'm always here alone and work long hours, so you aren't bothering me."

Mark smiled, "Thanks, if you hadn't answered, I would have had to sleep in my car last night. While that is alright during the summer, last night would have been too cold."

"I'm just glad you didn't need a designated driver from a bar, because I couldn't have done that," Shawn stepped out the door and pulled it to behind him.

Mark laid back down and fell asleep.

3

Everyone is conditioned to believe that Christmas is supposed to be the "Most Wonderful Time of the Year", but Christmas had never been a wonderful time for Mark. While most kids were coming to school after Christmas showing off the latest and the greatest gifts, Mark had never received the newest toys or the best clothes. But that had never bothered him. He didn't care about the nicest clothes and the most expensive toys.

Elizabeth did everything she could do to provide special presents for her kids. She always wanted to get them the most expensive gifts but was never able to get them what she felt they deserved. Her children always acted like they appreciated what she got for them. They were happy to have the used toys, and always wore hand-me-downs without complaining, but she felt that they were ashamed of the gifts she gave them. On the other hand, maybe it was Elizabeth who had been ashamed because she couldn't give them more.

Gorman had worked in construction all his life, and he made a decent income. However, most of it was spent on alcohol, so the family barely had enough money to pay their bills, let alone enough to buy special things for Christmas. Elizabeth did as well as she could with what she had. She would tuck away a couple of dollars of grocery money here, and some gas money there, so that she could save up enough to get her children something to go under the tree.

Every year, when Gorman gave her the meager allowance for presents the week before Christmas, he was always surprised at the gifts she would bring home. He never knew that she was squirreling away money throughout the year.

It hadn't always been like that. When the kids were little, he was always there for Christmas. Gorman acted like he wanted to be part of his children's lives. As they grew older, however, his addiction took over his life. Christmas became less about family, and more about finding just another reason to be at the pub.

Gorman's family had English roots. They had moved from the New York area in the 19th century to help settle the land west of the Mississippi River. For generations the homestead was passed down from one generation to another.

As a boy Gorman would play with his cousins at the old homestead, but he always felt like he didn't belong. His mother was Irish, and for some reason his grandmother hated her. Gorman was ten when his father died, in 1979. It had been a devastating blow for him.

Gorman had been very close to his dad. They had built a tree house in the back yard when Gorman was seven. His dad would even take him to work on the job sites when he could.

On the day his father died, Gorman had planned to go to work with him. His dad drove a bulldozer, and Gorman would often ride along on the dozer also. His dad would even let Gorman drive it sometimes when nobody was watching.

The morning that his father died Gorman woke up early to get ready to go but became very ill. He had gotten some type of "bug ", and so he wasn't allowed to go. He cried as his dad left the house. Gorman spent most of the day lying on the couch; he couldn't keep anything down.

Finally, he was awakened by a knock at the door. He knew something was wrong when his mother opened the door to find a Sheriff standing there.

Gorman couldn't understand. His dad was the best bulldozer operator that they had, but for some reason had hopped out of the dozer to move something out of the way. He didn't have it secured, so the dozer moved forward unmanned. There was no way that anyone could save him.

It was later hypothesized by some of the workers that there might have been a problem with the dozer. It had been reported to the company, but nothing was done about it. Right after the accident the problem had been mysteriously fixed. When Gorman's mom attempted to talk to a lawyer about suing the company, no one would take the case. Other than receiving a small settlement they never heard anything else about it.

As a child, Gorman had seen his dad climb out of the bulldozer many times. Gorman would make sure that it wasn't in gear. So, when he found out how his father died, he felt guilty, blaming himself. He believed, *If I hadn't gotten sick, I would have been there to help him.*

After his father died, his grandparents quit coming to visit, and he and his mother quit going to visit the homestead. His mother said it was because she was Irish, and his grandparents hated Irishmen and didn't want them around. As an adolescent, Gorman began hating his grandparents, and he felt abandoned by his father. Most importantly, he suffered from the guilt he felt because of his dad's death.

Gorman held on to his anger and depression. His dad had been his hero, and he was gone, and he hated it. The self-blame continued to grow inside like a cancer. It caused him to hate himself and never want to connect with anyone else.

Gorman's mother also suffered severe pain from the loss of her husband. She went from relationship to relationship and began to drink heavily. After a few years her life spiraled out of control, and she kicked Gorman out of the house. Without a home and food, he found himself scavenging on the streets. At first, he continued going to school because he received free breakfast and lunch. At night he would try to sneak into sheds or vacant buildings to sleep.

As time went on, he realized that he had to find a way to support himself. There was no way he could continue living on the street, so he began working a couple of odd jobs. He quickly discovered that he was good at construction, and so he started doing some "under the table" construction work. Nevertheless, he still struggled to survive. He was being paid very little and still had no place to call home.

Gorman decided that the only way to put a roof over his head and food in his stomach was to join the army. They would give him a warm place to sleep and three-square meals a day. His father had been in the army during the Vietnam War. He didn't talk about it much before he died, but Gorman felt it might help him connect with his dad if he went into the army as well.

He wasn't worried that he would be sent to war, because there were no major military actions taking place in the late 1980's. Instead, he felt that he would be able to put in his four years and be able to make a place for himself. Then when he got out of the military, he could find a house and settle down.

He was sent to Fort Jackson, South Carolina for basic training. Having to get up early to work out and run all the time left him exhausted but being in a place with people around helped him to build a new normalcy. The friendships and companionships that he began building made up for some of the pain that he had felt in losing his father and later being rejected by his mother. It gave him a place to belong.

After basic training he was stationed in Foot Hood, Texas. While there is met a beautiful red head named Elizabeth. She was working in a small diner right outside of the base. He noticed her one night when he and some other soldiers stopped by for a late supper, or maybe an early breakfast.

He was attracted to her blazing red hair. It was the same color as his mother's, which in his opinion was always her best attribute. It took about three weeks for him to finally work up the courage to ask the pretty young waitress out.

Every time he saw her, he couldn't keep from staring. She seemed to be getting more beautiful with each passing day. Her bright red hair and freckled complexion contrasted breathtakingly with her emerald green eyes. He had noticed her eyes the first time she took his order at the diner. They were different than any others that he had seen before. There was a slight hint of gray in the center around the pupil, and it was surrounded by the richest green he had ever seen. At night he would dream about them.

Gorman and Elizabeth began seeing each other every night. When they weren't together, Gorman was always thinking about her. He loved their time together.

After about six weeks of dating, he gave her a kiss. It was the greatest moment he had ever experienced. She was different than any other girl that he had dated, and he could see himself spending his entire life with her. He even began planning their lives together. He had it all figured out. After his tour of duty was over, they would find a home and build a family, something he never thought he would have.

All of that changed when on August 2, 1990, the world woke up to the news that Iraq had invaded the small neighboring country of Kuwait. The Iraqi leader, Saddam Hussein, wanted the wealth from the Kuwaiti oil fields. To save the nation of Kuwait, the world began sending troops to push back the Iraqi military forces. Within a few days a vast number of American soldiers would be on their way to the Middle East aid the Kuwaiti government. Gorman was one of the soldiers who would be sent.

With his impending deployment, Gorman made a drastic decision. There was a chance that he might not make it back alive. So, that night he asked Elizabeth to be his wife.

It was a very dramatic move on his part. Before meeting her, he never thought that he would get married, especially to a woman like Elizabeth. She was timid and respectful. She also was a very hard worker. She didn't like to party and went to church every Sunday.

Gorman had discovered that women often threw themselves at men in uniform. By the time he had been in the military three years, he had at least a dozen notches on his bedpost. Elizabeth wasn't like that. She didn't care that he wore a uniform; she loved him from who he was. She also had determined to remain pure until she found the person, she would spend her life with. She felt that it would make her feel cheap if she was involved in an illicit relationship. No matter how often Gorman tried to take advantage of her, she was determined to maintain her integrity.

Elizabeth was very excited when he proposed. She couldn't believe it because they had only been dating a short period of time. She accepted his proposal at once, and they agreed that when he returned from the Middle East, they would get married.

Gorman also felt like it gave him something to look forward to. The thought of their future together was something to keep him going while he was away.

Gorman really didn't know what love was. He remembered the strong love his father had shown him when he was alive. He thought that his mother also loved him, but the way she threw him out made him question that love. Of course, he had used the word "love" in relationships, to get what he was looking for from a girl, but his actions had never been motivated by love. He had used the term to gratify his needs.

Within a few days, Gorman would be on an airplane to a remote area of Saudi Arabia. Since Elizabeth knew that it would be a while before she saw him again, that night Elizabeth decided that it was time to ignore her inhibitions and give into the desire to consummate their love.

4

Gorman had never been out of the country before, and the people he saw there were completely different than any people he had been around. Not only did they speak a different language, but they had a completely different culture.

In the morning the soldiers would awaken to the eerie sound of the Muslim call to prayer, the Adhan. Gorman would hear the Arabic prayer leader's voice echoing across the desert sand. The sound was very disheartening. It had a haunting sound and left many soldiers on edge.

During the first few weeks they were deployed, the combination of the 110-degree days and the sun reflecting off the sand made everyone sick. It was impossible to keep cool, and it was difficult to stay hydrated.

The weeks went by, and Gorman began missing home. At night he would dream about Elizabeth. He wondered what she was doing.

He felt alone. Everyone else was receiving mail from home. Their parents and grandparents would send letters and packages, but Gorman was no longer in touch with his mother or his grandparents. However, one day a letter came. It was from Elizabeth. Gorman was so excited to see her name his heart skipped a beat.

He tore into the letter. He couldn't get it open fast enough. He poured over each heartwarming word. The more he read it, the more he missed being home. It made him long to be with her, to hold her in his arms and feel her head against his chest. He longed to smell her sweet perfume and the slight hint of lavender in her hair.

Each day Gorman would pull out her letter, reading it over and over. He would spend much of his time thinking about what they would be doing if he were home. While all the other men in his barrack left to find companionship in town, Gorman stayed in the bunk writing letters and thinking about home.

Gorman no longer wanted to go into town looking for girls. He knew not just anyone could offer him the satisfaction he sought. He wanted to be home so that he could be with the woman who would be his wife.

Something had blossomed in his heart. Elizabeth had become more than a challenge to overcome; now she was his connection with the real world. Every day he would write a letter to send home. He waited with anticipation for the post to come in, hoping to hear his name called.

Elizabeth's letters were the only thing that kept him going. Every few days he would receive another letter from her. They talked about the base, and about the things going on at home. She talked about her plans for the holidays and her desire to take some classes at the local college.

She also asked him if he had heard any news about when his deployment would be over. She asked questions about the fighting and if he had to shoot his gun. She also wanted to know if he had met any other women overseas.

Gorman would try to keep her updated as much as he could. He would tell her of the culture and the people. He wrote to her about weather, the craziness of the days, and the silence of the nights.

He didn't tell her anything about the war. It really wasn't a war. He hadn't seen much fighting and knew very little about what was happening everywhere else. She could get more info off the news on the television.

By the time November rolled around the desert temperatures had dipped into the mid 80's during the day and the low 50's at night. There was a dramatic difference between daytime and nighttime temperatures. Meteorologists said the temperature variance was due to the lack of humidity. There was no insulation to hold the heat in. Gorman didn't care why it got cold so fast; he was just tired of the weather.

Some time went by, and Gorman didn't hear from Elizabeth. Since he continued to send her letters regularly, he became worried because he hadn't received replies to any of them.

One day, a letter finally arrived in a pink envelope. He was so glad to see it. Before he opened the letter, he held it to his nose and inhaled the left-over smell of Elizabeth's perfume. He smiled as he closed his eyes to imagine her beautiful red hair and green eyes. Gorman laid down, clutching the letter to his chest.

Finally, he opened it up. She wrote:

My Dearest Gorman:

I'm so glad to receive your letters, and sorry that I haven't written you back, but I have been very sick. Over the past few weeks I have been unable to work and have been laid up in bed with what seemed to be a long-lasting stomach virus. I'm waiting with anticipation for the day that you return home to me, and we can continue our life together. But I have news that I need to share with you. When I went to the doctor because of my continued illness, he told me that it should go away in about nine months. We're having a baby, Gorm, and I wish you were here. I hope this doesn't change anything. I really wish I could see your face right now so you could tell me that everything is going to be alright. I'm very scared by myself. Please remember, I love you, and I'm looking forward to seeing you soon.

Gorman sat on his bunk in a daze. He didn't know if he should be happy or sad at the news. He didn't know how to be a father. He had been ten when his own father had passed away, and the only other male in his life was his mother's long-term boyfriend, Steve. He had shacked up with Gorman's mother for a while, but he was no father.

Gorman didn't know what he was going to do. This child wasn't part of his plan. Now he would be stuck with it.

He didn't reply to Elizabeth's letter. He was very angry and felt betrayed. He blamed Elizabeth and wanted to tell her to get it taken care of before he got back. He couldn't believe that this had happened. Even though he had been with a lot of other women, as far as he knew, there were no other "mini" Gorman Coopers running around.

How did he know that it was his, anyway? She worked right next to the army base. There were men going in and flirting with her all the time. She could have easily slept with anyone of them.

But Gorman knew deep down inside that she wasn't going to do that. It took her forever to give in to him. There is no way that she would have cheated on him now.

Needless to say, he didn't want a child. He had never planned on having children. He didn't want to start now while he was halfway around the world. Gorman tucked the letter away in his pack; he would have to deal with it later.

Days turned to weeks, and weeks turned to months. Thanksgiving came and went, and so did Christmas and New Year's. Every week or so, he received another letter from Elizabeth.

In the first few letters she talked about the pregnancy and how happy she was. She went on and on about the wedding possibilities and telling Gorman about her job and the changes going on in town. Gorman read every word, but he didn't want to write back. He didn't know exactly what to say.

Initially, Elizabeth believed his failure to respond just meant that her letters had been delayed, or maybe his letters were delayed on the way to her. Over time, however, Elizabeth realized that his lack of response wasn't due to a problem with the postal system. She realized that something was wrong. Around Christmas she wrote what would be her final letter.

In this letter she petitioned him to tell her why he hadn't responded. She begged him to at least let her know what was wrong, and that he was OK. She told him if he was breaking off their relationship, she at least deserved for him to respond and let her know. She had to know something.

It was mid-January before the letter finally made it to Gorman. As he read each word, he was saddened at her pain. He could see the tearstains and the smeared ink. He remembered the night that they were together before he was deployed. He remembered his happiness and the reason that he asked her to marry him. As his anger subsided, he realized that maybe a child was a good idea.

He decided that he was going to reply. As he pulled out his pen and paper from his pack, he heard the call. Something was happening. Gorman left everything where it was and headed out of the barracks.

5

The news called it "Desert Storm." All over the United States people were glued to their televisions watching the films of the bombardments of the American troops in Iraq. The Iraqi army continued to send Scud missiles into Israel and Saudi Arabia, trying to keep the war outside of their borders.

Over the next several weeks there was a lot of fighting. The US military was able to hold its own, but the Iraqi army was willing to do whatever it took to win the war. As a military tactic, the Iraqi military took drastic measures that would change the lives of many of those who were fighting for the freedom of Kuwait.

In late January the Iraqi fighters began setting fire to the oil wells in Kuwait. This method wasn't only an attempt to punish the Kuwaiti leaders for their overproduction of oil that affected the Iraqi economy but was also an economic attack on the nation at large. Over 6 million barrels of oil were lost a day among the 600 to 700 wells that were set ablaze. It would end up taking almost 10 months to extinguish all the fires.

To thwart the efforts of the military forces to extinguish the fires, the Iraqi Soldiers placed mines and traps around the wells. This action would prove detrimental for many of the firefighters who were trying to put out the massive blazes.

From the time the major fighting started Gorman hadn't had a
chance to think about anything but his responsibilities to the military.
The soldiers had little time to do anything. When they did have time,
they spent it relaxing and trying to get their minds off the battles
raging outside their doors.

One morning Gorman woke up very early. He was sick and
spent a while in the restroom trying to get over whatever it was that
was bugging him. By the time he heard the wake-up call, he was
feeling a little better. As everyone got cleaned up and ready to leave
their barracks, they were again surrounded by the thick black blanket
of smoke that filled the land.

The fires had been burning for several weeks, and Gorman's
company was going to the aid of the Kuwaiti firefighters who were
attempting to get the blazes under control. Dressed in fire retardant
clothes, breathing apparatuses, and oxygen tanks. It was very difficult
for them to get around. Moreover, the thick black smoke made it
practically impossible to see.

As Gorman's company got in place to begin their descent into
the valley where the well was located, something was bugging
Gorman. He hadn't thought about Elizabeth or the baby in several
days, but now he couldn't get them out of his mind. He wanted to
know how they were doing. He wanted to know if she had found out
the sex of the baby, and he wondered if there were any changes that
he needed to know about.

It had been several weeks since her last letter, and he hadn't
returned a reply to her. He had written the letter, but he was scared to

mail it. He just carried his reply in his wallet and read it over and over. He wanted his response to be perfect before he sent it out.

Something was not right, and Gorman had an overwhelming feeling of dread. He felt anxious and he did not know why. He wished he had mailed his letter, just in case something happened.

As his company got closer to the well, Gorman heard a noise behind him. Before he could turn, he felt someone push him out of the way. Suddenly, everything went dark.

Days passed and Elizabeth sat at the diner watching the TV before her shift. By this time, she was seven months pregnant, and her pregnancy was really showing. Since the major fighting started in January, she hadn't watched anything but CNN. Daily she waited for word from Gorman. It had been nearly two months since she sent her last letter. Considering the time, it would take the post office to get her letter to get him and the time it would take for her to receive a reply, she still had hope that a letter would be on the way. With each passing day that expectation was slowly fading.

Elizabeth was very worried about Gorman. She had just read in the paper about the scud attack at Dhahran that killed almost 30 members of a reserve group out of Pennsylvania, and there were around 100 who were severely injured. Elizabeth hadn't heard from Gorman in so long, she wondered if he was dead. All she could do was pray for him, which she did all the time.

Elizabeth had been feeling poorly for weeks. At the end of the day, her legs would be swollen and her back, hurting. At two o'clock in the afternoon she made the 6-block walk home from work.

When she finally got home and made it up the two flights of stairs to her apartment, she was exhausted.

It was very good to be home, and she was ready to put her feet up for a while. She flipped on the TV and stretched out on the couch. The newscaster was talking about the recent deaths in Iraq, and it made Elizabeth begin thinking about Gorman halfway around the world. She closed her eyes for just a minute and pictured Gorman in his Army uniform. After a few minutes she had fallen asleep.

When the phone rang, she didn't know how long she had been asleep. Slowly she made her way off the couch, trying to get the phone. It would be so much easier to get around without what felt and looked like a huge watermelon under her shirt. Eventually she made it to the phone after the answering machine turned on. *Stupid answering machine*, she thought, *I really need to get one that I can adjust the number of rings before it picks up.*

"Hello, this is Sergeant Crawford with the United States Army. I'm looking for Elizabeth Douglass," said a voice on the answering machine.

Elizabeth felt like her heart stopped. She hurried to the phone and picked it up. "Hello."

"Yes, hello, I'm looking for Elizabeth Douglass."

"Yes, that's me." She tried to swallow the lump in her throat.

"Yes, ma'am, this is Sergeant Crawford of the United Starts Army. Your name is listed as the immediate family for Corporal Gorman Cooper."

"Um, Yes, I'm his fiancé." She was trying to hold back the tears. She kept telling herself, if he had died then they would have come in person. So, everything must be all right. "Is something wrong?" She asked the caller.

"Do you know how we can get in contact with his parents?"

Elizabeth felt like he was avoiding the question. "Well, his father passed away, and his estranged mother has not spoken to him in over five years. I don't think he would even know how to get in touch with her. What is this all about?"

"Ma'am I'm very sorry to have to tell you this, but Corporal Cooper was severely wounded in an explosion. He is currently in a hospital in Germany. He should be transferred back to the states when he is stable enough for transport."

Elizabeth couldn't hold back the tears. "Oh, no! Is he ok? What happened?"

"Miss Douglass, I don't know the extent of his injuries. He was wounded when a mine exploded. He was lucky though that it did not take his life. He is currently in a coma, but the doctors are seeing some good signs. Someone will be in touch with you as soon as we know when he will be back in the states. Again, I'm very sorry, but that is all of the information that we have right now."

Elizabeth hung up the phone. She couldn't believe her ears. She was angry at herself for losing faith in him. Maybe his injuries were the reason he hadn't replied. She wondered if he had wanted to contact her but was too busy.

It saddened her to think about him being in a coma. Just that word "coma" gave her chills. She knew that some people stay in comas for years, and some never wake up. This news really frightened her. But she tried to stay positive about it and remind herself that at least he was alive.

Weeks came and went, and Gorman remained in Germany. He drifted in and out of consciousness, and the pain he suffered was unimaginable. They kept him medicated when he was awake to help alleviate the agony.

Ultimately, the severe damage done to one of his legs wasn't reparable. The doctors did everything that they could to save it, but they were unable to mend the portion of his leg below his thigh. The procedure that was required to remove the lower half of his leg took only a few minutes but would change his life forever.

The doctors kept him sedated for the first several hours following the surgery, continuing to check his vitals. After about a day they began decreasing the medication. Gorman found himself waking up to excruciating pain. Most of the medicine just took the edge off the discomfort, and the nurses were giving him the highest dosage they could give. The cycle continued for the next several days until the pain finally began to lessen, making it possible for him to return to the United States. They transferred him back to Texas.

Finally, Elizabeth's phone rang the day after Easter, which was, ironically, the first of April. When she answered the phone, the male voice on the other end of the line said, "Hello, Miss Douglass, this is Sergeant Crawford. I spoke with you in February about Corporal Gorman Cooper. Corporal Cooper has been transferred to Fort Sam Houston in Texas. He is conscious but is still in a lot of pain."

"When can I see him?" she petitioned.

"I'll have to check on that. I will do everything I can to get you in to see him." The warmth in his voice offered some comfort that everything was going to be alright.

Although it took a few weeks of negotiating, Sergeant Crawford was as good as his word and managed to get Elizabeth in to see Gorman. She was very nervous. The usual two-and-a-half-hour drive from Killeen to the hospital at Fort Sam Houston, which was located just outside of San Antonio, took longer because Elizabeth had to ride the bus. The more time she spent pent up in the stinky, stuffy seat right next to the on-board restroom, the more anxious she felt. She wanted to see Gorman more than anything, but she feared what she would find. Furthermore, she feared he wouldn't want to see her.

It was late in the day when she got to the hospital. Her legs were swollen, and she had had little to eat, but she was relieved that her trip was almost over. She didn't know what to expect, and even considering the doctor's warning, she was surprised at what she saw when she entered his room.

Gorman still looked rough. He had been burned over sixty percent of his body, and the stump of a leg that he had left caused him to feel incomplete. He never knew how much he would miss his leg.

Elizabeth found him asleep when she came in. His head was still wrapped, and she could see where his burns were still oozing. The doctor warned her that they would still have to do many surgeries to replace the damaged skin on his arms and legs.

She was saddened when she looked around the room. It was so sterile; the walls were off-white, and nothing made the room look cheerful. The television was set to a news station and turned down so low that she couldn't hear it. Unlike most hospital rooms there were no balloons and no flowers. There were no cards that said, "Get Well Soon," or "Thinking of You." There was nothing. It was as if Gorman had no one. There was no one who cared whether he lived or died, except her.

When Elizabeth walked over to the bed, all she could do was weep. Her heart broke for the pain that he was suffering. She saw the morphine drip that was hooked up to help rid him of pain, but it wasn't enough. While he slept Elizabeth could hear wheezing, which the doctor said was from the smoke inhalation. If he hadn't gotten the help when he did, he would have died.

As Elizabeth sat and watched Gorman, she prayed. Sitting in a very uncomfortable chair next to his bed she waited for him to wake up. After what seemed like hours, he finally did.

"What are you doing here?" Gorman moaned.

"I came to be with you. I want to be here, with you." She tried to reassure him.

Gorman was frustrated that she was seeing him like this. "You don't have to be here. I haven't needed anyone else to sit with me."

"I want to be here," she insisted. "I told you before you were deployed that I wanted to spend the rest of my life with you. As soon as I heard what happened, I did everything I could to get here."

"My goodness, you're about to explode." Gorman nodded toward her belly.

"Yep, we're coming up on the last month. The due date is on May the eighth. It's a boy; I want to name him after you. We can call him Mark." Gorman gave her a smile. She reached over and caressed the portion of his arm that was exposed. He tensed up, so she stopped, fearful that she might hurt him.

That night the hospital let Elizabeth sleep on a pullout chair, and she ate food from the cafeteria. While Gorman lay sleeping, Elizabeth stared at him. She didn't want to leave and return to home. She didn't have an extended contract on her apartment and had a little bit of money saved up. So, she made up her mind, she would move to San Antonio and so that she could be near the hospital.

Her plan only took about a week to execute. She really had no ties to Killeen, and, given the situation, her landlord released her from her rental agreement. She had no personal belongings really, except for her clothes, most of which she was able to fit into two suitcases. Luckily, she was able to find a small studio apartment that was relatively cheap. It wasn't the greatest, but it met her needs. It was on the ground floor, so she didn't have to go up the stairs like she had where she had previously lived.

Elizabeth stayed by Gorman's side every moment she could. It was the end of April, and the Texas weather was getting hotter with every passing day. She had been in Texas for several years, but this heat was becoming unbearable. Every morning she walked to the bus stop and rode to the hospital. Then in the evening she would ride the last bus back to her bus stop and walk back to her little apartment. She didn't know how much more she could take.

On May 3rd, Gorman was supposed to have another skin graft surgery. He had a couple already, and everything appeared to be going well. If things continued to go well, he shouldn't need any more grafts. Elizabeth's plan was to be with Gorman during his surgery, but baby Mark had something else in mind.

Early that morning, Elizabeth woke up, and noticed a lot of abdomen pressure. She tried to make it to the restroom, but before she could her water broke. Within about an hour Elizabeth was on the way to a hospital across town. Mark was on his way, and there was no stopping him. Eight hours of labor later Gorman Marcus Cooper was born. He weighed seven-and-half pounds and was nineteen-and-a-half inches long. He had a light shadow of red hair. Elizabeth couldn't wait to show Gorman the baby.

A few days passed before Mark could meet his dad, but Gorman was overjoyed. He never realized how much a parent could love a child. Hopefully, he wouldn't have to be in the hospital much longer. Then they could go home and be a family.

After a few weeks, Gorman was finally moved to a rehab center where they began working with him, helping him learn to use his artificial leg. It may not have been his permanent prosthetic, but it gave him the chance to get used to it. The Doctors said that his stump was healing well, but still had residual inflammation. It was typical for this type of surgery, but the inflammation made the prosthetic leg fit strange, but Gorman gradually became accustomed to it.

It was no longer the pain from the surgery that bothered him, but the dreams and memories that caused him to relive the trauma of his injuries. Gorman would wake up at night feeling the pain in his lower leg, just to be reminded that his leg was no longer there. The mental aspect of healing was the hardest. His doctor required him to go to weekly group therapy sessions with other recent amputees. He was reluctant at first, but it felt good to be around other people who understood what he was going through.

Elizabeth and the baby were rarely in the apartment because she wanted to stay with Gorman as much as possible. She had been living on the little bit of money that she had saved up, and it was running out.

She decided that it was time to return to her hometown in Northern Oklahoma. She had a house that had belonged to her grandparents. It had stood vacant for a while after her grandparents passed away and now it was time for her to make it a home.

When she arrived, she was overjoyed to have a place for her small family. It felt good for her to be back home. She remembered Thanksgiving and Christmas meals in the small kitchen and watching her grandmother bake cookies. Now she wanted to make those memories with her own children.

When Gorman was finally released from the hospital, he settled down in Northern Oklahoma with Elizabeth. There was a lot of work to do to get the house up to livable standards, but Elizabeth was up for it. Gorman also began helping clean up and fix things that needed to be repaired. He enjoyed having something to work on. It kept him busy and gave him something to think about other than the loss of his leg.

Finally, right before Christmas they were able to get married. Elizabeth couldn't believe that it had been ten months since she had been notified of Gorman's injury, four months since they had gotten to Oklahoma, and Mark was going on seven months old. Elizabeth believed that now their life would be perfect.

6

When Mark woke up in Shawn's living room, he realized that he had slept until 2:30 in the afternoon. He wasn't expecting to sleep so long, but at least he could feel at ease about returning home because he knew that Gorman would be out of the house by now. On Christmas Day, Gorman usually left soon after lunch to celebrate the Yule with his friends at O'Donnell's Pub.

The air outside the apartment was crisp as Mark walked out the door. There were icicles hanging from all the eaves and tree limbs. Mark could see his breath. He started the descent down the steps trying not to slip on the ice-covered staircase. He made it to the ground without incident and trudged through the slush towards his snow-covered car.

Mark sighed, realizing that he would have to clear the ice and snow from his windows. Since he had left his jacket at home, he would have to stand in the cold brisk air to scrape away the ice. He started his car so the warmth from the heater could thaw them from the inside, and then went searching through the trunk to find the ice scraper. He hadn't had to use it in a while, so he was unsure where it would be hiding.

After a minute of searching he accepted that it was nowhere to be found. Sadly, he also didn't have a blanket or shirt in the trunk.

He looked around in search of something else he could use. Noticing an old plastic drinking glass half buried in the snow nearby, he knew it would have to do.

Mark took a grease covered towel out of his trunk and wrapped it around his hand. Using the plastic cup, he began scraping the ice from the windows. He got as much of the snow from the window as he could. Even with the towel wrapped around his hand the chill stung his skin. Too bad he had not been thinking clearly when he left the house last night, or he would have grabbed some gloves. They were still at home next to his forlorn jacket.

The bitterly cold air didn't help his mood. If it hadn't been for his father, he would be home right now with his family. The more he scraped the ice, the more benumbed his hand became. He had to take a couple of breaks to sit inside the car to allow his hands to warm a bit before he could continue. Finally, after scraping for about five minutes and utilizing the warming defroster, he could see well enough through the frost covered window to safely drive home.

While he waited to get warm, he surveyed the scene around him. The apartment complex looked like a wintery wonderland. Some of the apartments had Christmas trees in the windows and Christmas lights around their doors. The winter snow made everything look tranquil and happy. There were kids playing in the snow, all bundled up to keep warm. They were building a giant snowman in the middle of the courtyard.

On the other side of the courtyard several children were having a snowball fight. Mark could remember when he was young how he and Ben loved to play in the snow. But Jessica, not so much.

She would rather stay in the house and watch them playing through the window.

Mark's brother Benjamin always moved a little slower than Mark. He was born with a twisted leg and had spent most of his life in a brace. At 17 years of age Ben no longer wore his brace. He had a definite limp when he walked, but it never seemed to bother him.

As Mark watched the kids throwing snowballs, he couldn't help but smile. He recalled how he and Ben would make forts out of anything they could find to protect their individual territories from the other's snowball attacks. One year, Mark gathered up all the bricks that his father had left lying around beside the house. He built a wall that was about three feet tall and four feet wide. Ben was on the other side of the yard hiding behind the woodpile.

They played all day. That afternoon when Gorman made it home from work, he saw that Mark's fort couldn't compare to the size of Ben's. He called Mark from the truck, and together they unloaded several large concrete blocks from the back of the truck. They used these to help reinforce Mark's wall.

Ben and Mark played the rest of the afternoon and on into the evening. They threw snowballs by the light of the streetlamps until their mother finally called them in for supper. It was the greatest day that Mark could remember, and the greatest memory that he had of his father.

Gorman was usually a good guy and seemed like he really wanted to be a good father when he wasn't drinking. When the kids were little, he would get down on the floor and play with them. He taught Mark and Ben about trains and helped them put models together.

As Mark grew older, he realized that Gorman wasn't as loving as he had been. It was harder for him to get down on the floor to play with cars and blocks. Mark loved his father, but he knew that something was wrong. Gorman began to drink more and would stay out later and later. When he would get home, he was usually drunk.

Gorman was receiving disability assistance from the military because of his amputation. He also was struggling with post-traumatic stress disorder. Since he had come to Oklahoma, after being released from the hospital in Texas, Gorman had been unable to find a support group. He had attended faithfully in the hospital, but there were no support groups locally. He never talked to his family about what had happened in Iraq, but still often woke up in the middle of the night screaming. No matter how Elizabeth tried to encourage him to open to her about his dreams, he ended up suffering in silence.

As his emotional pain increased, so did his drinking. He tried to avoid it his pain, both physical and mental, but it didn't seem to work. Even though he was disabled, Gorman did construction work from early in the morning to quitting time. Then all evening he medicated his pain with his favorite liquor.

As Gorman's "illness" grew worse, the anger-followed suit. He would come home drunk and would take his anger out on Elizabeth. He wasn't violent with the kids, if they stayed out of the way. But he was always hateful and angry towards Elizabeth.

Mark hated to see his mother being hurt, and as he got older, he would take up for her. He would get between his father and mother and try to calm the situation. This only exacerbated the problem.

At first Mark's father thought it was funny to see Mark get angry, until an eleven-year-old Mark punched him in the face the first time. This infuriated Gorman, so he made life much worse for Mark. Gorman began antagonizing Mark, attempting to start fights out of spite. He would force Mark to do more chores, push him around, and yell and cuss for no reason. Now every time that Mark thought of his father, he couldn't help but become angry.

When Mark got back to his parents' house that Christmas afternoon, his father's truck was gone. In truth, Gorman had probably been gone for several hours. He was most likely nursing a long neck bottle.

As Mark walked through the door of their house, he could smell the hot apple pie that his mother made for every special occasion. As he sniffed the air, he smiled. Because of his father's drinking problem, the family didn't have many friends. When the kids were growing up, they seldom invited people over to the house, and they never had family over for the holidays.

Mark always wished they had been able to celebrate the holidays with a large, extended family, but since that wasn't possible, Elizabeth tried to make things as special as she could. Mark remembered the times he had spent with his mother baking apple pie. She would separate all the ingredients into separate little bowls. Ben and Jessica would always fight over the chance to add the ingredients and stir them up. Mark, being the oldest, would always get to help mix the ingredients for the crust and then roll it out before they put the pie together. Helping prepare for Christmas was something the kids looked forward to.

The childhood memories made him smile as he slowly walked through the living room. Under their four-foot Christmas tree there were three presents. Two were wrapped in green paper with neat little bows on top. The other one was long and thin with a big bow right in the center. Mark could tell that the bow was homemade. His mom loved to take the time to make things at home. She always bought ribbon and created elaborate bows. She also made wreaths and holiday decorations. She would use magazines and green spray paint to make trees, and newspapers and glue to make papier mâché.

Mark slipped past the doorway into the kitchen. The table was decorated with Grandma's green tablecloth, and the gingerbread men candle sticks that Ben had made in the third grade. Mark could still see the place where Mr. Gingerbread's arm had been glued back on after his father had knocked it off the table.

Ben had been so proud of them and wanted them in the center of the table every year. One year when Mark was younger, Gorman got angry that that ham wasn't on the table to make it easier for him to eat. Out of frustration he made room by pushing everything off the center of the table, including the gravy boat, a pile of napkins, and Mr. and Mrs. Gingerbread. The gravy boat shattered and had to be thrown away. Mrs. Gingerbread was only chipped, but Mr. Gingerbread wasn't as lucky. He had to spend several days with a splint holding his arm in place until they were confident, he wouldn't fall apart again. The procedure was successful, but there was still a seam where he was broken.

Sadly, when Gorman got frustrated about something, he would act out irrationally. He would throw things or say very hurtful things impulsively. He would never think about the consequences of his actions before he did it. He didn't seem to care whom it would hurt.

Mark loved the time that he got to spend with his mom and siblings. They would sit around the table after lunch on Christmas day playing cards and board games. Sometimes late into the night, Mark would be winning at Monopoly or Clue and finally, Elizabeth would have to tell her three teenagers that it was time to go to bed.

It was important to her for the kids to be in bed by the time that Gorman got home. She didn't want them to witness his aggressive behavior when he was "sick," as she called it. She knew that they could hear it from the bedrooms, but at least she was trying to protect them from seeing the abuse.

Mark stood for a moment in the doorway between the living room and the kitchen, watching his mother doing the dishes. She was lost in her own little world, humming "Silent Night" with her back to him. It was probably the only solitude that she had enjoyed all day.

"Mom," he said as he embraced her from behind. He squeezed her in a deep bear hug. He could smell her perfume. It was the same perfume that she had worn since he was a little boy.

As he let go, she turned around. She was happy that he was home. After the fight with his father the night before, Elizabeth worried he wouldn't want to come home. "Mark are you alright?" she asked.

He sheepishly smiled as he ran his fingers through his hair, "Yes, Mom, I'm fine."

"Have a seat and I'll make you a plate." Elizabeth took one of her favorite Christmas dishes out of the cabinet and piled it full. She put freshly cooked ham and dressing. She added mashed potatoes and drowned them with gravy. She topped it off with two of her old-fashioned yeast rolls. Mark thought that her food was some of the best he had ever tasted.

Elizabeth had always wanted to become a chef. She had the ability to do it, but Gorman wouldn't allow it. Prior to having Mark, when she worked as a waitress in the café, she loved to cook. She would switch out with the cooks several nights a week. Even as a teenager she was designing menus and had quite a following in the area where she grew up. Mark always wondered what she could have done if she had had the chance to follow her passion.

Mark dug in as soon as the plate hit the table. He listened as Elizabeth hummed to herself, while she continued washing the dishes. As he ate, he wondered how she could be so cheerful even after the events of the night before.

His mind raced for something to say. He wanted to ask her why she wasn't willing to leave Gorman. He wanted to know why she would stay in a home with a man who treated her the way that Mark's father treated her. Mark wanted to know why Elizabeth was no longer angry at Gorman like he was.

With all these questions, Mark sat silent as he ate. He knew that his questions would go unanswered. She would say the same things she always said. "I still love him…I'm able to forgive him…He isn't a bad person…" Mark knew that she wasn't going to leave. She always said, "I promised, 'Til death do us part.'" Mark was scared that was going to be what happened.

Halfway through her second round of "Jingle Bells" Mark finally interrupted her. "Mom, this is the best Christmas dinner you have made in a long time. Why don't you see if you can find a job somewhere as a chef?"

"Baby, I have you, Ben, and Jess to worry about. I can't work." She continued to do the dishes, unfazed by his question.

"Mom, we're grown. I'm in college, and Ben graduates this year. Jess is in high school now. You need to start making some money of your own so you can set some of it back," Mark said as he swallowed a mouthful of potatoes.

"Mark, stop talking with your mouth full; anyway, I'm too old to go back to cooking. Why would I need to put some money back?"

"Ah… well, when you decide to get out of this house." Mark heard himself saying the words but couldn't believe that he was giving voice to what he had thought for a long time. It was his voice, but it sounded like it was coming from someone else.

For the first time, Elizabeth stopped washing the dishes. She looked down briefly. "Mark, I'm not going anywhere, this is my house. I have lived here forever. Your father loves me. He may not act like it, but he loves me."

"Mom, do you really believe that?" Mark probed.

Elizabeth put the bowl down that she was drying. It took her a few seconds to respond. She slowly turned to look at Mark. "Mark, he does love me, and I love him. I'm not going to run out on this. He has given me three beautiful children. He's getting better. You may not think so, but he is getting better."

"Run out on this? People get divorced all the time for things less important than this. You act like he's done something insignificant like complaining about your food, or he doesn't like his mother-in-law. This isn't about just running out on a relationship for some senseless reason, this is about leaving a man who has abused you for years. He comes in late every night after drinking away your bill money. Then he demands that you get up from bed and cook him fresh food. He knocks you around and treats you like trash…"

"Mark…You aren't going to talk to me like this about your father. He is a good man. He loves all of us, and he is going to change." Elizabeth's voice was stern and insistent.

This almost made Mark choke; he couldn't believe what she was saying. "How, Mom? How is he going to change? You have been with him all these years, and he has not made any effort to change. You really think he will get better?"

Elizabeth turned and sat down beside Mark. He could see the tears welling up in her eyes. "Mom, I'm sorry, I know you want him to change," he continued, "but he has done nothing to make you think that he is going to."

"Baby, your dad loves you. He just doesn't know how to show you." By now her tears were running down her face.

Mark regretted what he had said, but he couldn't see how Elizabeth could still believe that Gorman would ever change. He was hateful and angry, and the more he drank, the more abusive he became. There was no way that he would ever be any different.

Mark finished his lunch as Elizabeth went back to drying the dishes. "Well, Mom I need to run out to my car for a minute."

"Mark, you have got to stop smoking those things. It's going to give you cancer," She scolded, knowing the ulterior motive for running outside.

"OK, Mom," he replied sardonically.

Elizabeth was always nagging Mark about his smoking. She didn't want him to get cancer like she did. About six years earlier Elizabeth had to have a double mastectomy. She found out that she had stage four breast cancer and was given a couple of months to live. However, with the surgery and treatment, she went into remission and it had lasted for about three years. During the time she was receiving treatment for the cancer, she lost a lot of weight and all her beautiful red hair. When her hair grew back it was much duller and she never looked the same.

The doctor told her that the breast cancer had been caused by years of secondhand smoke. Gorman had always smoked more than a pack a day. Sadly, even her cancer didn't provide the impetus to change his habit. He continued to smoke more than he had before.

During her recovery Elizabeth was very sick. She spent hours throwing up after her treatments. She would sleep for days at a time. Mark took over the care of his brother and sister. He would get them ready for school in the morning and help them get to the bus.

Every night he would cook dinner and have the meal on the table when his father got home. During this time Mark and Elizabeth grew much closer. Sadly, since Mark took on the role of the parent, he began having severe anger issues regarding his father.

While he was outside smoking, Mark decided to call Shawn.

"Hello." Shawn answered.

"Hey, Shawn this is Mark, thank you again for letting me spend the night last night," Mark stated gratefully. He was very happy not to have to spend the night in his car.

"It was no problem," Shawn reassured him.

"Well, I wanted to ask you something. I was wondering if I could stay with you for a few nights until I can get a place of my own."

"Uh…well…sure, I guess. We can talk more about it later. I have a dinner planned with my parents tonight, but you're welcome to be there."

"I don't know. I may be at my folk's house a while, but I'll be there later." Mark was unsure how long her would be visiting his parents' house.

"Ok, I usually have to be in bed pretty early because of my work schedule, so try to be there before too late."

"That isn't a problem, I will make sure to be there early, I really appreciate it," Mark replied.

Mark hung up the phone as he threw his cigarette butt on the ground.

7

He went back into the house. Elizabeth was no longer at the sink. He could hear her humming in her bedroom. Instead of bothering her, Mark went down the hall and knocked on his sister, Jessica's, door.

"Come in," she called out. Mark pushed the door open. Jessica was lying on the bed reading. Mark couldn't believe how much she liked to read. He hadn't enjoyed reading in school. He spent most of his time just getting by. It wasn't until he began journalism classes in college that Mark began enjoying school. "Hey, bub, are you back?"

Mark sat down on the bed, "No Jess, I'm not back, I just wanted to come by to see you guys for a bit. Then I have to go."

Hearing Mark's voice, Benjamin came out of his room and into Jessica's room. "Hey Mark, you back?" Ben excitedly questioned.

"No Ben, he isn't back. He's just here for a little bit," Jessica snidely remarked.

"Hey, guys, I've just got to get out of the house for a while. I'm not gone for good, and when I get my own place, you guys can come and stay with me sometime." Mark tried to cheer them up.

"Kid's let's open gifts," Elizabeth called from the front room.

"Let's go open gifts," Mark repeated with mocked enthusiasm.

Ben and Jessica were still into opening Christmas presents, but Mark no longer cared. Since he became old enough to work, he had been working. Whether it was mowing lawns or working at a gas station, Mark had been making enough money to pay for all his own things for years.

When he was 13, his mother gave him a jacket. It was black leather with a soft interior. He was so excited to wear it to school the first day after Christmas break, to ensure he didn't forget it he laid it out the night before school resumed.

Everything was great until he got to the school bus, and one of the rich kids began teasing him. Mark tried to stay clear of the snob and his friends. They thought they were better than everyone else. When Mark got off the bus the rich jerk began taunting him and telling him that the jacket used to belong to him, but his mother had given it to Goodwill.

Mark tried to ignore him, until gym class, when the snob grabbed the jacket and turned it inside out. He pointed at the tag where someone had used a black marker to mark out the previous owner's name. He said, "See I told you this was mine." All the other students began laughing and calling Mark 'Goodwill'.

Mark never asked his mother about the jacket because he knew that it would hurt her to know how the other kids treated him, but he also never wore the jacket again. That summer Mark began going through the neighborhood with the lawnmower earning money for the things he wanted. His parents would take care of his basic needs, but he would buy his own clothes and school supplies. He wasn't going to be made fun of again if he could help it.

Mark pushed the memories out of his mind, Ben and Jessica were already on their way to the living room to open their presents. Ben beat Mark and Jessica to the living room. Their mother was already sitting close to the tree. "Mark, do you want to hand out the gifts?" she asked.

"No, let Ben do it," he remarked.

"Alright, Ben, you pass out the presents," Elizabeth said.

"Ho, Ho, Ho…let's see who has been naughty and who has been nice," Ben said with his best Santa impersonation.

It was strange to see a tall lanky Santa walking around with a limp, but Mark couldn't help but smile at his imitation. "Ho, Ho, Ho…this one says, Jessica. And this one says, Mark." Losing his Santa impression in excitement Ben yelled, "Ewwww! Look, this long one says 'Ben'. I wonder what's in it."

Jessica opened her gift to find a very nice pair of antique earrings that had belonged to Elizabeth's mom. She had kept them in a safe place since she was a teenager. Jessica was so proud of them.

She was a girly-girl and loved getting all dolled up. She would spend several hours every morning getting ready. She was prim and proper, and Elizabeth knew that she would love her grandmother's earrings.

Ben opened his gift and found his father's old hunting rifle. It had been stuffed in the back of the bedroom closet. Gorman hadn't used it in years and could care less what happened to it. On the other hand, Ben was into hunting and fishing and would go with his friends anytime that he could. This year he would be able to go hunting with his own rifle.

It was now time for Mark to open his gift. He didn't want to hurt his mother's feelings, but he didn't want to open his gift. It was a small package, covered in old wrapping paper. Elizabeth had to be as frugal as possible. Every year she would take the wrapping paper that wasn't torn up and save it for the next year. Mark believed that she was still using the same paper she used when he was a little boy.

"Mark, aren't you going to open up your gift?" Elizabeth prompted.

"Can I open it?" Ben begged.

"No, I'm opening it." Mark took his pocketknife out of his pocket and slit the tape that held the paper closed. He then carefully unfolded the wrapping paper to reveal the white tissue paper that incased his gift. Handing the wrapping to his mother he teased in a sarcastic baby voice, "Here is your precious wrapping paper." She smiled and took the paper. Flattening it out with her hand, she began pressing out the creases.

Slowly Mark turned over his little envelope of tissue paper. He removed the paper to expose a military issue wallet. It was a green canvas bi fold with a Velcro clasp. The word "Cooper" was stamped on one side. It was considerably worn and had dirt and stains on it. Mark was puzzled by the gift.

"Mom, I don't really know why you gave me this," Mark questioned, "I'm not really into old military stuff. I have a really nice wallet."

"I know, but there is something in it that you're going to want."

"I can't take your money," Mark protested.

"It's not money, just open it," She replied.

Slowly Mark began opening the wallet, when suddenly they heard, "Ho, Ho, Ho…Merry Christmas." Gorman burst through the door. He reeked of liquor and stumbled around carrying a large trash bag. "Merry Christmas, I've got presents."

Gorman threw the bag off his shoulder onto the living room table. Its momentum almost threw him over.

Excitedly, Ben tore the paper back, "What is it?"

Inside the bag was a really dirty box of old pictures and letters, some old clothes, and a small stuffed bear that was covered in dust.

"Well, I knew your mom was giving you a bunch of old junk, so I decided to get out one of the bags from the shed, thought you guys might want it." Looking at Mark, "Hey what are you doing here? I thought I sent you crying with your tail between your legs last night."

"Shut, up. I'm not here for you," Mark replied.

"I know you ain't here for me, you're here to spend time hanging on your momma's skirt tail while I ain't home. You ain't man enough to come while I'm here."

"Mom, I've got to get some stuff and go." Mark stood up and tried to squeeze between his bother and the table.

"There you go running away again, you stupid chicken. You run away from everything," Gorman taunted.

"Gorman, stop! You're ruining Christmas," Elizabeth cried out as she tried to push him back.

"I'm not ruining Christmas; he's the one running out of here."

Mark could hold it in no longer. "Really, you really want to do this? You come into this house drunk. You treat us all like this, throwing a trash bag full of junk in our laps expecting us to bow at your feet in appreciation. You're ruining Christmas. You always ruin everything. There isn't a holiday or event that you don't ruin. We try to do things without you so that we can enjoy our lives without your drunken games and abuse."

"If it wasn't for me, you wouldn't even have Christmas." Gorman started toward Mark but was held back by Elizabeth.

"Gorman, Mark, please, both of you, stop. Mark, go get your things." Turning to Gorman, "Gorman, calm down, come in the kitchen with me and I will make you a plate."

Gorman victoriously plopped down in his recliner and grabbed the remote off the table. He felt like he had won the argument and the mention of food took his mind off Mark.

Mark took his father's retreat as an opportunity to get some things from his room. As he walked down the hallway, he noticed the family picture that had been knocked down the night before was now hanging back up on the wall.

Mark came back down the hallway carrying his duffle bag and his jacket. "Mom, I'm sorry."

"Don't be," She replied as she handed Mark the wallet. Taking out some folded-up money from her apron she said, "Take your gift and this money. It's just a little, but it's all I can do."

"I can't…" Mark tried to rebut.

"You will, now go."

Mark slipped the money into the wallet and headed out the door. The snow was starting to fall again. Mark didn't know what to do. His mother was so absorbed in taking care of his father, and he couldn't understand why she continued to go through this every week.

He got into the car, throwing the old wallet and his bag in the passenger seat, and sped away.

8

ark woke up when the alarm on his watch went off at 6:30am. Shawn had been gone for an hour. He didn't wake Mark when he left. Mark was glad to be away from the dissonance at home. He was so tired of the fighting and the complaining. He could finally sleep through the night.

It was the third morning Mark had awakened on the couch at Shawn's place. The serenity of the silent apartment was refreshing. Most importantly, Mark didn't have to hear his father's yelling. He couldn't understand why Elizabeth would stay. Why would anyone continue to endure the abuse that she suffered?

No matter what happened, Elizabeth insisted that it was God's providence. She would always say that God would take care of it, and that one-day Gorman would work through his problems. Mark didn't know anything about God, but he did know that if God was really going to take care of it, then he was sure doing a lousy job.

As Mark left the apartment on his way to the office, he noticed a cool breeze blowing in. The snow was getting a little heavier but had still not filled in the footprints from all the people who had spent the last few days playing in the snow. The yards were littered with snowmen. Some of them resembled men, some looked like women, and a couple even looked like animals.

What had looked like a winter wonderland on Christmas, two days before, now looked like a muddy mess. Mark was surprised to see some children outside playing before 8:00 am. Most had taken their freezing toes and near frost-bitten fingers inside the night before and hadn't made it back outside.

Many of their snowmen were now mangled and leaning. It was obvious that some were being used as targets for rocks or snowball fights. They were left, abandoned, with only their ruins remaining.

It had warmed a little on Christmas day and caused the ice to begin melting. Then during the night, it froze again, leaving the roads icy. Mark had to drive very slowly. Luckily by this time of the morning, the temperature was already above freezing, so the ice had begun to thaw again.

Even though it had been two days, Mark continued to obsess over the Christmas Day conflict. As he drove past the dilapidated snowmen and the sludgy snow, he thought of his father's explosion. Something that was so beautiful was now chaos. Just like Elizabeth's attempt to have a beautiful Christmas was ruined by conflict.

No matter how much she tried, every Christmas ended the same way. Elizabeth would make a beautiful dinner and would prepare the best gifts she could. They would have a wonderful time until Gorman returned from the bar, and then all hell would break loose. And the sad part of it was that there was nothing that Mark could do about it.

When Mark pulled up to the newspaper office where he worked, there were only a few cars there. Most people had taken off a couple of days after Christmas to spend time with their families.

Mark didn't really care. He had spent all the time fighting with Gorman that he wanted to. He was ready to get back into the grind of everyday life. School would start in a couple of weeks, and he was looking forward to finishing up his degree in journalism. The only other car that he recognized was that of his boss, Robert Vance.

His work at the newspaper was Mark's dream job. He loved writing and research, especially when it came to writing articles and doing interviews. Since the day he had won first prize in the area-wide high school journalism contest, he couldn't dream of anything else.

Mark loved the college life. He enjoyed the time in class and worked very hard to maintain the best grades he could. Grades were very important to him. He felt that the only way he would ever make it anywhere in life was to get an education.

His father had very little education. His reading and writing skills were very weak. Mark didn't want to end up that way. Mark believed the better he did in school, the more he would be set apart from his dad.

Gorman didn't like it that his son was going to college, and he made that fact known. He called Mark a faggot and told him that real men found jobs and used their hands to make a living. He believed that real men were hard-working, and that journalism wasn't a job for a real man.

The more his father taunted him, the more he wanted to get out of the house; however, he couldn't get enough financial aid to be able to afford to live in the school dorms. Several nights a week Mark would sleep over at friends' houses or on the floor in the dorm rooms of people he knew. This usually followed a night of carousing.

When Mark started college, he wanted so badly to get out of his parents' house that he did everything he could to avoid being around his father. The easiest way to do that was go to every party he could. He would stay out late on the weekends and end up sleeping on the floor of his friends' apartments. The longer he was in school, the more parties he would find. Sometimes three or four times a week he would crash at someone else's house.

Mark didn't drink as much as everyone else. He rarely found himself hugging the porcelain throne. Nevertheless, his goal was to drink enough to forget all the problems at home.

Mark's drinking was his means to escape from the problems in his life. If he wasn't at a club, he would have a good time drinking and watching movies or playing poker at a friend's house. Mark was the type of person that could make himself at home anywhere. He didn't mind going in and kicking off his shoes in anyone's house.

Meanwhile, all of Mark's cohorts loved partying and barhopping except Shawn. He didn't act like everyone else. Shawn seemed to be happy even without all the partying. Mark didn't know what Shawn did for fun, but apparently drinking wasn't a part of it.

Fortunately, Mark never allowed his extracurricular partying to affect his grades. Even with little sleep he would strive for perfection and maintained a high-grade point average. His efforts and good grades eventually landed him a paid internship at the Chronicle.

A standard internship offered experience on a voluntary basis, but every year, because the college Mark attended was Mr. Vance's alma mater, the Chronicle gave an individual paid internship to a high-ranking student from Northeastern University. Mark didn't even apply for the position since it usually went to a graduate student, but one of his professors had contacted Vance directly. Mark couldn't believe it when he was called to interview for the internship; it was a dream come true.

For now, Mark assisted with stories. He would work with the reporters, proofread articles, and write small columns when the paper needed to fill space. He also helped obtain information through research, investigation, and interviews. The information that he collected would then be passed to a reporter who would put the story together. Mark may not have been getting the credit for the articles, but he knew that his research was vital, and he appreciated the experience.

By that evening, in the Cooper household, Elizabeth was busy getting everything cleaned up before she began working on supper. She was so excited that she had been able to spend time with all her children on Christmas day.

Every day except holidays, Mark was usually working, Ben played video games, and Jessica spent most of her time with her friends. The house always felt empty, and Elizabeth felt very lonely. To fend off her loneliness, she would spend her days cooking and cleaning. She would wash the dishes and sweep and mop the floors.

She would vacuum the carpets and clean the bathrooms. When the house was clean, she would sit down in the living room to read the Bible and pray.

Elizabeth seemed to really trust in the God they spoke about at church, and this annoyed Mark. He couldn't understand why she would put her faith in someone or something that never seemed to do anything for her.

She was constantly praying that God would bring about a change in their lives. She begged God to help Gorman and to defeat his addiction, but Gorman was still going out every night wasting their last bit of money on alcohol.

Mark couldn't understand a God who, if he really existed, would let this abuse continue. His mom always talked about the love of God, and how God was going to do a miracle. But no miracle had ever happened.

What made matters worse was that Elizabeth believed that God was trying to use Gorman's 'illness' to teach her patience and endurance. She said that when it was God's time to deliver them, He would. How could a loving God really use the pain that she was going through to teach her patience?

On this day, Elizabeth was sitting on the couch reading the Bible as she did every afternoon. The sun had already begun to sink lower behind the horizon, and Elizabeth was about to get up and begin cooking supper. She knew that it would be hours before Gorman would make his way home, but if his food wasn't ready for him when he got there, she would be in trouble.

As she usually was on most afternoons, today Jessica was out of the house. She was down the street at her friend's house, and tonight she was planning to spend the night. Ben was in his bedroom getting ready for a hunting trip, on which he could take his new gun.

The state of Oklahoma set aside time each year during the Christmas holidays for a youth deer hunt. Every year Ben would go with his friends and their fathers, but he would have to borrow a firearm from someone else, and this always left him feeling out of place. Typically, he and a friend would have to take turns using the gun while the other waited and watched.

But this year was going to be different. He now had his own rifle and would no longer feel like a charity case. He was so excited to have his own gun. Since he opened it, he continually sat in his room playing with it. He had spent time taking the rifle apart and cleaning it. He made sure that he could load it and unload it. He even tried to sleep with it. He wanted to make sure that he knew everything about this gun because he didn't want to go hunting and look foolish because he didn't know what he was doing.

Elizabeth was dozing off on the couch. She would sometimes catch herself napping instead of praying. Suddenly, she was woken by a sound that made her heart stop. She hesitated, unsure if she was truly awake or still asleep. Slowly she got up off the couch.

"Ben, what was that noise?" Elizabeth walked towards the kitchen door. There was no answer.

"Ben, what was that?" Again, there was no answer. Elizabeth could feel her heart beating in her ears. The sound was deafening.

Even though her heart was racing, she held her breath so that she could listen for Ben.

She hurried down the hallway, "Benjamin Franklin Cooper, don't scare me like this, what was that noise?"

She burst through the door, but Ben wasn't there. "Ben?" She came around the end of the bed. "Oh, my God!" she exclaimed.

She found Ben lying on the floor behind his bed; the rifle was lying right in front of him. There was a wound on the left side of his chest. "Baby, no!" she felt like everything she was doing was in slow motion. She grabbed him and pulled him to a seated position.

Ben opened his eyes just a little. He whispered, "Mom, I'm sorry."

"Ben, don't talk, you're going to be OK, just stay awake."

Elizabeth could hear his breathing was troubled by the slight gurgling he made every time he tried to expand his lungs. In a daze of desperation, she hoisted him up in her arms and ran down the hallway. It took every ounce of strength she could muster to carry him through the house.

She made it to the yard. The crimson color of his blood was staining her apron. She collapsed in the snow. She tried to hold pressure on his chest, not realizing that most of the blood was flooding out his back.

"Please, someone help me?" She cried out as she tried to save his life. His blood stained the snow causing a pool as red as the deepest rose. Ben still struggled to breathe. "Come on baby, you're going to be OK." Again, she cried out, "Please someone help me?"

9

Mark made it to the hospital just in time to see a helicopter taking off. As he walked into the emergency room, he found his mother sitting in the waiting area. "What's happening?" he asked her.

"They just flew him out to the Children's Hospital in Oklahoma City," she responded despondently.

"Why are we still standing here? Let's go!" Mark couldn't believe that Elizabeth was still sitting in the waiting area.

Elizabeth looked up; her face was stained with tears. "We're going to head down to Oklahoma City, but the doctor asked us to wait and talk to him first. He said that there were some things he needed tell us before we left."

"What? This is an emergency; we need to get going," Mark insisted. Her hesitation frustrated him.

"Mark, they are going to be taking him directly into surgery there, and the doctor had no idea how long that was going to take. We will probably be there before he gets out. We need to talk to the doctor here." Her pleading eyes begged him to calm down.

Mark relented and sat down with Elizabeth. It felt like hours passed while they waited for the doctor to come out to talk to them. Finally, the doctor who was on call in the emergency room came out and approached them, accompanied by a police officer and child protective services caseworker. Elizabeth and Mark rose to meet him.

"Mrs. Cooper, my name is Dr. Lambert; this is Officer Walker and Agent Jennings. We took your son immediately into surgery where we were able to get him stable enough to air evac him to the hospital in Oklahoma City. It was the closest hospital that might be able to save his life. I will tell you we have no way of knowing if he will survive. The next several hours are the most crucial." The doctor's words were cold and hollow.

"Did it damage his heart?" Elizabeth asked.

"Actually, the bullet barely missed his heart," He explained, "It damaged the pericardium that surrounds the heart. The problem is more with his lung. His left lung was punctured and deflated. The bullet broke his ribs and grazed his vertebrae. We're still unsure if there was any damage to his spinal cord. Normally, when a person has a deflated lung, he or she is still getting adequate oxygen from the other lung. In your son's case, he aspirated the blood that came up through his trachea. There is a possibility that he was deprived of oxygen due to choking on blood. We're unsure how long he may have been without oxygen. The doctors at the children's hospital will do everything they can, but he may have some brain damage."

"When will we know?" Mark asked.

"We aren't sure; it could be days or weeks. Also, if he has damage to his spinal cord, he may be paralyzed. That is really all that I know right now. I really hate to do this, but in these cases the police have a few questions for you." Doctor Lambert stepped out of the way so that Officer Walker could speak to Elizabeth.

"Mrs. Cooper, I'm very sorry to tie you up, I know that you want to get down to Oklahoma City to see how your son is doing, but before you go, I really need to ask a few questions in regards to our investigation." Officer Walker motioned for Elizabeth and Mark to sit down.

Elizabeth complied, but Mark stated emphatically, "I don't want to sit down. What investigation?" he inquired impatiently.

Officer Walker peered through his black-framed glasses. "And you are?" he said to Mark. Walker was in the typical blue police uniform. He was probably in his mid-thirties and had the typical police officer look about him. He was short and kind of stocky. He wasn't overweight but looked like he knew his way around the gym. His graying hair and mustache made him look older than he was.

Mark noticed that Walker was hanging on every word that the doctor had said, and it concerned him that the officer referred to this as an investigation. "I'm Mark Cooper, Ben's older brother."

"Well, Mr. Cooper, we currently have units at your mother's house. Anytime there is a shooting, we must investigate," he responded. Turning back to Elizabeth, he asked, "How long has your son been depressed?"

Elizabeth stared at the floor trying to process the information, "So you guys think that my Benjamin was trying to kill himself?"

"We have to rule out every possibility, ma'am," Walker answered.

"What? No, Ben wasn't depressed," Mark snapped back, "He wasn't trying to kill himself. He loved life, and he would have no reason to do that."

"I'm sorry to imply that, but what the officers are finding in your house seems to indicate that Benjamin may have intentionally shot himself," Officer Walker said matter-of-factly as he sat down next to Elizabeth.

"What are you talking about? He was getting ready for a hunting trip tomorrow. The gun must have gone off accidentally. He wasn't trying to shoot himself." Mark could feel his face getting hot; he knew that it was getting red. "I can't believe that you're trying to make my mother believe that her son would try to kill himself…"

"Mark…" Elizabeth tried to cut him off.

"No, Mom, I'm not going to let them make you feel…"

"Mark, stop," she again tried to intervene.

"This is a bunch of…"

"Gorman Marcus Cooper, stop acting like this!" Elizabeth blurted out in anguish. She stood toe to toe with her son.

Mark hadn't seen her get this upset with him in a long time. He couldn't understand why she was so upset. "Why are you acting this way?" He questioned her.

"Mark, I'm tired. I'm tired of you acting like this, becoming so angry and violent about everything." She sat back down in the chair, exhausted. "These officers are trying to help us. We don't know what was going on in Ben's room. We don't know what was in his head and what he was thinking. We don't know why this happened.

But I know that things are going to be alright. That Benjamin will be alright. That is all I can hold on to right now."

Mark could see the tears welling up in his mother's eyes. He knelt in front of her, and looked deeply into her eyes, "I'm not trying to upset you, but I don't want anyone to suggest that Ben was trying to kill himself."

Elizabeth reached up and put her hand on Mark's cheek, "Baby, God's going to take care of everything. We don't always understand why things like this happen, but God will take care of us."

Again, Mark felt the fire blazing in his eyes. He stood up pushing her away. "God…God will take care of everything! You need to quit thinking about God. What has he done for us? If God really cared, why did this happen to Ben? If He's going to take care of us, why is dad still drinking every night? Look, he didn't even care enough to show up here tonight. He's probably at the bar spending time with his real family. If God even exists, why are we left suffering? What did we do to deserve the pain he is causing us?"

Elizabeth couldn't believe what she was hearing. Instinctually, she stood up and slapped Mark across the face. "Listen to me Gorman Marcus Cooper, I don't know what has made you this angry at God, but this isn't His fault. I raised you better than this. Your brother is in surgery right now in Oklahoma City, but you would rather stand here and argue with me instead of letting this officer do his job so I can get down there and see how Ben is doing. You're reminding me more and more of your father."

Mark couldn't believe what she just did; moreover, he couldn't believe what she said. He was nothing like his father.

Gorman was an alcoholic who spent all his family's money on his own self-medication. Mark hadn't been to a party in months, and he only went to them as an excuse to keep from going home. He couldn't believe that his mother would compare him to Gorman. They were nothing alike.

Mark felt the tears welling up in his eyes. He knew that he had to get out of that hospital. He felt like everyone was staring at him, and he felt like his eyes were on fire. He turned to run and stumbled over the chair next to where his mother had been sitting.

He pushed the toppled chair out of the way and proceeded to the door. There was an elderly couple trying to hobble through the doorway. Frustrated, Mark pushed his way past them and rushed towards his car. In his hurry he ignored the snow that had again begun to fall. The day was warmer than the previous one, and so the ice had been melting. But after the sun went down, the temperature had dropped below freezing again, and the roads were becoming icy.

Mark didn't know where he was going when he peeled out of the emergency driveway at the hospital. He could barely see through his tears and the large flakes of snow. He found himself racing down Highway 62. All he could think about was his mother's words. The more he thought about what she had accused him of, the angrier he became.

There were only a handful of cars on the highway, and Mark flew passed them like they were sitting still. He didn't realize how fast he was going until he suddenly felt his car hit a large patch of black ice. His Mustang slid across the road and into the ditch. His car came to a stop, stuck in the snowdrifts that filled the ditch.

He tried to start his car, but the engine wouldn't turn over. He tried it again and again with no luck. In anger he punched his steering wheel. It was unbelievable; his brother was lying in a hospital in Oklahoma City. Now Mark was now stuck in the snow along the highway

Suddenly, he felt a shudder go over him as he noticed, out of the corner of his eye, someone walk past the passenger side window. He wondered, *Who on Earth would be walking out in the snow this time of the night?*

Mark struggled to open his car door. He wanted to find out who was walking past his car in the middle of the snow. It took a couple of attempts to clear the snow away from the door so he could get it opened. Finally, he escaped from his vehicle, and he trudged through the snow in pursuit of the person that he had seen.

"Hey, are you OK?" Mark called to the person who was walking a few yards in front of him. The shadowy figure didn't respond. Mark struggled through the snow to catch up, "Hey, are you ok? Were you in an accident? Do you need help?" Finally, he caught up to the man and grabbed him by the shoulder, spinning him around, "Hey, are you alright?"

The man pushed him away causing Mark to lose his footing, landing on his backside. As he lifted his hand, he noticed blood on the snow. Thinking he might have been injured when the car landed in the ditch, Mark quickly wiped the blood on his pants so he could examine his hand. He discovered that his hand wasn't bleeding. Instead, the blood must have come from the young man that stood before him.

This was the first time that Mark noticed that the kid was bare foot; all he had on was a pair of dingy socks. Then Mark noticed that the young man was wearing on old pair of red and blue flannel plaid pajama pants. He was also wearing a t-shirt and had blood seeping from just below his shoulder near his heart and running down to his stomach.

Mark didn't know if the guy had been in a wreck or had some type of accident. The snowflakes were huge and falling rapidly, obscuring the young man's face. As Mark struggled to see through the thick flurry, he was suddenly terrified. He knew this guy; it was Benjamin.

10

As Ben turned to go; Mark got to his feet. "Benjamin, what are you doing? How did you get out here?" Ben ignored his questioning and continued to walk away.

"Benjamin, what are you doing? You need to get back to the hospital, they can help you." Mark ran to catch up. He could no longer feel the cold night air, and he hadn't realized that it had stopped snowing.

Mark reached out to grab his brother's shoulder again, "Ben, please, we need to go back to the hospital where they can help you."

Yet again, he eluded Mark's grasp, Mark could feel the tears welling up in his eyes again. He wanted to do whatever he could to get Ben the help he needed. He had always wanted to protect his brother and sister.

When Ben was being bullied at school, Mark had always been there. He was there when Jessica was trying to get on to the volleyball team and was being made fun of. He would do anything it took to protect them.

This situation was a matter life and death. If he didn't get Ben back to the hospital, he would die. He made one last-ditch effort, "Ben stop walking and let me help you. What can I do?"

Ben stopped and slowly turned around, "If you want to help me, love Dad."

Mark stopped; he was speechless. Suddenly, Mark heard a voice from behind him. "Hey Kid, are you OK?" Startled, he turned to see a highway patrol trooper pulled up behind his car with its overheads on.

Mark turned again to Ben, but there was no one there. "Benjamin, where are you?" Mark began frantically looking for his brother. "Benjamin, where are you?" he called out hysterically.

"Hey kid, you alright?" the trooper called out again as he started walking towards Mark.

"My brother was just here, I don't know where he went," Mark said as he pointed into the night.

"Son, there was no one else out here. Was your brother in the car with you?"

Mark stopped for a minute before he spoke. He was confused, not quite able to wrap his mind around what had just happened. "No, he was in the hospital in Oklahoma City, but I saw him right here. You didn't see him?"

"No, son, but you do appear to have a pretty good bump on your head," the trooper replied.

Mark felt of his forehead, where he found a large knot. He hadn't realized that he had hit his head when the Mustang went off the road. He began walking back to his vehicle with the state trooper.

Mark couldn't help but look again over his shoulder. Benjamin was just there; where did he go? Shaking his head, Mark turned back toward his vehicle.

"Son come sit in my cruiser for a few minutes while I get some help out here," The trooper said as he ushered Mark to the back door of the black and white patrol car.

The only other time Mark had been in the back of a police cruiser was when he was younger, and he had driven some friends to the lake. They brought some beers. It was supposed to be Mark's first time to drink, but before he got the chance, a police car pulled up behind them with its lights flashing. The officer confiscated the beer and took the three teens home. Luckily, no one was charged with anything.

Gorman was very angry, nonetheless. Not that Mark was in possession of beer, but that he had to leave the car at the lake overnight. The next day Gorman and Elizabeth took him back out to the lake to retrieve the vehicle. At Gorman's request Elizabeth left the two men with the car and went home. Before Mark could say or do anything, Gorman plopped himself down in the driver's seat, started the engine and drove off, leaving Mark to walk all the way home.

At least this time Mark wasn't sitting in the cruiser because he had committed a crime. The state trooper sat down in the driver's seat, and Mark half-listened as he called for an ambulance and a tow truck. Mark was positive that Benjamin had just been standing there. Quickly he looked at his hand and then his jeans for any trace of blood. There was nothing.

It had to have been the bump on his head. There was no other reason why he would have seen or heard what he had just seen and heard. He sat in silence with his eyes closed listening to the hum of the cruiser's engine and the occasional crackle of the car's two-way radio.

After a few minutes resting in the patrol car, he could see the red flashing lights of the responding ambulance and the yellow beacons of the tow truck. Fortunately, it took only a few minutes for the tow truck to pull his car out of the snow, positioning it back on the shoulder of the highway. To the chagrin of the driver, Mark requested that he not tow it, instead he would pay cash for him to change the tire.

He sat in the back of the ambulance and watched as the tow truck driver replaced the flat tire with the donut spare that was in the compartment under the trunk. While it was already costing him a lot extra money because of the expense of calling a tow truck in the inclement weather, he didn't want the added expense of having to reclaim it from the impound lot.

He also refused to be transported in the ambulance but did allow the EMT's to check him out and make sure that he was fit to drive home. He was no longer seeing anything out of the ordinary, and other than having a severe headache, he seemed fine.

11

Mark awoke to the smell of bacon frying on the stove, and the sound of a coffee machine percolating. Last night, after his ordeal in the snow, Mark thought it was in his best interest to drive back to the apartment. He called the house to see if his mother had left town, but she must have left the hospital right after he did. Mark would have to get his tire fixed before he could head back out.

Mark still didn't know what to think about what had happened last night. He didn't know if he was hallucinating or if Ben had been there. It seemed so real, but it made no sense. How could Benjamin have been in the middle of the snow-covered ditch along the highway, when he had just been air evacuated to Oklahoma City?

At the time, Mark felt like it made sense, but now he could see no logic to it. Ben's final statement made it especially confusing. *Love Dad.* Why would Ben have told him to do that? Shaking his head Mark tried to clear his confused mind.

Mark sat up on the couch, stretching so hard that his back popped a couple of times. At the noise Shawn came around the corner from the kitchen.

"You're awake. Do you want some breakfast?" Shawn asked.

Yawning, Mark nodded.

From the kitchen, Shawn called out, "Do you want some eggs?"

Mark pulled his pants on. "Yes, scrambled please." Mark was very glad to be able to stay somewhere other than at his own house. The apartment was a great place to crash for a while until he could find a more permanent residence.

After making a quick stop in the restroom, Mark went into the kitchen to see what he could do to help. Everything was finished. The bacon was resting on a paper towel stretched across a plate. Two coffee cups were set out beside the coffee pot, which was waiting to be poured. Shawn and Mark filled their plates and sat down to eat.

Noticing Mark rubbing his neck, Shawn asked, "Is that couch comfortable enough for you?"

Mark had just taken a large bite of eggs, so he raised his eyebrows and smirked. He felt bad telling Shawn that the couch wasn't comfortable at all. *Beggars can't be choosers*, Mark's mom always said, and he didn't want to wear out his welcome.

"Well, I don't have to lie down on it much, so I really don't know," Shawn went on, "but I do have a second bedroom. It only has a bed and a dresser, but I would be glad to let you stay in there. All I ask is that you help with the bills and clean up after yourself. I would also appreciate it if you helped with the groceries."

Mark had a good job at the paper and could afford to pay his own bills. While living with his parents, Mark had helped with the groceries and given money to his mom when there was a need. He also had some money saved up. Paying half of the bills and helping with the groceries wouldn't be a problem.

"Yes," Mark replied, "I would really appreciate that." No longer did he have to bounce around from one friend's house to another trying to avoid dealing with the problems at home. He would have a permanent place to stay. But he would have to break the news to his mom.

Their conversation was soon interrupted when the house phone rang, and Shawn went to answer it. It was Elizabeth. After Mark was unable to continue his trip to Oklahoma City, he called the house and gave Jessica the contact number for the apartment. Jessica promised to give it to their mother when she called. She must have been good on her word.

Elizabeth was calling with an update on Benjamin. Mark was a little nervous when he picked up the phone; he didn't know what to expect. For all he knew, Ben may have passed away.

"Hey, Mom is everything alright?" Mark didn't know if he wanted to hear what she had to say.

"Right now, we still don't know if he's going to pull through." She tried to appear hopeful. "They were unsure how much damage was done to his spinal cord and had to put pins in his back. As Doctor Lambert told us, the biggest concern was the aspirated blood. He is breathing on his own, but it's still labored because of the collapsed lung. They still have him knocked out, and until they try wake him up, we won't know what type of brain damage, if any, might have been done. He does have brain activity that appears to be normal, but his spinal cord is swollen due to the irritation from the bullet. All we can do right now is pray."

"Wow, do they think he is going to be alright?" Mark didn't mean for his responds to sound heartless.

"Baby, they didn't say, but I believe that everything is going to be OK. God is going to work this out. We have just got to wait and see," Elizabeth responded.

"OK, when I get the tire changed, I will be headed down there." Mark felt bad that he hadn't made it to the hospital yet. He really wanted to make sure that Ben was going to be alright. Since Mark felt like the protector, he believed he needed to be there personally. He felt helpless being so far away from Ben right now. He couldn't help but feel responsible for Ben, and even a little guilty. Maybe if he had been home, it wouldn't have happened.

"Mark don't head to Oklahoma City yet. Benjamin is in good hands, and I'm here with him. Can you go stay at the house for a couple of days? Your dad is still working, and Jessica is staying by herself. I really don't care about her being there during the day by herself, but at night someone needs to be there. I asked your dad to get there early, but I never know when he will be home. Jess is going to be cooking and trying to take care of the house. I'm really not sure how long I will be here." Mark could hear the pleading in her voice, and he didn't want to let her down; however, he didn't want to be stuck in the house with Gorman. Who knows what could happen?

"Mom, I have something to tell you. I don't intend to go live at the house anymore. Shawn has offered me a room in the apartment, and I plan on taking it." Mark could hear the long sigh on the other end of the phone.

"Mark, I'm really proud of what you're doing, and I knew this day would be coming. Could you help me then, by going over to the house and spending a little bit of time with Jessica, at least until your dad gets home in the evenings? Ben is in the intensive care unit; they will only let a couple of people in at once. Last night I actually slept in the waiting room. Please help me with Jess. She really needs you right now."

Mark wanted so badly to tell her that he couldn't help, but before he could think he heard someone say, "Sure, I'll take care of it." Pausing for a moment he realized that it was his voice. He had just agreed to spend time at his parents' house.

"Thank you, I love you and will call you back later," Elizabeth replied.

Upon Mark's farewell she hung up the phone. Mark could hear the exhaustion in her voice. He knew she was tired, which caused him to worry more about her health. She hadn't been the same since the chemotherapy.

Mark didn't want his mother to overdo herself. Even though the cancer was gone, Elizabeth wasn't as strong as she once was. She got tired very quickly and didn't seem to eat much. She never regained the weight that she had lost when she was in treatment.

After the phone call, Mark finished his breakfast and then got ready for work. He didn't have a problem spending the time with Jessica; he just really didn't want to see his father.

When he came down from the apartment, he made a lengthy inspection of his vehicle. There was no noticeable damage except for the few scrapes around his bumper. There was also a little paint

missing near the previously broken headlight, from his last fender
bender. Other than that, nothing else was damaged.

12

On the way to work, Mark felt like things were calming down. The roads were slushy from the melting ice and snow, but they weren't slick, so driving wasn't so risky. The donut that was presently replacing his passenger front tire made it feel like his car was driving with a limp.

Mark pulled into the parking lot of the Chronicle. He could tell that life was getting back to normal because the parking lot was full, and everyone was returning from their holiday rest.

Mark was very glad that people were back in their regular places. He had spent yesterday rummaging through boxes, filing papers, and doing other busy work trying to make the day go by quicker. The editor, Robert Vance, had stayed in his office most of the day, so Mark had worked alone.

Today, his life could again return to normal. Every desk was full when Mark entered the building. The newspaper was a small area-wide paper and had a small staff consisting of a few writers and various other staff members, including reporters, photographers, and copyeditors. Some people were taking down the decorations that had been on their desks and cubicles for the past few weeks. Others were busy diving into the mounds of work that had accumulated over the holidays.

¶Mark settled into his chair and pulled his keyboard towards him. He hadn't decorated his cubicle like everyone else had, for obvious reasons. But before he could even check his email, he heard Vance calling everyone in for morning staff meeting.

The conference room was buzzing with excitement when Mark came through the door. Most of the staff apparently assumed that an announcement was forthcoming. Everyone knew that the lead journalist, Mike Jamison, had been asked to join the staff of the Fort Worth Star Telegram, and if he took the position, there would be a news writing position open. No one was certain as to whether Mike had decided yet.

It didn't matter much to Mark. He was a paid intern, and interns don't usually get full-time journalist positions. These positions go to people who have put in their time at the paper, like Sandra Farmer, who had been with the paper for years. She had spent time doing investigations and research for articles, like Mark was doing now. Her hard work ended up on the desks of other writers, who would put the finishing touches on the articles, but she never received the credit that she deserved. She also had experience writing about sporting events and various local festivals and activities. She had paid her dues and was working her way up the chain. This position would be perfect for someone like her.

Mark on the other hand, was just starting out. His dream had always been to be a professional journalist, but the chance that he would be given a position such as this was practically nil. Hopefully, someday his opportunity would come.

Vance stood at the head of the large conference table. Jamison sat at his right side. Most of the writers were seated around the table, while other staff stood around behind them to hear the announcement. The anticipation in the room was so thick you could cut it with a knife.

"Can I have your attention?" Vance called out, followed by a chorus of shushing. "As most of you know, Mike Jamison has been asked to join the staff writers at the Star Telegram in Fort Worth, Texas. He has decided that this opportunity is just too good to pass up. I have asked him to stay on with the Chronicle until the end of January so that we can have the time we need to decide who will step into his position."

There was a slight sigh as everyone in the room realized that they wouldn't find out today who was taking over Jamison's duties. "I know everyone is very curious about who will be taking his place, but we need to take a couple weeks to see who is the most qualified for the position. If you're interested in the position, I would like for you to stop by my office so that we can talk for a bit."

After hearing Vance's announcement, Mark knew that there was no chance he could get the position. So, when the meeting was over, he slowly walked to his desk. It was a tempting idea, but he knew everyone must work his or her way to the top, and Mark was just starting out.

As the day went on, several people stopped by the editor's office and visited with Vance. As Mark expected, the first person who went in to talk to him was Sandra Farmer. She sat in the office for about half an hour. When she left the office, someone else ambled into the office and stayed thirty minutes, or so, talking to Vance about the position.

This parade of aspiring journalist continued for the rest of the day. As the day ended, Mark wrapped up his work and packed up his things, getting ready to go. From over his shoulder he heard, "Hey Mark, can I see you in my office for a minute?" Vance's voice caught him off guard.

"OK," Mark answered as he slowly walked toward his boss's office.

"Why don't you shut the door and have a seat?" Vance offered from behind his desk.

Vance was a nice-looking man. He was in his mid-fifties, with salt and pepper hair. He always wore a pair of slacks with a buttoned-down shirt. Instead of a belt, he wore a pair of red suspenders to hold his pants up. Some days he wore a suit jacket, and other days he didn't, but he always wore his fire-engine red suspenders.

Mark respected Vance. When Mark had started working at the paper, Vance had taken him under his wing and offered Mark special opportunities that many young writers could only wish for. As the editor, Vance had given Mark the chance to help with projects that were usually given to the lead writers.

Vance also knew a lot about Mark's life. He would often stay after hours with Mark talking about home life and the problems that the young writer was facing. Vance understood Mark's situation; he, too, had grown up in a house with an abusive father.

He had a slight hair lip which was covered by his gray mustache. Unlike many people who were born with a split upper lip, Vance's was caused by his father. When Vance was 8 years old, he was helping his dad hold up a 2 by 4. Vance was struggling to keep the board up, after several attempts his father lost his temper. He swung the board hitting Vance square in the face. It split his lip almost to his nose. The doctors stitched up the cut, but it left a permanent scar. Today doctors would have contacted child protective services, but that was seldom done in that day and time, so Vance's mother told the doctor that he had fallen and cut his lip.

In the office Mark looked around at all the awards and pictures that Vance had displayed on his walls. There was a picture of himself with Walter Cronkite, with "Old Iron Pants" signature written in red ink on the bottom right hand corner. He also had a picture with Katie Couric, whom he had met in New York in the late 1990's. The picture that Vance was most proud of was an autographed picture of Truman Capote. It sat on a shelf right behind the desk.

Displayed at the front of desk were several pictures of his family. One of the pictures showed him and his kids when they were younger on a trip to see the redwoods in California. The next picture was of Vance when he had taken his two boys hunting up north. In the picture the three of them looked so happy. There was a large caribou on the ground in front of them. Vance stood holding its antlers, and his boys were both standing behind it. The animal was so large that it dwarfed his two boys who were eight and ten years old at the time. Mark was amazed that a man, whose home life as a child had been really bad, could have the kind of relationship that Vance had with his kids.

His children were now grown, and had gone their own ways, but Vance was still involved in their lives. He often left work early for little league games his grandsons were playing in, and was at every ballet recital that his granddaughters participated in. Every year he flew to Alaska with his two boys to hunt caribou. He couldn't wait until his grandsons were old enough to come along.

"Well Mr. Cooper, how is your family?".

"Ah…well…my brother had an accident and shot himself in the chest."

"What, seriously? What happened?" Vance sat up in his chair. He leaned forward on the desk, "Is he alright?"

"He was preparing for a hunting trip, and somehow the gun went off. The doctors flew him to Children's Hospital in Oklahoma City." Mark told Vance about the experience that he had in the hospital and how the officer tried to say that Ben had attempted suicide. He also told Vance about the vision of Benjamin that he saw out on the road after his car had landed in the ditch as he was headed to Oklahoma City to see about Ben. Vance sat listening to every word, nodding occasionally, like he was taking it all in. Mark couldn't help but wonder if Vance thought he was crazy.

When Mark finished describing the whole situation, Vance sat there for a moment before he spoke. "Wow, I'm surprised that you came in to work today. You could have let us know and headed down to the hospital. No one here would have been upset about it."

"Yeah, I had thought about it, but when I talked to Mom this morning, she told me to stay here. Ben was still unconscious, and she needed me to help with my sister here in town. My father usually stays out really late, so I'm needed to sit with Jessica until he gets home." Just discussing it caused Mark's chest to feel tight. Just the thought of Gorman made him feel anxious.

Vince smiled, and his smile helped Mark relax a little. "Well, I know what you mean. Let me know if you need any time off and keep me updated on how he's doing." Mark smiled and started to stand up. "Hold your horses," Vance continued, "I needed to talk with you."

"Sorry, I thought we were done."

"It's OK, I actually wanted to know why you didn't come in and talk to me about Mike's position."

"I really didn't feel like I had worked here long enough to try to get a position like that." Mark was very surprised that Vance was even talking to him about it.

"Why not? You're quicker than many of the other interns that we have had. You may not have the experience that some of the other people do, but this may be the position for you."

Mark couldn't believe that what he was hearing. He was just an intern; why would the Chronicle offer him a lead writing position? "Yeah, I would love to have the promotion, but I just felt that you would probably promote someone who has been here longer, someone with more seniority."

"Mark, you know that I'm the first to base my decisions on seniority. As the editor, I have a responsibility to everyone who has worked with me the longest. However, also as the editor, I must know who the best for each position will be. For this newspaper to stay in business, I must give our readers articles written by someone they can relate to. I have to hire writers who will produce the best writing."

"OK, then yes, I would love to have the position. What do I need to do?" Mark replied.

"On Monday morning, I will be meeting with all of the potential candidates in the conference room at 9:30. If you're serious about wanting this position, be there then."

13

Even with the news of his possible promotion, Mark dreaded going to his parents' house. He didn't mind helping his mother, but just the thought of seeing his father caused him to feel sick. Slowly, he drove through town. Most of the cheerful decorations that had recently filled the store windows were gone. Only a couple of random businesses still had their lights and trees up.

Mark pulled into his parent's driveway. He could still see the lighted tree through the window of the house. Knowing Jessica, it probably hadn't been turned off since his mother went out of town. As Mark went through the front door, he could smell chili-macaroni cooking on the stove. Jessica was down the hallway talking on the phone. It seemed very strange not to have Ben and Elizabeth at home. It was an eerily quiet.

Mark checked the food cooking in the pan on the stove. He could tell the cheesy noodles were starting to stick to the bottom of the pan. "Jess, food's burning." Mark called out as he moved the pan off the stove and turned the fire off. He could hear a commotion coming down the hallway. Looking up he saw Jessica with the telephone glued to her ear, walking on her heels holding the brush from her nail polish in one hand.

"I know, but I don't have a cell phone," Jessica spoke to the person on the other end of the line, "so I can't text him. Can you please text him for me and let him know that I'm looking forward to seeing him, too…I know my parents are lame, but I don't figure I'll be getting a phone anytime soon."

"Who are you talking to?" Mark questioned her.

"Jen," she whispered before she continued with her phone conversation. Jennifer Bradman was Jessica's best friend. They had known each other since childhood. They met in first grade and had been close ever since.

Jennifer had dark brown hair and green eyes. If she were older, she would be the type of person that Mark would want to date. But she was way too young for him. He always felt like he was her big brother, too.

Jennifer was an only child. Her mother had passed away when she was very young, and her father couldn't raise her by himself because he was a truck driver. So, they moved in with Jennifer's grandmother, who keeps her company while her dad is out of town.

Jennifer used to spend the night with the Coopers, but as she got older, she began to ask questions about the fighting between Gorman and Elizabeth. Her grandmother thought it best to have Jessica spend the night at their house instead. This kept the Cooper family secret safe from their neighbors.

Mark got a couple of plates out of the cabinet and began his own plate. He left Jessica's sitting on the table. She didn't cook often because Elizabeth was always home. Their mother did the cooking, and they ate it without complaint.

However, Mark had to admit, Jess had done pretty good for someone with no experience. The cheese was a little scorched. Other than that, it wasn't bad.

Jessica finally came back down the hallway with the phone removed from her ear. The polish must have dried because she was no longer walking on her heels. "How's it taste?" she asked.

"Mmmmm, it's delicious." Mark responded with a smirk.

"Don't lie to me," Jessica scolded.

"No, seriously, it's not bad," Mark reassured her, "have you talked to Mom?"

"Yeah, she called a little bit ago. Ben is doing about the same. He is still unconscious and isn't responding to anything. His heart is still beating, and he is breathing on his own, but they don't know when he will wake up."

Jessica set her plate down on the table, "Mark, do you think he will ever wake up?" The tears were already welling up in her eyes.

Mark didn't have an answer for her. He wanted to say, *Yes, of course he's going to wake up*. However, Mark didn't know if he was going to be alright. He remembered the way the doctor was acting at the hospital and the police officer's questions. Mark tried to picture in his mind what happened to Ben. He tried to see Ben's face when the gun went off. He tried to force himself to see what really happened.

He wanted so badly to find out if Benjamin's injury was intentional or if it was accidental. He couldn't help but remember what Ben said the night that Mark slid off the road.

Mark didn't know the best words to say to Jessica. Suddenly, he heard his mother's words coming out of his mouth. He told her,

"Everything is going to be alright. It's all going to work out." He took a paper towel and gave it to Jess so that she could wipe her eyes. She smiled at his comforting words, but they were more of a comfort to her than they were to him.

After eating his supper Mark found his place on the couch and began flipping through the channels on the television. Jessica curled up in the recliner with a tiger striped blanket.

They spent the evening vegging out in front of the TV. Time passed, and before Mark knew it, he had dozed off on the couch. He was awakened by someone coming through the front door. Mark had intended to leave before his father got home, but it must be too late.

Mark slipped his shoes back on, as his mother came walking through the door. He was surprised to see her home. She should have called before she left the hospital. Elizabeth shook the rain from her hair and took off her coat. Mark could hear the thunder outside. It had been raining for a while, but Mark wasn't sure when it had begun.

"Mom, what are you doing home?" Mark asked her. She began to cry; tears were running down her face in a torrent. She couldn't breathe between her sobs. Seeing the state that she was in, Mark helped her to the couch. "Mom, what happened? Why didn't you call us?"

Elizabeth composed herself and took a deep breath. Mark wasn't sure what to expect, but he felt like he already knew the answer. Fighting back the tears, she finally spoke, "He's gone."

Mark felt like his throat was closing up, "What? When? Why didn't you call?" He couldn't get the words out of his mouth. They sounded hollow and stale. As if he were talking to himself.

"I'm sorry, I didn't know what to do. Tonight, he just stopped breathing, and everyone came rushing in. The doctors did all that they could, but finally told me that he was gone. I left the hospital. I didn't know where to go, so I just came home."

Mark couldn't make sense of what was happening. He looked at Jessica who was still asleep as if nothing was going on. She looked like she had when she was a little girl, curled up with her blankie. He also noticed that he was wearing his pajamas, but he didn't remember putting them on.

"Mom, do you know what happened? Did they tell you why he quit breathing?"

"No, they didn't tell me what was wrong. BEEP, BEEEEP," when Elizabeth opened her mouth out came the sound of a car horn. "BEEP, BEEEP, BEEEEEP."

Mark jumped awake just as Jessica did. He shook his head to clear his mind. The car horn kept honking outside. Mark grabbed his coat and threw open the door. The rain was coming down in sheets.

Mark couldn't see through the blinding downpour. He squinted, hoping that it would make it easier to catch a glimpse of the vehicle. Then he realized who was honking. Gorman was sitting unconscious in his car, leaning on the horn.

Jessica grabbed her jacket and raced outside in the rain. She opened the door to her father's green Chevy Malibu. She began struggling to help Gorman out of the car. "Mark, hurry he needs help."

"Why, he can get himself out?" Mark scoffed at her attempts. She was daddy's little girl and always wanted to do everything that she could to help him. She waited on him, much like her mother did. There were times that Jess would even be angry at Mark for arguing with him.

"Mark please, we need to help him."

Mark relented and ran out to the car. He tried to pull Gorman out of the vehicle by grabbing him from behind. Gorman smelled of Jack Daniels, cigarette smoke, and soured sweat. This wasn't the first time that Mark had had to help Gorman into the house when he was drunk. The last time was at the request of his mother.

Mark began dragging his father backwards in the cold, trudging through the mud. Jessica slammed the door to the car. Gorman jumped awake.

"Hey, what are you doing? Give me my beer," He pulled loose from Mark's hands and stumbled face first onto the ground. "Why did you push me?"

"I didn't, you're drunk." Mark had known all along that he shouldn't have tried to help Gorman. Mark grabbed Gorman and pulled him to a standing position. Again, Gorman pulled away.

Jessica grabbed his hand, "Come on, Daddy, let's go inside and get you dried off."

"I said, 'I want my beer.'" Reaching the car, he pulled the door open, rescuing his half-empty bottle of beer from the console. "See, I haven't finished my beer." Gorman stumbled toward the front steps, but he made it only three steps before he fell again.

The beer bottle fell on the concrete and broke, leaving the neck and a long-jagged edge. Mark and Jessica tried to help him up.

Gorman picked up the broken bottle by its neck he lunged forward with it almost slicing through Mark's arm.

"Look what you made me do. Now I can't finish my beer because you two made me fall. What good are you stupid kids?" Gorman snapped with anger and hatred in his voice.

Mark stepped out of the way and let Gorman again attempt to make his way to the front steps. Throwing the bottle aside, Gorman stumbled to the porch. He pulled himself up the steps and through the front door, only to collapse on the floor inside the house, unconscious.

Jessica followed and attempted to lift him up on her shoulder. "Mark, help me get him to his bed."

"Sorry, sis, I'm done. I've got to grab a few things, and then I'm leaving." Mark stepped over Gorman's body on the way to his room. He grabbed some more clothes and stuffed them into his pillowcase.

As Mark moved back through the living room, he again had to step past them, and tried to ignore Jessica's frustrated stare as she sat on the floor beside their father. As he shut the door behind him, he could hear her mumble some hateful remark. Nevertheless, he was through helping his old man. This was the second time he had tried to stab him, and Mark wouldn't take it anymore.

Lighting up a cigarette on the way home to Shawn's apartment, he took a deep breath. He was ready to be home. Home is a word that brings the feeling of happiness and acceptance. He was truly headed home. Mark had not felt like he had a home in a long time, until now.

14

It had been three days since Mark was over at his parent's house. He told his mother that Jessica would have to stay over at Jennifer's house until their father got home the rest of the time that Elizabeth was out of town. For all Mark knew she may have stayed the night over there. It would be safer for her than staying at the house with Gorman.

The past couple of mornings Mark had been so glad to wake up in an actual bed instead of on the couch. His back wasn't hurting, and he no longer had a crick in his neck. The bed was much softer and a lot newer than his twin-size mattress at his parents' house. He didn't know where his parents had dug up that bed, but it was like sleeping on a lumpy pile of rocks.

His new room was small, but serviceable. Alongside the full-size bed stood a dresser and a nightstand. The closet was at the far corner of the room sharing a wall with the bathroom and hall closet. The carpeting was the same as that in the rest of the house, a light dingy taupe, and the walls were sterile white. The room was a great place for a bachelor.

Unlike the master bedroom which had its own in suite bathroom, Mark's bathroom was the common bath. Its door was across from his doorway. Between the two doorways was a cleaning closet that also housed the furnace and hot water heater.

The bathroom wasn't very big, but it did have a tub and shower combo. There was a small veneer-covered cabinet above the toilet that allowed space for towels. The vanity in which the sink sat was also made of veneer-covered particleboard. It was too small to hold much more than cleaning supplies and extra toilet paper, so Mark chose to keep his personal items in his room.

Mark was glad that today was New Year's Eve. Tomorrow would be the first day of 2012, and he would be that much closer to graduation. He also knew that Monday morning was the big meeting with Vance and the other applicants for the lead writer's position at work. It was going to be a long weekend, and Mark was filled with anticipation.

He got a quick shower and headed out of the apartment. Since he heard Jessica's conversation with Jennifer Wednesday night about the cell phone, there had been only one thing on Mark's mind. A cell phone would really help him out, and he knew that Jessica and Elizabeth could both benefit by having one, too. Mark would even get one for Ben to use later.

All the snow had melted, and other than the chill in the air, there was no other sign of the previous weeks of ice and snow. As he walked around his car, he was reminded of the donut that was still replacing his passenger front tire. He needed to get that fixed before he had any other problems.

After spending an hour and $150 in the tire shop for a new tire, Mark was ready to find somewhere to buy a cell phone. He had never had a phone of his own and didn't know where to begin. Finally, he found a store that wouldn't only give him adequate coverage, but also set up a family account for up to five people. The cost was a little more than he wanted to pay, but he would now have a way to get in touch with his family when he needed to. Mark even bought a blue flip phone for Benjamin.

Mark couldn't wait until Ben was better. He missed his little brother. The day before, Benjamin had been moved from ICU to his own room. He still wasn't responding to touch, but he did seem to notice when Elizabeth was speaking to him. He even winced when the nurse was changing the bandages. The doctor had no idea when he would awaken.

The doctor had advised Mark's mother that Ben was stable, and if his condition continued to improve, he might be able to be moved to a rehab center closer to home. Right now, they were very concerned about his spinal cord. When the bullet went through his back the damage to his spinal column caused his spinal cord to swell. They had him on steroids to eliminate the swelling. Even with treatment, they were unsure if there was any spinal cord damage. Ben wasn't reacting to touch on his lower extremities. They were concerned that there might be some paralysis.

As Mark headed back to the apartment, he was excited about the plans that he had for the evening. Shawn had invited him to go out, and New Year's Eve was always a night for fun. Maybe he would hook up with a nice girl for a long kiss at midnight.

Mark didn't have a girlfriend at present. Actually, he very rarely dated. How could he date a girl and bring her home to meet his mother just to let her see his mama get knocked around all the time? What type of an impression would that make? So, Mark just avoided the problem altogether. Every so often he would get interested in a girl, but without being fully conscious of it did everything he could to sabotage the relationship before it started.

It didn't matter; Mark wouldn't know how to be a husband, anyway. The only thing his father had taught him was how not to act. Maybe if he just acted the opposite way his father did, then everything would be perfect.

Mark felt like a dog waiting by the door for its owner when Shawn got home. Mark was all ready to go, sporting his nice button up shirt and a pair of blue jeans that he had ironed. Mark had never ironed before. Since his mom did all the housework, he never had to. Now that she wasn't around, he had to do it himself.

It was a very interesting experience. He had a burn on his arm where the iron fell while he was positioning the pants on the board. He also didn't know how to set the steam, so he scorched himself while trying to do it. Nevertheless, even with the mishaps, he was pleased with the outcome.

By the time his roommate arrived, Mark had been watching TV for a couple of hours. When Shawn came through the door, he was still wearing his green scrubs, and so he went straight into the bedroom to get ready. Mark didn't know where they were going; he just knew that Shawn said he would enjoy it.

"So how was your day at work?" Mark questioned.

"Long. No matter what I did, I couldn't seem to get everything done. I have this Director of Nurses working over me who really seems to think I'm stupid or something." Shawn came out through the living room in his boxers carrying his clothes to throw into the dryer for a few minutes to de-wrinkle. "I just don't understand why she thinks that I can't do my job without her standing over me the whole time."

"Sounds delightful," Mark replied.

Shawn smirked, "Well, it gets on my nerves. I see you're ready to go. Let me get my shower, and we can head to the church."

"What? Church?" Mark followed Shawn into his bedroom. "What do you mean, church? I thought that we were going out. You know, close down the bars?"

"Well I thought you might want to go to church with me tonight. It really is a good place. And we're having a special service to ring in the New Year," Shawn told him while he was shaving in the bathroom mirror. "Give me just a few minutes, and I'll be ready to go." Shawn pushed the door to, and Mark went back into the living room.

He couldn't believe it, all day he had been psyching himself up getting ready for a night out on the town. He thought maybe they would meet a couple of ladies, and they would have a good time bringing in the New Year, but apparently Shawn had something else in mind.

He could feel the disappointment. Why on earth would Shawn want him to go to church? Mark didn't even know if he believed in God. Even if he did believe in God, why would he want to go to church? What had God ever done for him? God was his mother's God, and she could keep him.

As he sat in the living room Mark began trying to find some excuse for not going. He wanted to let Shawn down easy. He thought about telling him that he wasn't feeling well or maybe that he had forgotten about prior plans that he made. Maybe he would tell Shawn that he had to go stay with his sister until his father got home. That wouldn't be lying; his mother had asked him to help watch his sister. There had to be some way to get out of going to church.

Even the word "church" made him feel uncomfortable. Wasn't that a place filled with a bunch of faceless, brainwashed disciples who came to listen to a man scream at them for hours telling them how bad they were? Didn't they play with snakes and drink poison in their fruit drink?

No matter what, Mark didn't want to get involved with them. He could see it now, the gossipy, backbiting old women who thought that they were more spiritual than everyone else. The elderly gentlemen who would sit around the front judging everyone who came in. And the preachers who just wanted to molest all the little boys and demand everyone's money. Mark didn't want to have anything to do with them and their cult.

15

Even after pulling out all his bag of tricks to get out of going, Mark found himself in the car with Shawn, pulling up to a large strip mall where several of the stores had been renovated into a church building. There was a sign on the front that said, "New Hope", in bright green letters with a sun in the place of the letter "o".

Mark couldn't believe that he was there. He felt the same tightness in his chest that he felt when he saw his father. He tried to breathe slowly to calm himself down, while he kept thinking, *I could use a couple of shots about now.*

They walked through the door of the large building that had once been a department store. The store had been closed for probably ten years, and even though the city had attempted to get new businesses in the area, no one would take the location. The double glass doors across the front and the brick facade were original to the building.

Inside there was a large foyer with a small coffee shop at one end. Near the coffee shop there was a sitting area surrounding a baby grand piano. The walls in the cafe were painted green and brown and had the typical coffee-bar feel.

There were signs everywhere announcing different events and classes that could be taken. Television monitors displayed the upcoming services, and there was a directory in the middle of the foyer to help direct visitors to the various amenities that the church offered. An arrow pointed in the direction of the children's church and another guided guests to the welcome booth, which was filled with information. There were smiling people all over the place.

Mark looked around as he walked into the main auditorium. No stained-glass windows greeted him, and no elderly men stood there looking to judge everyone who came through the doors. Very few elderly people were there at all. Most of the church was made up of individuals who looked to be college aged and young professionals. The congeniality of the people made him feel at ease. It was nothing like what he expected.

On the stage a rock band played electric guitar riffs. Everyone greeted one another while they found their seats. They had chairs, not the old wooden pews that were in the small Baptist church that his mother had taken him to. These were actual chairs with cloth cushions. It was nothing like any church he had ever seen. It offered a bright and happy atmosphere.

"Hey, Mark I want to introduce you to some people," Shawn said as he led Mark into a center row. "This is Marie Mills. Her father owns the Mills Insurance Company here in town."

"Hello," Mark said sheepishly. Marie nodded back and smiled.

She was a beautiful Latina with auburn hair and hazel eyes. When Mark looked at her, she smiled and lowered her gaze. He thought she was beautiful, but she didn't act like she knew how beautiful she was.

If it hadn't for her light-colored olive skin, he would never have known that she was Hispanic. She was wearing a pair of jeans that flared at the bottom of the leg around her black boots. She had on a purple shirt that was tight around her midsection and had a slight V-neck. Dark-framed glasses covered her eyes. Her hair lay in wisps framing face. She had a very soft voice that Mark enjoyed hearing.

"And this is my girlfriend, Trisha Brown," Shawn pointed to a beautiful African American girl with long black hair.

"Hi, Mark," she greeted. "You guys want to sit somewhere else, or is this OK?" Trisha seemed to be very outgoing. Mark could now see why Shawn liked her; she was his complete opposite. Opposites attract they always say.

Nothing about this church was what Mark was expecting. Colored lights hung from the ceiling trusses. While the stage was dimly lit, the theatrical lighting splashed color on the walls. It added a more modern feel than the stuffy business-like churches that Mark always pictured. The atmosphere set Mark at ease, reminding of the clubs that he was accustomed to.

As the worship service began, Mark stood watching the people. Many had their hands in the air or swayed back and forth to the music. Others were seated or kneeling in front of their chairs. It seemed that the people were free to express their worship in whatever form they felt they needed. They all seemed to know every word to every song. Mark couldn't believe it. The atmosphere in every church he had experienced had been bone dry. Too often the music was dead, and the people went through the motions of worship without enthusiasm. These people acted like they wanted to be in church. Their praise and worship seemed genuine.

Furthermore, the preacher didn't get up and yell and scream. He didn't get up and tell Mark that he was going to Hell. He didn't try to force God down his throat. There was something completely different about this view of God.

Mark had always imagined God as hateful. Elizabeth had told him that she believed God gave her Gorman to teach her patience. But Mark couldn't understand why God would have planned for her to be abused just so she could learn how to be patient.

Nevertheless, this minister presented a God filled with compassion. This God loved people so much that he sent his Son to die in their place. Mark couldn't help but feel overwhelmed. He had never been around anything like this before. Maybe Elizabeth needed to become acquainted with this version of God.

About 170 miles away, Elizabeth sat in the chair beside Benjamin's bed, where he lay motionless. The TV was on, but she wasn't watching it. She had spent the evening reading the Bible and praying. She didn't know what God wanted to do, but she knew something had to happen.

Since they had gotten married, she and Gorman had had never been apart this long. This time alone had given her time to think and to pray. She found herself feeling lonely, and without purpose. She was a caretaker, watching out for everyone else. But right now, she wasn't at home taking care of the kids, and she wasn't cleaning the house and washing the clothes. She was sitting in a hospital room next to her son, waiting.

She knew there was a solution to his problems, but it was beyond her ability. The nurses were in and out like clockwork checking blood pressure and oxygen level. They cleaned Benjamin up and made sure that he was comfortable. All Elizabeth could do was watch.

The nurses had offered Elizabeth a cot the first night, but she chose to sleep in the chair instead. She refused to leave Ben's side, much less the hospital, so the nurses felt sorry for her. Even though Benjamin was still asleep, they had meals delivered just in case Elizabeth was hungry. She would nibble on the dessert or the mashed potatoes and veggies, but her appetite was negligible.

She sat there reading her Bible. As she read, she found herself praying, "God, please work this out." Slowly she read word after word, searching each syllable hoping that some new revelation would emerge. But there was nothing. They were the same words that she read every year, over and over, and had ever since she was fifteen. She couldn't help but ask herself, "Is this really what it's all about?".

She felt the tears begin streaming down her face. There had never been a time in her life that she doubted what she believed. She never questioned why Gorman had lost his leg, or why she had gotten pregnant so young.

She had never petitioned God about Gorman's alcoholism, or about his continued abuse. She always felt like it was God's way of teaching her to be submissive and obedient. She always accepted it and moved on, but this was different. Her son lay on the bed, unresponsive. What could God be trying to teach her this time?

She lay her head down on Benjamin's chest. She could hear his heart beating. As she listened, the tears began to flow uncontrollably. She was overcome with grief, and with anger. She cried out, "Why, God? Why would you do this to me? I have tried to teach my kids how to live. I have honored my husband, and I have done everything that I can to be a good mom. Why would you do this?" The sound of her voice echoed in her ears.

The sound of another voice startled her. "Mom, why are you crying? Where am I?"

Elizabeth jumped back, "Baby, are you really talking, or am I dreaming?"

Benjamin tried to reposition himself in the bed. He winced in pain. "I think I'm talking. What happened? Why am I here?"

Elizabeth responded, "Honey, you don't remember?" Ben looked puzzled so she went on to explain. "You had an accident. You were getting ready to go hunting and your gun went off."

"No, I want to get up." Ben was beginning to get agitated. He started to throw back the covers and to pull on the line in his arm. His monitors began going wild, and quickly the room was filled with nurses and aides who rushed in trying to calm him down.

One of the nurses gently escorted Elizabeth out into the hallway while they helped Ben. After a couple of minutes, the nurses made their way out of the room, and Ben's nurse led Elizabeth back to her son's side. Ben was calm, he looked as if he could go back to sleep, but he was no longer trying to remove the IV from his arm.

"Mrs. Cooper, I wanted to let you know that we will have the neurologist in as quickly as we can get him up here." The nurse continued, "We gave your son a mild sedative to calm him down."

"So, he is alright?" Elizabeth asked. She was so relieved that Ben was finally awake.

"This is a very good sign. We still have tests to run, but things are definitely looking up."

Ben looked at his mother and asked, "What is today?" while fighting the sedative and trying to stay awake.

"It's New Year's Eve, Benjamin. Do you know what year it is?" The nurse responded.

"I don't remember."

"That's alright, Ben you just rest; there is a doctor coming to talk to you in a little bit."

"Can I watch the ball drop?" Ben interrupted.

"What, Baby?" Elizabeth asked.

"The ball on TV, can I watch the ball drop? We always watch the ball drop," Benjamin petitioned.

"Yeah, that's fine." Elizabeth handed him the television remote. "He doesn't remember what happened. Is that alright?" Elizabeth asked the nurse.

"Yes, that is normal in some cases. Some of his loss of memory may be caused by his medication, and some of it may due to his injury. With most people memory comes back within a short period of time, although it may be sporadic." The nurse finished jotting some notes down on Ben's chart and then checked his vitals. "Ok, everything is looking really good. Ben, are you hungry?"

"Yeah, can I have a pizza?" Ben answered, his mouth already watering.

"I'll have to see. Would a sandwich be OK? The cafeteria is closed." She responded.

"Yeah, a sandwich will be great," he replied with a big smile on his face, "any food would be great."

"Ok, I'll get you something. I'll be back in a few minutes," the nurse responded as walked out into the hallway.

"How are you feeling, baby?" Elizabeth asked.

"I feel like I have to pee, but I didn't want to tell that nurse." Benjamin was still squirming a little.

"Well, they actually had to put a catheter on you. You have been asleep for a few days," Elizabeth responded.

"What, you mean she saw me, you know, down there?" He was mortified. His face turned red. The only time that Benjamin's Irish blood came through was when he was embarrassed and angry.

Elizabeth couldn't help but chuckle. "Baby you have been asleep for several days, and they had to make a way for you to go to the restroom. It's alright, she's a nurse and is used to that."

"Why do I still feel like I have to go to the restroom?"

"Well, it's just pressure from the catheter, but you're OK. Just rest, and they will bring you something to eat." Elizabeth reached out and took his hand.

Elizabeth finally felt like she could relax. It was the first time since the accident that she felt like things really were going to be alright. She ran her fingers through his hair, as she silently offered a prayer of gratitude.

16

As soon as he woke up, Mark had a lot on his mind. He couldn't get the vision of Marie Mills out of his head. Her sweet smile and beautiful hazel eyes kept him awake most of the night. When he was finally able to go to sleep, he continued to dream about Benjamin's accident.

Upon waking, the preacher's message resounded in his ears. Being the last day of the year, the message was about letting go of past hurts. The preacher's words stung. While Mark figured that he could ignore what the preacher said like he had done many times when his mother tried to talk to him, the words edged their way into his heart. The more he listened, the more the words penetrated deeply, past his attempts of evasion. It was as if the preacher had been discussing Mark's entire life.

By the time the service was over, Mark was crying. This was no "Ouch, I stumped my toe" type of crying. This was all out, uncontrollable weeping. Mark had never found himself this upset, but the tears were good, bittersweet.

Mark had constantly carried around his anger. He was mad at his father and mad at himself. His anger arsenal was full, and the tears helped to ease the built-up tension.

Now Mark felt much better than he had in a long time. Just having the chance to flush out his emotion helped him to believe that things were going to get better. He always tried to ignore his mother's incessant positive reassurance that everything would work out, but now he wondered if maybe she was right.

After taking a quick shower and getting dressed, Mark noticed the light on his new phone blinking. It was a voicemail from Elizabeth. She could hardly contain the excitement she had felt since Benjamin had awakened. Happy to hear the good news, Mark called the hospital. Ben was wide awake and eating breakfast.

The best part was that the doctor had said that Ben should be released soon. The most recent tests showed that his brain function hadn't been affected, and he was able to talk without slurring his speech. The only remaining concern was the possible damage to his spinal cord. Ben still couldn't feel his legs. While the MRI didn't show any damage, the swelling interfered with the nerves to his lower body.

The doctors feared he might never be able to walk again. For the time being, he would be undergoing physical therapy to keep his muscles from atrophying. Mark didn't care if Ben ever walked again, he was just glad that Ben was getting better.

As Mark drove to work, he struggled to maintain his excitement about Benjamin's continued improvement. He turned his radio up and rolled the windows down. The cold air whipped against his face. At the top of his lungs, He sang every song that came on. Even with passersby staring at him, he didn't care, and just gave them a big smile.

As he pulled into the newspaper parking lot, his excitement quickly become anxious anticipation. The big meeting was today, and he had been waiting for it all weekend. He had no idea what to expect. The air was buzzing with conversation. People were discussing what they had done on New Year's Eve and their new year's resolutions.

Mark smelled the fresh coffee brewing in the break room and saw a box of fresh donuts sitting on the table. He wasn't a big donut eater. Mark was used to big breakfasts at his parents' house: eggs and toast or pancakes and bacon. Elizabeth's food was his favorite, and Mark missed it now that he was no longer at the house. But at least he had his fruity flakes.

When Mark entered the board room from the newsroom, he found it empty. He was so excited about the opportunity to try for this new position. It would be his dream job; moreover, the chance to work closer with the lead writers would be invaluable. Mark was a stickler about being early. He didn't want to waste time and chance run the risk of being late.

The conference room had the typical long, brown table surrounded by brown leather office chairs. In the middle of the table was a telephone and a triangular shaped intercom used for conference calls. Every time Mark saw the intercom, its shape made him think of a small UFO.

A glass wall with ceiling-to-floor venetian blinds separated the conference room from the newsroom. Opposite the glass wall were several large windows that overlooked the parking lot. Mark could see his car basking in the sun light.

At one end of the room there was a large flat-screen television that was always tuned to some news channel. Underneath the TV was a table with a coffee pot and basket filled with creamer and assorted sweeteners. Bookshelves covered the wall on the opposite end of the room.

Mark had been in this room several times before. The first time he saw it was when he was hired as an intern. He could feel the butterflies moving around in his stomach. For some reason this room did that to him. To calm his nerves, he sat down in one of the chairs, watching the silent newscast and reading the subtext that scrolled across the bottom of the screen.

After a few minutes, the other applicants filtered in. A handful of people were applying for the position. Each had a few years of experience, and Mark felt very intimidated. Seniority was very important to most people, and he didn't know if he would be able to keep up with them.

Sandra Farmer had the most experience. She had paid her dues by years of working under other difficult editors. She looked the part of a reporter, with dark hair pulled back in a bun. Her glasses had black plastic frames, and she had a mole on the right side of her nose. Every time that Mark looked at her, he couldn't help but think that she had something on her face that didn't belong. He thought he saw it move once.

A retired naval officer named Roger Norman was also applying for the position. He began working at the paper part-time a few years prior. While in the military he had worked with information management and public relations. He had written press releases and helped to disseminate information to the public regarding the Naval Corp and its work throughout the world.

Roger was in his late fifties and had retired from the Navy with full honors, but he was not as skilled in his personal life. He had two divorces, and his three grown children no longer talked to him. Originating in northern Oklahoma and Roger returned to help his aged mother who had been ill for several years following a stroke. When she passed, Roger found the position at the paper to keep himself busy.

He still had the starched look of a naval officer, no wrinkles in his clothes, and pleats ironed perfectly. He even had the same structured lunch of a ham and cheese sandwich with a diet cola every day. His silver crew cut was always trimmed precisely with no hair out of place, and his rugged face was always clean-shaven. Roger rarely talked, but when he did, everyone stopped to listen.

Other applicants, Jason Lambert and Willy Benson had both been at the Chronicle for about two years. Like Mark, they had previously been interns, and were hired fulltime after graduation. Mark didn't know them very well.

Jason was a few years older than Mark. He had dark hair and a full beard. Most of the time he wore khakis, a button-up shirt and a tie, but today he sported dress slacks topped by a sport coat.

Willy, on the other hand, could be considered a young hippie. He had shoulder-length blond hair and a dark patch of hair right below his lower lip. His dark eyes were typically hidden behind a rounded pair of light-blue, tinted glasses. His lackadaisical appearance belied his impressive intellect. He was always reading journals and research articles and had graduated magna cum laude from the University of Oklahoma School of Journalism.

The last applicant was Angela Wilson. She was in her mid-thirties and had sandy-blond hair that she kept pulled back in a messy bun with a pencil sticking out of it. Her bright blue eyes were framed with smile lines and small crow's feet. She usually wore a pair of slacks and a button-up shirt. She also wore a slightly tattered gray sweater. Her attire reminded Mark of a kindergarten teacher.

Angela worked very diligently. She was passionate about her job and did everything she could to provide professional-quality work. Part of her drive was the result of severe dyslexia. While in school, she had to learn techniques to overcome her disability. She determined at a young age that she wouldn't let it keep her from achieving her goals, so she pushed herself to work harder and accomplish more than those around her. This made her stand out above her peers.

As Mark looked around the room, he noticed that everyone sat quietly trying not to make eye contact, except for Jason and Willy who whispered back and forth to one another. Angela sat with her open notebook tapping her pencil on the table. Sandra was checking her voicemail, and Roger looked to be playing a game on his phone. The silence was deafening. It made Mark feel even more out of place.

Mark stared at the large clock at the end of the room. The hands pointed to five minutes after nine. It disheartened him that Vance had yet to emerge from his office. His punctuality was matched by no one. The extended wait exacerbated Mark's anxiety.

Earlier, a man dressed in a dark suit, white shirt, and bright red tie joined Vance in his office where they now sat. In between the slats of the vertical blinds, Mark could see Vance reclining in his office chair with his feet propped up on the desk. They seemed to be enjoying themselves, unaware of the stress that Mark was experiencing.

Finally, he noticed that Vance and his comrade standing. Mark took a deep breath. Vance and Mr. Red Tie left his office, on their way across the news floor towards the conference room.

"Hello, everyone," he addressed his staff, "I would like to introduce you to Martin Vasquez. He graduated with me from Northeastern many years ago. I have invited him to help me choose the best candidate for this job." Vance took the head seat at the table, and Martin sat next to him. "Marty, tell everyone about yourself?"

Martin straightened his tie, and smiled, showing his pearly whites. "Well, I'm from the Sacramento area. I spent some time in the military during the early 1990's. I came out here for school and then returned home. I finished my Master's in Educational Leadership from UCLA and have spent the last several years teaching at a local junior college."

Martin looked to be close to Vance's age, maybe a little younger. He appeared to be African American, but his name indicated that he may have been at least partly Hispanic. He wore a three-button black suit with thick white pinstripes. As he was seated, Mark noticed that his belly kept his white shirt taut. His red tie added color to his ensemble.

The presence of Martin Vasquez put a different twist on things. Not only was Mark going to have to impress Vance, but now he would have to impress Mr. Vasquez, as well. Mark could feel his stomach begin churning at the thought. He shuffled in his seat, looking around at the others in the conference room. They seemed to feel confident, but Mark didn't know if he would be able to compete with his opponents.

"Over the next few weeks you need to get your portfolios ready," Vance continued. "Your portfolio is very important, and you should always keep it up to date. It needs to include your best writing. We will need to see columns, samples of investigative reporting, and feature articles. While you're working on this, you will also be expected to keep up with your current and future assignments. We will also be watching to see how you work with other employees, especially those in this room."

Mark wasn't so sure about working with the other applicants. He wasn't very social at work, especially since he was the youngest in the group, and was very intimidated by the others. However, Vance had asked him directly to apply for this position.

"You need to find your very best work. As you know, there are many articles that go into making a good newspaper, and it takes contributions from a lot of people for the paper to be successful." Martin explained, "Your Portfolio needs to demonstrate your best work, but it should also demonstrate a diversity of work. As a professional you will be asked to do many different types of writing; we need to see that you can write different types of articles and in diverse styles. We will need everyone's portfolios by 9:00 a.m. on

January 23rd. You can turn them in earlier, but that will have no bearing on our choice for the position. However, a late portfolio will result in the removal of your name from consideration.

"When you look through the articles you've written, if you find that some may be lacking in one area or another, please take time to rework them," Vance restated. "Also, if you're missing your feature articles, this should allow you enough time to put something together. Are there any questions?"

Mark again looked around at the others in room. Of all of them he had the least experience. He had written only a very few articles for the newspaper. Most of his writing had been done as assignments for school. Slowly he raised his hand.

"Mark, you have a question?" Vance asked.

"Yes," Mark sheepishly replied, "most of my work was done in school. Is it alright to use that in my portfolio?"

"Mark, is it?" Martin answered.

"Yes, sir," Mark replied.

"Mark, your writing is your writing. Whether it was published or not, you'll need to put together everything that you have. Even if it's schoolwork, blog entries, or anything else that shows the best of your writing…"

"Yes, thank you, Mr. Vasquez."

"Any other questions," Vance asked to no one's response. "OK, get back to work. If you have any questions, feel free to stop by my office. Martin and I will also be doing interviews on Friday the 27th after we get your portfolios."

Mark knew that he had to find all his schoolwork. He remembered that he had it on a jump drive somewhere but hadn't used it since he got out of school in December. Everything else would be on his computer here at work.

As they left the room, he overheard Jason and Willy mocking his question. Since Mark was younger and less experienced, they obviously felt that he shouldn't even be in the running for a full-time journalistic position. He could feel his ears turning red and becoming hot. Jason and Willy seemed like they were jealous of his relationship with Vance.

When Mark returned to his desk, he closed his eyes briefly to calm his nerves. At work Mark didn't want to lose his temper. He had worked too hard to be where he was, and the last thing he wanted to do was lose his job over something stupid.

"Are you taking a nap?" Angela queried as she peeked around the cubicle wall. Her question startled Mark. "Wow didn't mean to scare you. I just wanted to say good luck on this position."

"Oh, uh, thanks, good luck to you, too." Mark was very surprised that she had come to talk to him. He couldn't remember ever hearing her speak, except when she was on the phone.

"Thanks, so do you have any feature articles? I will have to go through my file cabinet. I have a hard copy of everything I have ever written. I even write stuff when I'm bored. I may decide to write something else since I have time to do so." Mark was struggling to keep up with her. She talked faster than anyone else he knew.

"Uh, yeah, no, not really, I will have to look through my records and see," Mark answered.

"I don't know yet what all I will include. You know, I really want to do my best, and so I may end up doing something different. I was thinking about doing an article about the economy. But you can't steal that from me." She scolded, punching Mark in the arm. Angela then laughed with a snort.

Mark rubbed his arm. He didn't know if she was joking or not, either way it was very awkward. "No, I wouldn't. I don't know. I will just have to do some research." Mark smiled at Angela and then turned to his computer, hoping she would go away. She acted like she was going to say something else, so Mark picked up the phone like he was going to make a call. Dejected, Angela walked back to her own computer.

Mark didn't know what to write about. He had many ideas. There were tons of things that interested him, but he wasn't sure where to start. He thought about talking to Vance about it, but Martin Vasquez was still in his office. They were both laughing. Mark decided to hold off on his search for a little bit and take a smoke break. He would have time to prepare, but he had a phone call that he needed to make right now.

The air outside was warm, probably the warmest that they had seen since before Christmas. Before Mark walked around the end of the building, he realized that someone else was outside. He could hear the voices as he came out the door. Sandra and Roger must have felt that it was time for a smoke break, also. Mark lit up his cigarette and stood in a small cleft at the corner of the building so as not to be noticed by the other smokers.

"You know, I really feel like this position is going to go to one of us. We both have a lot more experience than any of these kids that are applying," Sandra whispered. "You know that one kid, Mark, he won't even graduate until May. Why would he think he would even have a chance?"

Roger scoffed, "Well, if one of those babies gets this position, I'm going to be leaving. I'm not going to work under any of them as a lead reporter."

Mark flipped his lighter open, Sandra looked around the corner. Mark smiled sheepishly. Rolling her eyes Sandra snuffed out her cigarette on the side of the building and then headed back inside. Roger quickly did the same. Mark began to wonder, *is this worth it?* Maybe he should just wait, but then again Vance was the one that recommended that he apply for the position.

Pulling his phone from his hip, he dialed Shawn's number. After a couple of rings, the voicemail answered. "Hey," he said, "I was wondering if you wanted to see if Trisha and Marie want to go out tonight. Text me when you can."

17

Mark was very excited about the opportunity to show his journalistic prowess. At the same time, he was humbled. He was very unsure of himself and felt like he had to prove that he was the right person for the job. He had always had a problem believing in himself. Even though Elizabeth was very supportive, Gorman wasn't. This left Mark feeling unsure about his abilities. He knew he was able to write, but was his writing good enough for Vance and Mr. Vasquez?

Nevertheless, this was something that he had wanted since he began writing. He was ready to prove himself. If he didn't get the position, it wouldn't be from a lack of trying.

Mark looked at the clock when he got back to the apartment. It was fifteen after five, and it would be another hour before Shawn got home. They had arranged to take the girls to go to a movie, and Mark had a while to get ready.

He was about to get in the shower when he looked in the mirror. He was getting a little shaggy around the chin. It had been a couple of days since he had shaved, so he might need to clean up his face before tonight.

Mark's face was "follicly" impaired with just a few patches growing sporadically at his chin and jaw line. Unlike some people who show a five o'clock shadow by 9:00 in the morning, it would take Mark a week to get anything growing.

As he looked at himself, he couldn't help but think, *maybe it's time for a change*. Instead of a complete shave, he would start growing a goatee. It may take a while but with all the other changes happening in his life, why not?

It felt good to get a quick shower. His work wasn't that rigorous, but he always felt like he was washing the cares of the day away when he stood under the hot streams of steaming water. After scrubbing himself head to toe, he stepped out, dried off and got dressed. Checking his phone to see what time it was, he sat down on the bed to put his shoes on. It would still be a few minutes before Shawn arrived home, but Mark already being dressed meant that he had a little time to burn. Stretching out on the bed he called his mother.

"Hello," she answered.

"Hi, Mom, how's everything going?" Mark asked. He figured that there hadn't been much of a change, but you never know.

"Everything seems to be going well," she responded, "but we're ready to come home. Ben won't eat this hospital food anymore, and I keep telling him that I don't have the money to go buy him a hamburger or pizza."

Mark could imagine the look that Elizabeth was giving Ben right now. He had seen that look many times. It was a cross between a scolding scowl and a sarcastic smirk. This was her non-confrontational "you know better" look.

"Mom, do you need some money? I can send you some to help out for a few days," Mark offered. He knew that Elizabeth was only eating the leftovers from Ben's meals. She would give her last bite to anyone of her kids and let herself starve if she didn't have enough for both to eat.

"Honey, I don't want to take your money. You need it now that you now have bills to pay and your car payments. I'm fine." Elizabeth was never willing to accept charity from her kids. Not that she was too proud, but she would rather do without so her children could have what they needed.

"Mom, I have some money in savings, I don't have any problem helping you guys out. Are you eating?" Mark didn't know if she would tell him or not.

"Yes, Mark, I'm eating. You know Ben won't eat breakfast, so I usually have my choice of eggs and sausage or pancakes with bacon. Then he won't eat the fruit or salads with his lunch, so I eat that as well. The past several days, the kitchen has been sending an extra supper tray, and instead of throwing it out, the nurse has been bringing it to me. It's kind of odd, that they make the same mistake every evening. I'm eating more than I do at home." Elizabeth responded.

"How is Ben?" Mark asked.

"He seems to be doing better. They took the catheter out today." When Elizabeth said that, Mark could hear Ben's embarrassed scolding her in the background. "Well, he is doing better. He can tell when he has to use the restroom, but if he begins having any problems, they may have to put it back in."

Elizabeth sounded very tired, and almost like she was forcing herself to be optimistic. Mark could hear Ben asking to talk on the phone, and then he heard a rustling sound.

"Hey, Mark, I'm sorry that she told you everything about me having to go to the bathroom. She embarrasses me so much when she says stuff like that. So, what's going on?" Ben sounded like he was getting back to his old self.

"Everything is good here; you need to hurry up and get better. I want to show you the apartment, but I can't bring you up in a wheelchair. Your heavy butt would be too heavy to carry in a wheelchair." Mark joked, trying to lighten the mood.

"Hey, I'm not that heavy," Ben rebutted.

"I know you're not; I just want you to hurry home. Even if I had to carry you up the stairs I would." Mark didn't want to cry but could feel tears welling up in his eyes.

"So, what have you been doing? You know I'm not doing anything fun," Ben quipped.

"Not much, just working. That's what I do most of the time," Mark answered with a smile.

There was a knock at the bedroom door. Shawn opened it. He was wearing a towel and was drying his hair. "Hey, I just got out of the shower; I'll be ready to go in a few minutes."

"Ok," Mark got up from his bed, "Hey, Ben let me talk to Mom really quick; we're about to leave."

"Hello," Elizabeth came back on the line.

"I have been looking through all of my things at the apartment. Have you seen a jump drive at the house anywhere?" Mark asked.

"What's a jump drive?" Elizabeth sounded confused.

"Well, it's a little blue rectangular thing that you stick into a computer. You can use it to save off the computer anything you need to keep. I have all of my school stuff on it, and I need to create a portfolio." Mark knew that Elizabeth was behind the times but didn't realize it.

"Sorry, I don't know. You may have to go check at the house." Elizabeth's response wasn't what Mark wanted to hear.

"Ok, I'll have to run by in a few days to check," Mark responded. "Thanks. Give Ben my love and hope to see you soon."

Mark didn't want to go to the house. He wanted to avoid the probable conflict with his father any way possible, but his mom didn't even know what he was talking about. He would have to find the thumb drive, himself.

18

Shawn and Mark decided to take Shawn's sports utility vehicle instead of the Mustang. There just wasn't enough room for everyone in the Mark's car. They arrived at Trisha's house, and Shawn went up to get the girls while Mark stayed in the car.

The girls lived in a one of the cookie cutter townhomes close to the school. The house was brown brick with a chocolate color trim. There was no porch on the front; only three steps from the ground level to the front entry. The townhouse was in a nice area of town where a lot of college students lived. Mark had slept on the floor in a couple of them following weekend keggers that he had attended.

Shawn knocked and was quickly greeted by the two ladies who were ready to go. Mark couldn't help staring at Marie as she walked down the sidewalk to the car. She was so beautiful with her hair was pulled back from her face. She was wearing a pink button up blouse, blue jeans, and a pair of boots. She also had a white wrap around her shoulders. Mark couldn't take his eyes off her. He continued to stare from inside the car.

Suddenly, Shawn shifted his position to intentionally block Mark's view snapping him out of his daze. Shawn covertly pointed to the back seat, but Mark didn't understand what Shawn was doing. Shawn more overtly, motioned for Mark to get in the back seat, but Mark remained in his thoughts.

Finally, Shawn opened the car door, and pulled Mark out by his arm. "You're in the back," he said as he shoved Mark towards the back door.

Mark quickly realized his err opened the back door to get in. Marie thought he was opening the door for her, so she smiled and got in. Mark was caught off guard, so he stood there for a second with the door open. Regaining his composure, he smiled and shut the door, before walking around to get in on the other side.

Just as Mark got to the driver's side rear door, the SUV lurched forward. Mark stepped back and peered inside. Shawn's pearly whites were gleaming bright from inside the vehicle. Mark again approached the door, and again the car lurched forward. Mark could hear Trisha scolding Shawn for messing around.

Mark reached out and grabbed the door handle and swung the door open. Without saying a word, he got in. Mark was a little embarrassed and if the ladies hadn't been there, he would have had some choice words for Shawn, but he had to keep his cool.

Mark's hands were sweaty, and he felt like an awkward teenager. He kept his hands tightly grasped together and continued to stare down at his knees. Every now and then he would catch a glimpse of her and would smile and look back down. Mark could hear Shawn and Trisha talking, but he wasn't paying attention to their conversation, until he heard his name.

"What?" Mark perked up.

"I told her that you wanted to go to some fast food place for supper," Shawn responded.

"No way," Mark retorted, "I didn't say that."

"I know you didn't say that," Trisha said in her sassy voice, "Shawn always wants to go there because they have a dollar menu."

"I like their chicken nuggets, thank you," Shawn argued.

"What are you talking about? The last time we went out to a nice place, I had to pay for my own food," Trisha countered.

"OK, I'm frugal, is that a problem?" He asked.

Mark and Marie sat listening to the conversation. He turned to Marie, "Are they always like this?"

"No," She replied, "normally he wants to just stop by a convenience store and warm food in their microwave. Actually, they pick on each other all the time, but I think it's a form of affection or something."

"Oh, OK," Mark had never seen this side of Shawn. He was being playful and couldn't get the smile off his face. Trisha's hand was enveloped in Shawn's. As Mark watched, he kind of longed for that same type of relationship.

Marie butted into their spat, "Do you guys want to watch the movie and then go to Dixie's afterwards?"

Trisha agreed, "Dixie's Diner, now there is a good place for us to go. It's better than the fast food dollar menu."

"What is Dixie's?" Mark asked. Mark lived in the area all his life but didn't go out to eat much. He had never heard of it.

"It's a little diner downtown. It's been there forever. They have old-fashioned milk shakes. You'll like it." Marie smiled at Mark as she talked. She then shyly brushed her hair behind her ear.

Mark couldn't help but smile, also. He looked back down at his hands. They drove the rest of the way to the theater just listening to the conversation between Shawn and Trisha. It was good to go out to something more than just a party.

The theater was packed with couples. The girls insisted that they just had to see the new romantic comedy that had recently come out. Mark didn't really mind going to a romance movie. It was better than the foreign movie that his last girlfriend took him too. That movie had been the beginning of the end of their relationship.

The movie was just about to start when the two couples finished getting their popcorn and drinks. Shawn and Trisha were sharing a tub of popcorn, Mark and Marie both had their own smaller cups. Marie insisted that she pay for her own, since Mark paid for the movie tickets. They quickly found seats at the back of the theater before the opening credits began. Mark could feel his feet sticking to the floor laden with spilled soda and stale popcorn. He hated to come into to the movie after the lights were down, he felt like everyone was staring, wishing he would move out of the way.

Finally, the movie began and from the first scene the theater was filled with waves of laughter. Mark had his hand sitting on the armrest. Marie laid her hand on his. Mark was unsure if she consciously did it, or if it was an accident. She didn't pull her hand back. It felt good. It felt natural.

By her actions Mark couldn't tell if she was even aware of his hand laying there. Mark spent most of the movie watching her. He wanted to know if she was intentionally trying to hold his hand. He hoped she was but wasn't for sure.

At one-point Mark had to move a little because of the uncomfortable chairs. Marie became aware that she was holding his hand. She quickly pulled it back. Mark spent the rest of the movie wondering if her reaction was instinct or if it made her feel uncomfortable. By the end of the movie, Mark had no idea what had happened. He was too caught up in the enigma that sat beside him than he was the movie.

As they walked out to the car, Mark could tell that Marie was embarrassed. Shawn and Trisha went on ahead.

"I'm very sorry that I had my hand on yours, I didn't think about it," Marie began.

Mark walked toward the car with his hands in his pockets. He replied, "No, it's fine, I didn't mind."

"Well I just normally don't do that. I wasn't thinking about it," She continued.

Their conversation was cut short. Two children were running down the sidewalk being trailed by their mother. They bumped into Marie pushing her into Mark's arms. He could smell the sweet smell of her hair. He took a deep breath.

"I'm so sorry," the mother said to Marie and Mark. She called out to her kids, "You're both going to bed when we get home!" She continued her chase.

Marie stepped back and dusted herself off. "Sorry, I don't really date much and so I'm kind of awkward."

"That's ok, I enjoy being awkward, I mean with you." Mark smiled at her.

She returned the smile and ducked her head brushing her hair behind her ear. That drove Mark crazy. She was so beautiful.

19

Dixie's Diner was only a short drive from theater. It had the typical diner look to it. Across the front were long rectangular windows framed in a metal veneer. There were booths along the front wall and down each side. A diner bar ran down the center; behind it was the workstation and a large service window where the cooks served up the orders. All the booths were empty minus a table of college students and a couple of elderly coffee drinkers.

Though the restaurant probably needed some updating, Mark could tell that it was well-maintained. He felt like he was walking into a diner from the 1950's. He expected to see a soda jerk behind the counter. For that matter, it was probably like the diner where his mom had worked at when she met his dad. That thought put a smile on Mark's face.

The two couples ordered a round of burgers and fries. Shawn and Trisha shared a shake, but Mark had a soda, and Marie asked for water.

"So, Mark, Shawn tells me that you're going to be a journalist?" Trisha enquired. "Does that mean that you want to go to remote places looking for a juicy scoop?"

"Uh, well, kind of, I'm working at the Chronicle right now and should be finishing my degree this semester. Then I'll probably stay around here for a while until something opens in a larger area," Mark replied.

"Wow, isn't journalism a very tedious job filled with tight deadlines and forcing you to travel all over? Do you think that will pull you away from your family? I always pictured the news writer stuck at his desk until all hours of the night and having to fly out of town at the drop of a hat to interview a politician or some dignitary. Does that worry you?" Trisha's attempt to play devil's advocate made Mark a little uncomfortable.

"Uh, well yeah, I guess that would, but at least for now that's not the case. Here the paper is smaller. There will be occasions when we're required to interview local people or maybe a politician who is coming through the area, but most of the time we write about all the local news that people from this area want to know about. What are you majoring in?" Mark returned, wanting to divert the attention from himself.

"Well I have another year before earning my teaching certificate. Next fall I should be student teaching. I want to stay in the area. I'm not in any hurry to get out of town. More particularly, I don't want to leave my little Cherokee warrior here." Trisha ran her fingers through Shawn's straight black hair.

"Cherokee… I knew that you were something," Mark blurted out before he even thought about what he was saying. He paused for a moment to collect his thoughts as he surveyed the faces around the table. He could feel the sudden heat on the nape of his neck and his face was probably turning read. He clarified, "What I mean is that I knew your ethnicity was different than my Irish-American roots."

Shawn just laughed, "You didn't know? I just figured you did. Yeah, I'm half Cherokee and half German American. Mom was full Cherokee and Dad was a transplant from New Jersey."

"How is your mom?" Marie asked.

Shawn's demeanor changed, "She's OK I mean it's been eight months; you know. She is starting to move beyond it. Dad had been sick for a while. He is the reason that I decided to go into nursing to start out with. After he got sick and was unable to take care of himself, I began bathing him and helping him go to restroom. He was sick for six years, and he was ready to go; he didn't want to suffer anymore."

"I'm sorry, I didn't know that either," Mark said. He had no idea what Shawn had been through.

"It's fine;" Shawn assured him. "The last year of his life pushed me to get into church. I couldn't have done it without my friends at church. My mom is a devout Catholic. It comes from her upbringing in the tribe, and she is faithful to go to mass and confession. But I was never able to connect with their beliefs. I mean, it's good for her, but not for me. I found a family at New Hope." Shawn took a deep breath.

"That's not all you found," Trisha said as she took his hand in hers. She leaned in for a quick kiss.

"Ahem," Marie cleared her throat, "So, Mark, what are your folks like?"

"Well, my mom is nice. She is a homemaker and takes care of my younger brother and sister, Benjamin and Jessica. My father is a Gulf War vet with PTSD, who works construction on the side, and when he isn't working, he drinks," Mark was very blunt about the situation.

"Sounds like you don't like your dad that much," Trisha observed.

"Trish," Marie scolded.

"No, that's alright," Mark responded, "Actually I don't really like him. You know, I love him, but I don't like him. He is a drunk, and if something doesn't happen to change him, I'm scared he is going to kill my mom. He was great when we were kids, but he has just gotten steadily worse, and I don't know what to do to help him."

"I'm sorry," Marie said as she reached out and took his hand.

"Don't be," Mark responded, "that is just the way it is, and there in nothing that I can do about it. I've tried but nothing has helped."

"Well, all I can say is, don't ever give up on him, Mark," Shawn's words were sharp but comforting. "I led my dad to Christ the day before he died. He wasn't the best father; he didn't abuse us, but all he did was work himself to death. My mom would tell me not to give up. When he came down with lymphoma, I began to study and see what could be done, but even with treatment he never really went into remission. Sure, the treatments prolonged his life, but never really made it better. I hated God, until I found him, and then I poured it all out to him. Just don't give up. You would miss him if he were gone."

Shawn's words rang in Mark's ears. He pricked his heart a little. However, he had given up on his dad long ago. He wondered if it was too late now for their relationship to ever be repaired.

When they were done eating, Mark looked around and noticed that the diner was empty. It was getting late and was time to take the girls home. Mark didn't say much on the drive home. He was deep in thought; he really didn't know what to say. He didn't want to lose his father, but he didn't know how to help him.

That night he lay in his bed trying to sleep, but there was no use. His alarm clock showed 2:30 a.m., but Mark's mind was wide-awake. He didn't know what would happen. His heart was in turmoil. He heard Shawn's words, but how was he supposed to act on them? He had sounded like Mark's mother when he said, 'Don't give up on him.'

Mark couldn't take it anymore. He got up and knelt beside his bed. "God, if you really care about me as much as everyone says you do, I need you to do something for me. Change my father. We can't continue to live like this. It's too hard for my family to keep going through the pain that we have been forced to go through. God, if you can't change him, then change me."

Mark found himself weeping just like he had done in church a couple of nights before. He was engulfed in a feeling of comfort; it was almost like someone had put their arms around him and was holding him. He was reminded of when he was a little boy and had fallen and skinned his knee.

He ran to his dad crying. He felt his dad scoop him up and hold him tightly in his arms until he stopped crying. That was how he felt now. It was like someone had picked him up and was holding him in his arms. He fell asleep kneeling at the side of the bed.

20

ark continued to search all over for the missing jump drive that had his school portfolio on it. Without it he had none of earlier writings to present to the newspaper. He figured that it had to be at his parents' house, but since his mother didn't remember seeing it, Mark knew he had to go look for it, himself.

As he pulled up at the house; he was relieved to see that Gorman's work truck wasn't in the driveway. As Mark opened the front door, he noticed that Jessica was asleep on the couch covered in a shawl that Elizabeth had draped over the back. The volume barely audible on the Saturday morning cartoons that were on the television.

Mark tiptoed through the house to avoid waking his sister. He noticed that the house looked clean even though Elizabeth wasn't home. The dishes were drying in the rack, and the floor looked swept and mopped. The trash had recently been taken out, and the cereal boxes were put up on the shelf. If he didn't know better, he would have thought they had hired a maid.

As Mark started down the hallway that led to the bedrooms, he noticed the family picture was still hanging on the wall. Someone had taken the broken glass out of the frame, but the picture was still intact. He stopped for a moment to straighten it before glancing at the gallery of family memories that were displayed for all to see. The pictures had been hanging on the wall since he was little, but it had been years since he had paused to look at them. Each photograph brought a different set of emotions that he hadn't felt in a long time. He broke away after a few minutes of reflection so that he could continue his search for the lost jump drive.

As he opened the bedroom door, he noticed that Benjamin's room was still in a state of disarray, nothing having been straightened up since the night that Ben had his accident. The police had made marks on the wall showing where the blood had splattered on it, and there was still dried blood on the wall and the ceiling. Looking around the room gave Mark chills.

Mark crept through the room stepping over trash and clothes that had been left in the floor. It appeared this was the first time that anyone had been in the room since that night. The room had a strange odor that Mark had never smelled before. It could only be described as earthy, kind of metallic, and it made him a little nauseous. He was relieved that the odor wasn't worse than it was. He had imagined it would smell more putrid, like a decaying animal left in the summer sun on the side of the road.

He began rummaging through items in the closet trying to find his backpack from the previous fall. He usually kept the thumb drive in a small pocket on the side of the bag. Shoved into a corner of the closet was a pile of Ben's dirty clothes. They smelled like sweat and stinky feet. Mark couldn't help but think, *If Mom only knew, she would tear Benjamin a new one.*

Finally, in the back of the closet he located his bag. Taking it to his bed, he dumped it out and began scavenging through its contents. He found all his books and a bunch of wrinkled up papers from the previous semester. He also found a folded-up copy of his upcoming semester's classes. There were pens and pencils in every pocket, but no jump drive.

Where can it be? He wondered as he looked around the room. There was stuff piled everywhere, drawers were left open, and the trashcan was overturned. Mark figured it was the result of the police pilfering through it, looking for drugs and other weapons. They had confiscated the rifle and remaining bullets that Ben had been given for Christmas. There was no telling what else they had picked up. Mark could tell that the only way to find anything in this room was to clean it up.

Since they would no longer be needing two beds in the room, Mark decided he would begin by taking his bed apart. He pulled the mattress off and carried it outside to the shed, where he found a hammer that he could use to dismantle the bed frame.

Piece by piece he separated the head and foot boards from the old metal frames. It was a very old bed that didn't have box springs. Instead, the springs were attached to the frame itself. Mark tried to carry each piece out of the house as quietly as possible to store it in the shed.

He discovered a ton of stuff under the bed: a baseball, a school notebook, and a lot of trash. Mark grabbed the broom from the kitchen and began sweeping up the mess. He picked up all the trash that had spilt out of the can and swept the rest into the dustpan to throw away.

Next, Mark began putting the items back on Ben's dresser. He organized the trophies and pictures on top. He also made sure that the two top drawers where his own clothes once lived were cleared out. He sorted through everything and boxed up items of his to put in storage.

Within a few minutes he heard Jessica coming down the hallway and going into the restroom. When she came out, she peeked in at Mark. "Hey, bro," she said and went on into her room. A second later she came back out of her room, with her eyes as big as saucers. "What are you doing here?"

"I came to look for a small jump drive that has all of my schoolwork on it. I decided that I would never find anything in this pig sty, so I was going to clean it up," He replied.

"Ok, I'll help," Jessica said as she left to grab a clothesbasket. She grabbed as many as she could find and brought them back into the room. She started filling them up with all of Ben's clothes that were strewn about. It didn't matter if they were dirty or clean, she believed it would be better just to wash all of them just in case.

While Jess was washing the clothes, Mark started gathering all the video games and putting them back on the shelf under the television. He straightened up the clothes in the closet that had been pulled down in the police search. And if it didn't have a hanger on it, he took for granted that it was dirty because he wasn't going to check it. At least if it was rewashed, they would know it was clean.

Then Mark moved Ben's bed against the wall where his had once stood, and he heard something fall from underneath the bed. As he pushed it over, he noticed a small tin box lying the floor. It was small enough to fit between the mattress and the springs, not much bigger than the size of a mint container. He popped the lid off and dumped its contents out on the bed. There were about fifteen pennies, a couple of paper clips and a broken pencil. Flipping the box over, Mark looked inside and saw a folded piece of paper wedged against the bottom. Slowly he pulled it out, and what he found written on it made him shudder.

Mom, Dad, Mark, and Jess:

If you're reading this, it's because I have decided to take matters into my own hands. This decision wasn't made quickly, but for a long time I have been thinking about the effect that my leaving would have on y'all. I love you very much, but I'm so tired of the constant fighting. I'm so tired of Dad being drunk and hurting Mom. I'm so tired of Mark fighting with Dad. All I can do is hope that my death will help you see the importance of family and will help you know what it's like to lose someone. Then maybe you won't have to lose anyone else. I'm sorry, but know I love you.

Benjamin Franklin Cooper

Mark was suddenly sickened. This couldn't be true. It had to be a bad prank. Had Ben really been planning on hurting himself? That wasn't possible; he was happy. He had everything he needed, so there was no way that he would intentionally shoot himself.

Just then Mark heard Jessica coming down the hall. He quickly folded the letter, shoving it into his pocket, and then he swept the other items back into the box and put the box in the top drawer of the nightstand.

"Hey," Jess asked, "Do you want me to go ahead and strip the bed and wash the sheets and stuff, too."

"Uh, yeah, sure, that would be good." Mark was still in shock over what he just discovered. He moved out of Jessica's way so that she could pull the sheets off.

Mark sat down at the small desk in the corner of the room. "Hey, Jess, do you think Ben is happy?"

"Yeah, I guess. He always seems to be. Why?" She inquired.

"No reason, I was just curious if you thought he was. I know as crazy as things have been here, that it can be disheartening. I just wanted to know what you thought," He replied.

"Yeah, I think he is," Jessica repeated as she left the room, her arms filled with sheets.

Mark sat in disbelief, his little brother was hurting, and he had lived in the same room with him, and never knew. He never even thought about it. He slept in the same room with a guy who wanted to end his life, and somehow, he had missed all the signs. Mark had been so absorbed in his own dissatisfaction with life that he was unable to see the pain that the other individuals in his family were feeling. What made it worse was that he was partly to blame. It all felt surreal, like the night in the hospital. Mark took a deep breath trying to process it all.

As Mark looked up, he saw the blood on the wall and on the ceiling. He took his finger and tried to wipe it off the wall, but it had stained the paint. Even trying to scratch it off accomplished nothing but damaging the topcoat.

"Hey, Jess, can you bring me some water and a sponge to clean this wall?" He called out to his sister who was in the laundry room.

She came down the hall with a sponge, a bowl of water, and some cleaner. Nothing that they tried would take the blood from the wall. Mark sat for a moment wondering what they needed to do.

Jessica brought in the first load of laundry, already folded, and ready to be put away. She placed it back in the drawers and took the basket back into the laundry room.

Mark heard someone coming back down the hall. Since Jess was the only other one at the house, Mark called out to her, "Hey, this isn't coming off of the wall no matter what I do."

"Then we should paint it," Gorman's voice rang out from the bedroom doorway.

Startled, he turned around to see his father standing there. "Uh, yeah, I mean, I guess we could," he replied.

"I didn't mean to startle you," Gorman said.

"No, it's alright, I just thought you were Jess, that's all," Mark tried to make an excuse for his reaction.

"Well, come on, I have some blue paint out in the truck. It was left over from a job, and so I was bringing it home just in case we needed it. It should be just enough." Gorman motioned for Mark.

Mark followed his father down the hallway, and they walked out to the truck where Gorman handed Mark a couple of rollers and pans. He grabbed the almost full can of blue paint, and they headed back into the house.

Gorman and Mark spent the afternoon painting the room and getting it ready for Benjamin when he was able to come home. Jessica helped make up the bed, and they moved the desk to the opposite wall so that Ben could sit in the desk chair and watch television or play video games. As the last bit of paint finished drying, they pushed the bed back into place. Unfortunately, even after searching the whole room, Mark hadn't found the jump drive anywhere.

He accompanied his father and Jessica to the kitchen to get something to drink. Jessica made herself some tea and went to the living room to see what was on television. Mark sat at the table, and Gorman grabbed a beer from the fridge.

"You want one?" he asked Mark.

"No, I would rather not," he replied.

"Suit yourself," Gorman answered, "I thought you liked beer?"

"Nope, I've never had a taste for it," he explained.

"Then what do you drink? I know you drink something because I can smell it in your clothes when you come home after those parties you go to," Gorman charged.

"Well, actually I prefer shots of tequila, but I have never been a beer drinker," Mark rebutted.

"You know something that I think is crazy? You get so angry when I drink, but you're as bad as I am. You spend nights out all the time, partying and having fun drinking with your college friends. It's no different than what I do," Gorman prodded Mark.

Mark could feel his ears getting hot and knew that his face was turning red. However, he knew he had to remain calm. Gorman's words hurt, but deep inside Mark knew he was right. He took a deep breath and let it out slowly.

"Dad, do you remember when I was six, and I was out in the street playing ball, and I missed the ball and fell. When I did, I skinned my knee and got gravel in it," Mark began.

"No, not really, why?" Gorman responded.

"I ran to you because you were out in the yard mowing. You picked me up and held me in your arms. You talked to me and help me calm down. Then you took me in and sat me on the side of the kitchen counter and used the sink sprayer to wash the dirt and rocks away. Then you sprayed me in the face and made me laugh. You took out your pocketknife and asked if I needed you to cut off my leg and that you would get me a fake leg so I could be like you. I laughed and told you, 'no'. But inside I told myself that I wanted to be just like you," Mark continued.

Gorman smiled at the recollection.

"Dad, back then I wanted to be just like you. But now, I'm not like you. I don't have to drink to live. I do it so that I can get away from you. I have a little, but not usually enough to get wasted. I just want a place to stay the night so that I don't have to come home. So no, I'm not like you." Mark stood up and walked out the front door and got in his car and returned to the apartment.

21

The weekend was gone before he knew it since Mark had spent all of Saturday redoing Benjamin's bedroom. The conversation with Gorman still rang in his ears, and he couldn't seem to move past it. He didn't want to be like his father, but the more he thought about it, the more he recognized that he was walking in his father's footsteps.

Mark had a rough past, and he was still working through the abandonment that he felt because of Gorman's lack of attention and caring as a result of his addiction to alcohol. Mark also had a strong Irish temper that was made worse when he did drink. Like Gorman, he used his drinking to avoid the problems in his life.

Especially, since the church service Sunday morning, Mark had been doing a lot of soul searching. He didn't want to end up like his father. He remembered what it was like when he was a child when Gorman wasn't a violent person. Sadly, for Gorman, while there had been good days, many of his days were filled with pain and frustration. The more frequent the bad days, the worst the drinking became.

Through searching his heart, Mark realized that he would end up exactly like his father if he didn't change the way he was living. He could very easily become an alcoholic if he continued to use alcohol as his medicine of choice. Mark could never really understand why his father was like he was. He never understood what led to Gorman's alcoholism, but now Mark realized that he was headed down the same road.

The spring semester classes were beginning, and Mark's schedule was going to require him to go to class in the mornings and then work in the afternoons. Mr. Vance was always willing to work with the interns around their class schedules, so it wasn't a problem for him to work in the afternoon and evening.

On the first day back at school, his cell phone rang. It was Elizabeth. They spoke at least once a day; either she called him, or he called her for updates. "Hey, Mom," Mark answered.

"Hello, son," Elizabeth replied, "I just wanted to let you know that we should be back in town by this evening. They are moving Ben to a local rehab center in town."

"Wow, they should have him here this evening?" Mark questioned.

"Yes, he's going to be staying at the Northwest Nursing and Rehabilitation Center. It's right by the hospital." Elizabeth's voice was filled with relief. She was tired and missed being with the rest of her family. The only other occasion she had spent this much time in the hospital was when she was waiting for Gorman to recover when he had first returned to the states.

"Mom, isn't that the old folks' home?" Mark teased.

"No, it's a rehab center. There will be elderly people there, but it's for anyone who needs twenty-four-hour care. The doctor doesn't think that he is well enough to go home, so this is the best option. It's better than keeping him at the hospital," Elizabeth answered.

"Alright," he responded, "just let me know, and I will come up for a visit. I start classes today so I will be working late."

"Did you ever find your jump thingy?" she asked.

"What?" At first Mark had no idea what she was talking about.

"I don't know, that jump thingy, you said it was attached to your school papers and you needed it for work," Elizabeth tried to explain.

"Oh, the jump drive… no I didn't find it. I looked all over the bedroom, and it wasn't there," Mark answered.

"I'm very sorry. Do you know anywhere else it could be?" Elizabeth paused for a second, "You know the police took several things from your room that they thought might help them figure out what happened. They took the gun and the ammo, but there were some other things that they took as well. I don't remember what all it was, but your drive thingy may have been among them."

"Ok, I'll see if I can talk to them about it," Mark replied. "Let me know when you're back in town."

***

Mark's first day of classes went by quickly. He had three classes on Mondays, Wednesdays, and Fridays, and two classes on Tuesdays and Thursdays. After school he headed into the office.

Mark had a lot on his plate. He had to work on his portfolio in order to have it ready to turn in the next week. He also had to research and write a feature article, in addition to keeping up with his normal workload. Moreover, Ben and Elizabeth would be in town soon.

Nevertheless, before Mark could get to work, he had an important call to make. He had to see if his jump drive had been confiscated by the police. Since he was a child, Mark had done everything he could to avoid a run in with the police. As he dialed the number his stomach was filled with butterflies.

"Police and Fire… how can I help you?" said the pleasant-sounding individual who answered the phone.

"Yes, this is Gorman Marcus Cooper; my brother had an accident and shot himself in our parents' house several weeks ago. The officers confiscated some items from the house, and I was wondering if I could find out what was picked up." Mark could hear his voice waver, as he tried to suppress his nervousness.

"Alright, let me transfer you to the property division," the cordial individual responded.

What if they won't let me have it back? he worried.

After a couple of minutes, an officer came on the line, "How can I help you?"

"My brother, Benjamin Cooper shot himself right after Christmas. I was told that when the officers confiscated the gun, they also picked up some other items. I was trying to see if they picked up a blue jump drive. It has my college papers on it. Can you tell me if you have it?" Mark asked.

"Let, me see," the officer put Mark on hold for a couple of minutes. "Well, I know we had several things from the location. The firearm we need to keep for safekeeping, since he used it to hurt himself. How is he doing?"

"Well, he is actually doing alright. He will be moved into a local rehab facility today," Mark responded.

"Do you know if they are going to get him some help for his depression?" The officer asked.

"Well, I don't know much about that. We're still trying to get that worked out." It was very alarming to Mark that the police were investigating this like an attempted suicide. Could that mean that Benjamin would be in trouble, or on some list of people that they think may be suicidal?

"Well, until we know that it's safe, we will need to keep the firearm and the hunting knife here. We don't want him to attempt to do anything else. Next time he could try to hurt the rest of your family."

That frightened Mark. He thought this would be a onetime occurrence. He had never thought about the possibility that Ben might do something like this again. If he did try again, he might succeed. Worse, he might try to take the whole family with him.

He could hear the officer rummaging through the box. "Ok, here we go. There is a blue jump drive, and it appears from the report that there was nothing on the drive except a few files…but nothing suspicious I should be able to release it to you."

"Ok, that's great! Can I pick it up after class tomorrow?" Mark asked.

"That should be fine, just ask for property when you get here," the officer responded.

22

It was late in the evening before Elizabeth called back. They had just made it to town, and she was going to run by the house and check on Jessica before she would be able to go up to the rehab center. Mark thought that while his mother was otherwise occupied might be a good time to talk to Ben about the letter.

As Mark pulled into the parking lot of the rehabilitation center, he parked close to the front door. There was a man in a wheelchair sitting right outside smoking a cigarette. Mark went into the foyer where a couple more people were sitting in wheelchairs. One elderly man kept calling out for help.

The nursing facility had a strong stench of a cleanser mixed with a musty smell of urine. The dining area was empty except for the few patients who were still eating their supper. Mark continued down the corridor to the nurse's station.

"I'm looking for Benjamin Cooper's room," Mark informed the lady behind the desk.

"Cooper? Is he a new resident?" she asked without looking up from her computer.

"Yes, they just transferred him into the rehab center," Mark answered.

"Ok, he is going to be in the west wing of the facility. Go down the hallway to your left, you will see the entrance on the right." She pointed to the hallway.

Mark headed down the hall. He passed the activity room, where there were people making crafts at one table. At another table they were playing dominoes. He passed several rooms where elderly patients were watching television or talking on the phone. Finally, he came to a door on the right side of the hallway that had the words, Rehabilitation Services, in big black letters.

He pushed the door open. This hallway was much shorter, and it didn't smell like the other hall. There was a large open room with workout equipment and tables where patients received their physical therapy. There was another nurse's station near the center, but no nurses were there now.

Unlike the main nursing facility, with its many rooms, this wing had only a few. Mark noticed a physical therapist helping a middle-aged man move from his wheelchair into a leg extension machine. Mark followed the corridor around the corner. There were names written on a dry erase board by each door. Mark continued until he found the room with his brother's name. It was almost at the end of the hall.

Mark knocked on the door. Someone said, "Come in." But it wasn't Ben's voice. Slowly, Mark pushed the door open and found Gorman sitting in a chair by the bed. "Hey, Mark, how are you doing, son?"

"I'm good. I guess this is the room," He replied. Mark was a little disappointed to see his father there. He reasoned that, at least for the time being, he wouldn't be able question Ben about the letter.

"Well your brother is in the bathroom. He does well getting in and out of that wheelchair. Maybe since he is here, they can help straighten out his crooked leg," Gorman laughed until he started coughing.

Mark heard the toilet flush in the restroom, and a minute later Ben pushed the door to the bathroom open. "Mark, you're here," Ben said excitedly.

"I wanted to see you," Mark replied as he bent down to give Ben a hug. Mark was so happy that his little brother was safe. While it had only been a few weeks, he felt like they hadn't seen each other in a year.

"Isn't this cool? I have my own room, and I can watch television if I want. Also, I'll have my physical therapy right here, so I no longer go all the way across the hospital for therapy," Ben excitedly explained.

"Yeah, it's nice. You're in the old folks' home," Marks teased squashing Ben's excitement.

"Actually, this isn't the old folk's home. They're next door. This is the rehab wing," Ben snapped back. "There are other people in this wing that are in their twenties and thirties. I'm the youngest, but today I met a college guy who got his back broken playing football. He must learn how to live without use of his legs. He's your age, Mark."

There was another knock at the door, and Elizabeth slowly pushed it open. "Benjamin are you decent?" she asked as she peeked in the room.

"Mom, really, why would you say that?" Ben complained.

"Oh, Mark you're already here," she greeted as she walked over and gave him a kiss on the forehead.

"I couldn't wait to see my little brother," Mark taunted Ben as he gave him a noogie.

"Well I don't know about you kids, but I'm starving, I'm going to pick up some pizzas," Gorman said as he stood up and stretched. His shirt came untucked slightly, showing off his pale stomach. He pushed the corners of his shirt back in his waist band as he walked across the room.

"Finally, pizza, Mom wouldn't let me have real pizza in the hospital. It was just that hospital food. Dad get some with pepperoni," Ben requested.

"Alright, I'll grab some drinks, too," Gorman replied as he headed out the door.

"We brought some games from home if you want to play," Jessica offered. She pulled several games from her bag.

"I want to play," Ben exclaimed, "This is like a family reunion."

It was like a family reunion and reminded Mark of being a little boy. His family spent the next couple of hours hanging out in Ben's room. Gorman brought back the pizza and drinks, and they played games and watching television. It was the first family time that they had enjoyed in years. Mark had begun to look at his father differently. He hadn't gotten past everything that had happened, but he wasn't feeling angry at the sight of Gorman anymore. It was the first time that Mark had called him "Dad" and didn't feel awkward doing so.

By nine o'clock it was time for everyone to go. Benjamin had a tutor coming in the morning from the school to help him get caught up with his classes, so Elizabeth declared that his visitors had to leave so he could rest. Everyone said their goodbyes and walked out the door.

Mark turned to go back through the nursing facility door. It was then that he discovered that there was a direct entrance into the rehab center near Ben's room. It would have been so much easier if he had known that before. He would have been able to bypass the nursing home, altogether.

Mark followed his family outside the main rehab doors even though he would have to walk all the way around the building since he was parked around front. Gorman left in his work truck, probably to head to his favorite watering hole, so Mark stood outside talking to Elizabeth. He pulled the two phones out of his pocket. He had given Jess her phone previously, but this was the first time that he had seen Ben and Elizabeth since the accident.

"Mom, I wanted you guys to have these just in case you need them. Jessica has one, and the blue one was is for Ben," Mark explained. He was very happy to be able to help his family, knowing that having a cell phone was something they couldn't afford, but would help them in an emergency. If his mother had had a cell phone the night Ben was injured, she might have been able to get help for him faster.

"What about your father?" Elizabeth asked.

"At the time, I hadn't planned to get him one. I didn't think that he would need one, or even care to have one," he shrugged.

"Oh, well, I don't think I can take this, then." Elizabeth tried to hand the phone back to him.

"Mom just take it. Keep it put up in case you have an emergency. You never know when something will happen and you will need it," Mark replied.

Reluctantly, she put it in her purse. She didn't want Gorman to find out about the phone. It could start a war in her household, and she wanted to avoid that anyway that she could. She thanked her son for the gift and promised to give the other one to Ben, when she came back in the morning.

After one final hug and a kiss on the cheek he walked around to car.

23

Mark woke up extra early the following morning. He needed to stop by the police station before he went to class. He decided that he wouldn't have time to go by during the interval between school and work.

The police department was practically empty at 8:00 a.m. There was no one behind the window for him to talk to, so he sat down to wait in a small lobby area opposite a glass window. Officers walked back and forth behind the glass, but no one seemed to notice him. Class started at 9:30, so he couldn't afford to spend all day waiting.

Eventually, a female officer sat down behind the window. She had her dark hair pulled back in a bun, and her bangs were reminiscent of the hair styles popular in the 1980's. She had a freckled face and just a little bit of makeup around her eyes. She wore a blue police uniform with a shiny brass badge on the left side of her chest. Her nametag said, *Anderson*.

When she motioned for Mark to come up to the window, he explained his problem. She called the property clerk and told Mark to have a seat out front. Mark was again waiting in the lobby.

After a few minutes a heavyset black officer invited Mark into a small room. There was a long brown table in the center of the room. At the end of the room was a large plate glass window. On the other side of the window was a darkened room with parallel lines on the wall with markings for different heights. It reminded Mark of police sitcoms where the victims would pick the suspect out of a line-up.

Sitting on the table was a cardboard box with a case number written on the side. Opposite the table was another officer who looked familiar, but Mark couldn't remember where he had seen him before. There was a second man, possibly in his forties also sitting at the table looking through the box. He had graying hair, and a gray mustache. Instead of wearing a uniform, he had on a button up shirt and a pair of khaki slacks.

When Mark walked into the room, the property officer motioned to the box, and Mark began to look through the items which were left. Ben's clothes from the night of the shooting where laying on top. The shirt had jagged cut marks where the paramedics had cut it off when they first examined him. The jeans seemed to still be intact but were bloodstained as well.

Mark saw a couple of spiral notebooks and a small journal as well as a couple of Ben's video games. Underneath it all was Mark's blue jump drive. He took the jump drive out and put it in his pocket.

"You can actually take everything with you," the older officer told him. "By the way, my name is Detective Burks, and I work in our Crimes Against Persons division. This is Officer Walker; you might remember him from the hospital. We wanted to take a few minutes to talk to you while you were here."

"Is everything ok?" Mark questioned.

"Yeah, we're just doing some follow up," He responded.

"Do you usually take all this stuff when someone accidentally shoots himself?" Mark questioned.

"It's typical for us to take things that we think could be evidence. That was why we took the drive, the notebooks, and journal…just in case they contained any information that we need to know. As you can tell, we aren't a large agency, and so we sometimes do things a little differently than other agencies. Nevertheless, I'm really concerned about your brother," the detective continued, "Any time that a child attempts suicide, we don't take it lightly. Does your brother have a history of drugs or alcohol use?"

"No, not that I know of. Don't you guys send off his blood to have it tested anyway? I'm still trying to understand what he was feeling. He may have been depressed, but I don't think he wanted to die," Mark was emphatic as he explained the situation to the officers. He couldn't grasp the idea that his little brother would intentionally try to take his own life. The more Mark explained, the more he felt like he was trying to convince himself.

"Mark, I remember at the hospital you said that your brother wouldn't have wanted to hurt himself, but now you think he was depressed. What changed?" Officer Walker asked.

"I don't know," Mark responded.

"Mark, if there is something that you know, you need to tell us. Has someone been hurting your brother?" the detective asked.

"No, I don't think so. But I cleaned out his room the other day, and I found a letter that he had written. In the letter he apologized for what he was going to do. I just can't believe that he would do something like that. He's seventeen years old with his whole life ahead of him." Mark was visibly frustrated.

"We're not trying to upset you, but we want to help your brother. People don't do this without a reason. If he needs help, we want to see that he gets that help. Is there anything that you can tell us? Is there anything that you know that might have caused him to hurt himself?" the detective's tone calmed Mark's frustration.

"I really don't know why he would want to do this. But if he wanted to kill himself, why would he shoot himself in the chest? Don't most people who are bent on suicide shoot themselves in the head?" Mark asked.

"Yeah, but just because he shot himself in the chest doesn't mean that it wasn't a suicide attempt. Think about it, he was using a long gun. The only option he had was his chin or his chest. We're still not sure how he pulled the trigger, but apparently, he must have found a way. We just want to make sure that he is getting help so that nothing like this happens again," the detective responded.

"Ok, I will keep watching for anything else, but I have class in a few minutes, so I need to go," Mark picked up the notebooks and was led out of the room by the property clerk.

He would have to find time to talk to Ben, but with his family around that would be almost impossible. However, he had to do it, or he would never know what was going on. For right now, that would have to wait. He barely had enough time to make it to class as is. After class he planned to head straight to work so that he could see what he had on the jump drive.

That afternoon he hurried into the newsroom. The desks were half full. He sat down at his desk and popped the jump drive into the computer. As he looked though all his writing, his fear was confirmed, there was nothing he felt comfortable using as a feature article. There were a lot of columns and basic new stories, but nothing that grabbed his attention. He searched the computer hard drive at work and found several interviews that he had done, but he could find nothing there that would impress his boss.

Mark wanted something that would be grab people's attentions and at the same time demonstrate his writing skills. He wanted to show his best work. It needed to be something that said, *I can do this job better than all the other applicants.*

In the back of his mind Mark continued to think about his meeting with the police. He closed his eyes for a moment and pictured what it would have been like to have lost Ben. The funeral, the mourning that his family would go through, and the way it would affect his future. He could see his father spending more time and money drinking. This would exacerbate the fighting and the abuse. Ultimately, his father would either go to jail or drink himself to death. Life would have been completely different if Ben had died.

Suddenly, it was like a light bulb came on in his head. He knew what he would write about. He opened a web browser and typed in, The Effects of Teen Suicide. Mark would write about how teen suicide affected the lives of the families and friends that were left behind. Most of the other applicants would probably provide articles about local events, biographical works about important people, or even special interest stories. Mark's story would be something different. For him it would hit close to home. While no one ever wants to suffer from this kind of tragedy and most believe that it could never happen, anyone who has a teenager in his or her life is susceptible.

Mark started his research and quickly became absorbed in it. He found a lot of information regarding the causes of teen suicide, the methods used, and the aftermath. He couldn't believe the staggering statistics involving the number of teenagers who had attempted suicide.

This was a different world for Mark. He had dealt with his own depression but had never really considered the idea that killing himself was a possible solution for his problems. He understood that some people suffer worse than others, but never would have guessed the overwhelming number of teenagers who suffer from severe depression with suicidal ideation and tendencies. It concerned him however, that many youths who have attempted suicide once, would wind up attempting it multiple times in their lives, until they either received help or were successful.

So, if Ben *had* been trying to kill himself, he might try it again if they didn't do something to get him some help. That was why the police were so emphatic about finding out the facts surrounding the injury and getting Benjamin the therapy, he needed.

Mark was sickened at the thought. If Ben's actions had been intentional, there would be a greater chance that he would succeed if he tried it again. Mark wanted to do whatever it took to get Ben help before it was too late.

That evening, Mark climbed the stairs to the apartment. As soon as he opened the door, he could hear Shawn in the kitchen cooking.

"Honey, I'm home," he called as he came through the doorway.

"Great, you can help me cut up the vegetables. We have some people coming over tonight," Shawn responded as he handed Mark a knife.

"Who's coming?" Mark hadn't been told about a party, "Do I need to go pick up anything, a couple of six packs, or some chips?"

"No, I think we have everything, there are a few sodas in the fridge, and Trisha will be here soon to help with the burgers." Shawn threw Mark the head of lettuce and two tomatoes.

Mark felt like a juggler trying not to drop the flying produce. As he began cutting up the vegetables, he asked, "How many people will be here?"

"I'm not quite sure. During the school year we normally have a small group here at the apartment. A handful of people come over, we eat, and have a Bible study," Shawn explained.

Mark didn't really know what to expect. He had attended many parties, frat house shindigs, and mixers, but nothing like this. Mark didn't really want to stay. He had never been to a gathering that didn't include alcohol. Since they were having a Bible study, he figured there would be no liquor served.

Mark enjoyed parties from time to time. He liked hanging out with other people. He liked seeing the crazy things that people do when they have had a little too much to drink. However, now he wondered if he shouldn't avoid drinking all together. Since the argument with his dad, he hadn't wanted to drink. He didn't want to become like his dad.

There was a knock at the door, but Trisha let herself in followed by Marie. Mark was glad to see her. The last time they had been together, she acted very awkward, so he was concerned that she might be upset. Now however, she seemed fine.

As other participants arrived, Mark was introduced to about eight people he had never met. All were young singles. Some were apparently involved in relationships with someone else in the group, but most appeared to be unattached.

There were people from different backgrounds and different races. Some were right out of high school, while others were about to graduate from college. Even with such an eclectic group, they all had one thing in common; they all were looking for a deeper relationship with God.

The leader of the small group was a guy named Jerry Miller. He was a recent college graduate who planned to begin working toward his graduate degree in psychology this next fall at Oklahoma State University. Mark was intrigued by Jerry's field of study and wondered if he would good resource for information regarding teenage suicide.

While waiting for the Bible Study to begin, Mark found an opportunity to talk to Jerry. He had so many questions regarding suicide and teenage depression and hoped to get some answers. Mark could tell by the expression on Jerry's face that the more questions he asked, the more concerned Jerry became; however, before he could explain the situation with Ben, it was time for the Bible study to begin.

That night Jerry taught on the love that God has for people. He read verses in the Bible that showed how God loved the Jews even when they turned their backs on Him. Jesus even loved the soldiers that crucified him even praying that God would forgive them for what they had done.

Mark had never heard anything like that. He couldn't imagine the kind of love that would be able to pray for the forgiveness of someone who had done him harm. Mark wondered if that was what his mother always did. If she prayed that God would forgive Gorman for all the times he had hurt her. If so, that was probably why she still hoped that he would change.

Jerry said something that really amazed Mark. He stated that God loved people beyond their past. God was even willing to overlook someone's past and offer forgiveness no matter how bad they had been. Moreover, he also explained that Christian love should look beyond a person's past and recognize the fact that God has a future planned for them. Mark had never thought about that. Sadly, he didn't know if he could do that when it concerned his father.

That night as everyone was leaving, Jerry pulled Mark aside and asked him if he had been having problems with depression. Mark casually smiled and answered, "No, I'm not having problems with depression. I was worried that you might have come to that conclusion."

Jerry smiled, "Then what were all of the questions about?"

Mark explained that he was doing an article on the effects of teenage suicide on the families of the victims. This answer seemed to satisfy Jerry. Mark didn't want to explain what had happened to Ben.

That night after everyone had left and he was going to bed, Mark found himself battling his own demons. He continued to think about Gorman and the problems that he had. He also thought about his own drinking. Suddenly, Jesus' prayer while he was on the cross came to mind. Mark closed his eyes, and as he dozed off, he prayed, "God, forgive my dad, and help me forgive him, too."

24

The air was filled with the sweet aroma of fresh flowers. It was reinforced by the damp smell of freshly cut grass. A light breeze rustled the leaves on an old oak tree nearby. One of the leaves broke free from its home and floated effortlessly under the tent where everyone was seated.

Mark looked to his left at the row of men standing next to him. All were adorned in dark suits, with white shirts and ties. On each man's chest was a single carnation. Shawn was standing beside him. Shawn put his hand on Mark's shoulder. As Mark turned to look at him, Mark felt a tear run down his face and off his chin. Shawn smiled slightly.

Mark couldn't speak. It was surreal. He felt like everything was moving in slow motion. He could hear the sniffling from those who were seated in front. He could see his mother on the front row. Her eyes were puffy, and she had a box of tissues. Jessica sat next to her. Jess's eyes were red, and Mark could tell that she had been crying, also.

As Mark looked around, he felt as if couldn't breathe. He couldn't believe that this was happening. He knew that it was possible, but never expected it to be this soon. But things don't always work out like they are planned.

The officiating minister was standing to Mark's right. He also was wearing a single white carnation on his left lapel. Beyond the preacher, Mark could see Trisha. She was wearing a lacey slim-cut dress. Mark saw her wave slightly to Shawn, and out of the corner of his eye he saw Shawn secretly wave back.

Turning to Mark, the preacher cleared his throat; he said in a low voice, "It's time."

Mark nodded and took a deep breath.

As the singer began singing, the whole congregation rose to their feet. Mark looked down the aisle and standing at the back of the tent stood Marie being ushered in by her father. She was in a beautiful white dress that flowed down to her feet. She had a short train and a long veil that covered her face.

As they reached the front of the chairs she turned to her father, who lifted her veil and gave her a kiss. Mark looked over to his dad and Ben who were sitting by Elizabeth. They were smiling. Mark turned back to the preacher who had stepped forward to take Marie's hand and lead her to the altar.

As Marie looked toward Mark, he peered deeply into her eyes. He was filled with joy and excitement. He couldn't believe that it was happening.

Suddenly he was awakened by the loud beeping of his alarm clock. He reached over and turned it off and stretched. He wanted to go back to sleep and finish the dream, but he knew that it was time for him to get up.

Elizabeth had agreed to go with him to church today, and he wanted to take her out to eat. Maybe he would have the chance to talk to her about Benjamin. Maybe she had noticed something, a sign or symptom of his depression.

Mark could hear Shawn in the kitchen cooking breakfast. As he stepped out of his room, he noticed that Shawn was already dressed and ready to go. Mark wasn't a morning person, and it bothered him that Shawn was so chipper at this hour of the day. However, being a nurse, this was getting up late for Shawn.

Mark turned the water on in the shower. He brushed his teeth and shaved his face. His attempt at a goatee was coming along slowly. It seemed that Shawn never had to worry about shaving. His tan skin seemed to remain hair free for the most part.

Mark quickly got his shower and began drying off. He was in a hurry because he knew that Elizabeth would be waiting on him. She was notorious for getting up extra early. She would get up before the sun, cook herself an egg and some toast. She would then get dressed and sit in the living room reading her Bible until everyone else was ready. This was her routine. If anyone else woke up, she would cook breakfast for that person as well and then go back to reading.

Elizabeth tended to be the one who was calm amid madness. She was the constant that helped the family connect. It didn't matter the amount of chaos the family suffered, Elizabeth could maintain her poise and lead her family through it. Years before, when she found that she had cancer, the family was shaken to its core. That stability was being tested.

During that time, Mark had to grow up fast. He had just turned sixteen and was about to start his junior year in high school. It was supposed to be a year of football games and parties, but he was stuck at home taking care of the little kids. He was supposed to be working towards graduation and hanging out with his friends. Instead he was taking care of his mother and making sure that his father had what he needed.

Mark didn't resent his mother for the upheaval in his own life caused by her illness. He knew that she couldn't be held accountable for the situation. She was ill, and there was nothing that she could do about it. Gorman, on the other hand, could have stepped up. It still infuriated Mark when he thought about his father's unwillingness to help.

Gorman always had an excuse. He would say, "I'm the bread winner, so I should be able to rest when I get home."

Before she got ill, Gorman's alcoholism had increased, but it seemed that her illness was the straw that broke the camel's back. The later Gorman came home every night, the more Mark had to take on parental responsibilities. Mark would cook supper for his siblings and make sure they were bathed and in bed. He would then get them up early and make sure they were ready for school the next morning. It was his father's fault that Mark couldn't have a normal, teenage life.

25

ark pulled up to his parent's house. Gorman's truck was still in the driveway. That meant he was probably still in bed. That was Gorman's typical Sunday morning ritual. He would get up around 10:30, have a couple of cups of coffee and watch television in his underwear.

Mark approached the house and opened the door to find his mother exactly as he expected. She was sitting on the couch reading her Bible. The house was silent. Jessica had spent the night with a friend, and Gorman was still in bed.

Elizabeth wore an older dress. Mark hadn't seen it in a long time. It was white with pink and purple flowers. She had a thin purple jacket laid out to wear over it. The jacket had 1980's shoulder pads. Elizabeth had her hair pulled back in curls. It seemed the older she got, the duller her hair looked. It was thinning as well. Mark was very worried about his mother's health, but he could only do so much.

Elizabeth was very excited that she was going to attend a service with him. Jessica informed him that their mom had been talking about it all week, which excited Mark. Nevertheless, we were concerned that she would dislike it, so he explained that it was more contemporary than what she was used to.

For years Elizabeth had tried to get the kids to join her in church. She wanted to attend services anytime she could. Gorman never went with her. In the beginning he made no effort to restrict her from going. Yet as time went on, he began demanding that she be home by noon so she could have lunch ready. Slowly her chances to fellowship with other believers became fewer and fewer as Gorman expected more and more of her time.

The kids would sometimes go to Sunday school because they enjoyed being away from home. The church bus would pick them up and take them home after services. Mark remembered that old bus. It was a short, yellow school bus with the word "School" blacked out and painted over with the word "Church". It was an older bus with a more rounded backend and badly faded paint. It wasn't equipped with seat belts, so the children would bounce out of their seats every time it hit a pothole.

Above all, Mark remembered that it smelled like feet. He would sit in the back next to the emergency door. The bus would pick up him and his siblings first every Sunday morning, which also meant that they would be the last to be returned home afterward. The kids liked it, but Gorman didn't.

When Elizabeth got sick, they all quit attending. At first the two younger kids wanted to continue going, but Gorman needed Mark home to help around the house. He felt that if Mark wasn't going Benjamin and Jessica didn't need to leave the home either.

After a while, Ben stopped petitioning to attend Sunday School, but Jessica, on the other hand, started going to church with her friend's family. Every Sunday morning, she got up, got dressed, and walked two houses down so she could ride with them to service. Mark always figured that she was getting enough "Jesus" for the whole family. Now she wasn't the only one enjoying the connection to a body of believers.

During the service, Mark watched Elizabeth. Even though he was worried that the contemporary form of worship would make her uncomfortable, she loved it. While it was different than the services in the small white church that she was familiar with, Elizabeth really seemed to enjoy all of it. From the first strum of the guitar to the final prayer, she wept. She couldn't help herself, and her crying made Mark cry as well.

Elizabeth was glowing as they left the building. Her smile stretched from ear to ear. She reminded him of an angel, and Mark was delighted that she came with him. Just a few weeks earlier he had told her that he didn't believe in God, and now he was the one taking her to church with him.

"I guess you liked the service," Mark asked.

"It was really nice," She replied, "I'm so glad that you asked me to go with you. I'm really glad that you're getting into church. It has been a long time since you wanted to go."

"Yep," he replied, "there is girl that I wanted you to meet, but she was out of town today. I will have to introduce you some other time."

"She's not the only reason that you're going, is she?" Elizabeth gave him an inquisitive gaze.

"No, I actually met her at church. She is a friend of Shawn's girlfriend. We actually have a small group meeting in our apartment," He replied.

"What is a small group?" she asked.

"Well, it's a group of people who meet in someone's home to study the Bible," he didn't want it to sound too cliché.

"Oh, that sounds nice. I would like to come to that," she smiled.

"Uh, well, it's actually for young singles. I don't think you would fit in. But I'm sure they have a group that you can get involved in." He smiled hoping that he didn't hurt her feelings.

"Oh, that's fine, I'm sure it's nice." She smiled, then looked out the window.

Mark knew that he needed to talk to her about Benjamin. He didn't want to ruin her day, but this might be the only time that he would get to talk with her when no one else was around. It was now or never.

"So, how do you think Ben is doing?" he asked. "I'm glad that he is close to home."

"Oh, he is, too," she replied, "You wouldn't imagine the change that he has made since we have been back. He was really upset to be that far away from home, mainly, because he was away from you."

"Was he depressed?" Mark questioned her.

"I don't know if I would say he was depressed," she responded.

"Did he ever talk to you about what happened in his room and how he shot himself?" Mark pressed.

"Not really, he didn't talk much about that night," she answered. He could tell that she was a little concerned about his line of questioning. "What is all this about?"

"Mom, I'm worried that Ben may have done this intentionally," he said. Elizabeth looked perplexed. The expression on her face showed that she was visibly shaken and was trying to wrap her mind around what he said. "Mom, I don't want to upset you, but I'm really concerned that there was more to his accident than we want to believe."

"Why would you think that?" Elizabeth was starting to fidget in her seat.

"I went to the police station and they talked to me about what they found. Mom, there are some inconsistencies about what happened, and it really looks like Ben may be dealing with more than we know. I really think he may have done this on purpose." Mark tried to explain to her without upsetting her.

"You're wrong; he would never do anything like that. He has been very happy," she answered defensively.

"But there were so many things that make it seem like there is a problem…" He tried to explain.

Elizabeth interrupted him, "No, it was an accident. He told me it was. Those police officers are just stirring up trouble. They want to get everyone on medication for things that they don't need, but he is fine. There is nothing to worry about. That's enough; I don't want to hear anything else about this. And don't say a word to your brother about this. He looks up to you, and it would devastate him if you started making accusations."

"Fine, but just keep on a look out for anything that seems weird." Mark didn't tell her about the note that he found. She wasn't ready to believe it, and it would be bad for him to continue pushing it.

The rest of the drive was silent. She didn't say much when he dropped her off, and she went into the house after giving him a slight smile. Mark could tell that she was thinking about the conversation, but she didn't want to imagine that her little boy would do that. Mark could only pray that she would listen to what he said and keep an eye on Ben's actions.

26

Today was the big day. Everything that Mark had been working for culminated in the portfolio that he had printed to give to his boss. He arrived early as usual. He would have to leave for class, but he wanted to make sure that is writings were on Vance's desk before anyone else's.

The news floor was empty, except for the few workers who stay overnight to get the next day's paper published. At night only a handful of lights stay on, so it was relatively dark when Mark came through the door. He could see that Vance's office light was off. He usually wouldn't be in for about an hour.

Mark went to his computer to finish printing his final article. Most of his writings were short articles, so he had printed everything that he could find. Out of all the articles he had written, he was proudest of his article on teen suicide. If anything would help him to get the position, it would be this article.

Mark was always confident about his work. He took time to meticulously research everything that he wrote. He wasn't willing to turn in anything that was below par. Whether it was a school assignment or a project at work, he labored diligently to give it his best. It wasn't in his nature to halfway do his job. He felt that his reputation was at stake and wanted everything that he did to be a representation of who he was.

Mark's desire for perfection could prove sometimes to be a problem. Any time he made a low grade or was asked to make corrections to a column, he would be left feeling defeated. Since he considered his work as an extension of who he was, if there was a problem, it tore down his self-confidence. For this reason, he worked very hard to make things perfect.

Mark slipped into Vance's office and laid his folder on the desk. It appeared that he was the first person to submit a portfolio. He took a long, deep breath and let it out slowly. He then left the office, shutting the door behind him. He went back to his desk to gather up his things to get ready for class.

Within a few minutes he noticed Sandra and Roger coming in together. Both had large binders filled with papers. Sandra's was neat and tidy, but Roger's was messy. He had newspaper clippings sticking out every which a way.

Roger put on the persona of professionalism. He looked prim and proper with not even a hair out of place, but he cared very little about his work. His desk was always cluttered with notebooks and folders. He had baskets piled high with notes and scraps of paper with writing scribbled all over them.

Roger had an arrogance about him that Mark really didn't like. He would make statements about his clutter as a sign of his high intelligence and would talk down to others whom he deemed to be inferior to himself. This part of his personality annoyed many of his coworkers, except Sandra.

Sandra took Roger's notebook and laid it with hers on Vance's desk. Mark watched her very carefully. She looked around to see if anyone could see her. Mark's desk was at just an angle that he could see her, but she couldn't see him. She picked up Mark's folder and thumbed through his articles. Mark could feel his ears turning red. They felt like they were on fire. He wanted to say something but knew that he lost his temper too easily.

He had an idea. He picked up his phone and dialed Vance's extension. The phone rang and startled Sandra, who dropped the folder in the floor. Quickly, she scooped up the papers shoving them back into the folder. She adjusted her dress and walked back out of the office.

As she and Roger walked past Mark's cubical, Mark could hear them talking about his writings. He could tell by the tone that they made a snide remark but couldn't actually hear what it was. Mark took a couple of deep breaths and then grabbed his bag off the back of the chair. He left the newsroom and headed for class.

Unusually that morning, class seemed to drag on, and Mark couldn't stop thinking about Sandra rummaging through his writings. She had no reason to even look at it, and for sure not to talk about him to Roger. He tried to focus on class work, but he continued to wonder what she was talking about.

If anyone thought he or she was better than everyone else, it was Sandra. She snubbed everyone in an obvious way. She had very little tact about her. While most people subtly showed their disapproval, her condescending attitude was blatantly displayed. He could just imagine what it was going to be like if she got the position of lead journalist.

On his way from campus, Mark pulled into the gas station next to the school. He had been milking the gas tank for couple of days, driving on fumes. It was time to get gas, or he wouldn't make it back home that evening. He watched the numbers on the gas pump as they turned, his dehydrated car drinking it in. With the constant fluctuation in gas prices, it had been a long time since his Mustang had been filled up.

He stopped the pump when the display read twenty-five dollars, closed his gas tank and sat back down in the car. Looking at his phone, he noticed the back light was lit up. He had a message from Vance emphatically requesting a call. Mark's stomach sank. It seemed like something was wrong and he had no idea what it could be.

"Hello," Vance's voice rang out from the speakerphone.

"Yes sir, I noticed that you called, and I wanted to see what you needed," Mark responded.

"I wanted to check on everything. I noticed that you left your portfolio on my desk. I read your columns and your stories, but there is no feature article. Was everything alright?" Vance sounded very concerned. "Is everything alright with your sister?"

"Yeah, my sister is fine, it was my brother that was in the hospital," he replied.

"Sorry, that's what I meant," Vance corrected, "*Is* everything alright?"

"Yes, he's good. No, everything is good. It was in the folder this morning. I even came in early to print it out and left it on the desk." Mark felt the tension in his head. What happened to his article? "I'm on my way to the office? I will reprint it for you."

Vance agreed.

Mark couldn't breathe. His face was hot, and his ears were on fire. He couldn't imagine what happened to that article. It was his best work. At least he had it saved.

As he pulled into the parking lot, he noticed a different car in Vance's parking spot. It was a new tan Chevy four door truck. Mark had never seen that truck before. Vance must have traded up.

27

He walked into the office. Vance was sitting at his desk, and Martin was sitting opposite him. They were engulfed in reading. Mark went to his desk and turned on his computer. This was strange; he always left it on. For sure it was on this morning. He put his jump drive in and reprinted his article. There had been some computer issues the week before, so he backed up all his work to the jump drive just in case there was a crash.

As he approached Vance's office, he felt like all eyes were on him. As he looked back, Roger quickly put his head down, hoping that Mark hadn't noticed him peering over the top of the cubical. Mark stepped into Vance's office with a new copy of his article.

"Boss, did the computers crash today?" Mark asked.

"Not that I know of," Vance replied, "Why?"

"You know most of us leave our computers on; my computer was off when I came in. It's probably nothing." Mark tried to shrug it off, but he had an uneasy feeling that someone had been messing with his computer files.

Seeing Mark, Martin asked, "Is there some reason you're late on your article submission? When kids come into the class without their homework, we mark off points. You can imagine what we do when you're applying for a job."

"I understand, completely, but I truly printed this and left it in my folder when I put it on the desk." Mark replied.

"Do you know if anyone else came in and messed with the stuff on my desk?" Vance asked.

"Actually, yes, I was sitting at my desk. Sandra and Roger came into your office to drop their portfolios off. Sandra picked up my folder and was looking through it." Mark could feel his ears getting hot.

"Did you see her take anything?" Martin asked.

"No, but I felt uncomfortable with her looking through it, so I called your extension. The ring startled her, and she dropped the papers on the floor. Maybe it's under your desk." Mark was hopeful.

Vance looked under the desk and did find one of Mark's columns, but there was no sign of his feature article. "Well, it looks like something was dropped on the floor, but we really don't know if anyone took anything out after that," Martin replied.

Again, Mark's stomach fell, he wanted to throw up. This would ruin his chance at the position. He went back to his chair and sat down. He knew it was only business, and everyone must follow the rules. Nevertheless, he was so frustrated because of the situation; and there was nothing that he could do but wait until the interviews on Friday.

As the day dragged on, Mark really wanted to do something to get his mind off the situation at work. He even considered heading to the local watering hole on his way home so he could drown his sorrows in some of his favorite spirits.

Luckily, as he finished up his work, he noticed that there was a text on his phone. Jessica wanted to remind him about her concert at

7:00 p.m., and he had promised that he would be there. Maybe it was good that he couldn't stop by the bar; he didn't really need it anyway.

Jessica had been waiting weeks for her winter choir concert. It wasn't really Mark's cup of tea, but he wanted to support Jess. She had had to go to every football and basketball game that Mark played in, so the least that he could do in return was to hear her choir sing.

Just a few weeks prior, Jessica had won first place in an area-wide vocal contest for school, and she told everyone about it. She even had a gold metal to demonstrate her accomplishment. This was her first real achievement.

Tonight, she would be performing her solo piece accompanied by the choir. It was the grand finale of the program. She was busy practicing every time that Mark called her. Mark didn't want to go to the concert because he was depressed about work; but she would be devastated if he missed it.

Mark still couldn't imagine why someone would go into Vance's office and take his feature article out of the folder. Roger and Sandra were hateful, but he never would have guessed they would actually do something to sabotage his chances of being promoted. Granted, they were cunning and thought they were better than everyone else, but would they seriously steal something he, himself, had written?

That evening Mark left work late with caused him to be running late when he pulled into the high school parking lot. There were no parking spots open which left him unsure if he would be able to find a seat inside. He sneaked into the back of the auditorium. The lights were down, and music was playing. There didn't appear to be any open seats anywhere, so Mark stood at the back along with all the other late comers, a man with a large video camera, and several people trying to record the program on their cell phones.

He scanned the crowd to see if he could find his parents. Close to the front of the center section was a guy sitting in a wheelchair. He was in the aisle, which made it easy for Mark to see. Mark squinted a few times. It looked like Ben sitting in the chair, and his mom sitting in the aisle seat next to him. Mark couldn't help but smile. It was good to see Ben outside of the rehab center.

Mark had never been to a choir concert before, and he really didn't know what to expect. They sang songs that he had never heard before. This was almost what he would picture an opera being like. Most were in English, but there were a couple in foreign languages, and he didn't understand what they were saying.

Finally, it was time for the big final number. A young lady stepped from the side of the choir. She was beautiful. Her long black dress sparkled in the light. Her hair was fixed in ringlets cascading off the back of her head.

She opened her mouth to sing. Mark had never heard her before. She had the voice of an angel. Her tone was flawless, and her vocal range was spectacular. Mark was no music aficionado, but her singing was out of this world. She sang an old-time Negro spiritual. Mark closed his eyes to listen, and it would have been easy to have mistaken her for Aretha Franklin or Mahalia Jackson. She was incredible.

When the song was over, there wasn't a dry eye in the place, and everyone was on his or her feet, clapping and cheering. As the concert concluded, the director received one more round of applause for the choir before releasing the audience. While everyone was pushing, trying to get to the back, Mark attempted to make his way to the front. He found Elizabeth trying to push Ben's chair up the steep incline to the back of the auditorium. He took hold of the handles and helped get him up the incline and out the door.

"Wow, could you believe the voice on that last singer?" Mark told his mother.

"She was very good, wasn't she?" Elizabeth replied.

"Do we know her?" He asked.

Elizabeth turned and looked at him in surprise.

"What? I'm serious," he continued.

Very surprised, Elizabeth replied with almost a sarcastic tone, "Well, that was your sister."

"No way," he replied, "How is it that I have never heard her?"

"I think the real question is 'Have you ever really listened?'" Elizabeth retorted.

"I don't guess so," Mark answered.

Jessica came out of the choir hall door and found her family waiting for her. She had the biggest smile on her face. Elizabeth silently clapped for her as she came their way. Jess ran up and gave them a big group hug.

"I can't believe that voice. I never realized that you had such a talent," Mark commended her.

"It's not that good," she shyly responded, "I just really enjoy singing."

Mark couldn't help but be astounded by her voice. She was possibly the best singer that he had ever heard, and he still couldn't believe that he didn't know. It was so good that he actually forgot about the promotion and the portfolio mess up. For sure he had forgotten about going to the bar.

"Thank you so much for coming," Jess said as they walked towards the car.

"I wouldn't have missed it for the world," Mark responded.

28

The entire week while waiting for the big announcement, Mark's anticipation level was through the roof. He was barely able to contain himself. He wanted so badly to talk to Vance and see what was going on, but Martin was always there with him. There had also been a lot of new people in and out of the office every day. Mark thought this constant flow of new faces was very suspicious.

Friday finally arrived and Mark was filled with emotions. He was very nervous to have his final interview and was anxious about the final decision. Sadly, the day seemed to be dragging by. Mark watched Vance and Martin in the office going through each portfolio. They had repeatedly done this over the past several days, and Mark wondered what they were discussing.

Martin came to the door and called Sandra into the office for her interview. Mark wished that he could hear their conversation, but Martin shut the door and closed the vertical blinds. Mark turned back to his desk and continued to work.

Sandra sat in the chair opposite Vance's desk. She didn't seem nervous. She wore her typical gray pantsuit and had her hair pulled back in a ponytail. She also had her plastic-framed glasses on. Mark had often wondered if the glasses were all a show. There were several times that he saw her working without the glasses. She seemed to have them on only when she was around someone she was trying to impress. The rest of the time they were clipped onto her shirt.

As she sat in the office, Vance watched her closely. He noticed that she had her typical smirk on her face. Martin went on with the interview. Sandra answered every question flawlessly. She explained how she would oversee the department. She talked about her knowledge of writing and what she would do when she got the position.

Vance noticed that she spoke a lot of herself but was very derogatory about the other applicants. Vance decided to push the envelope a little bit, to find out how she really felt about the people she would be over seeing. He asked her if she thought that Roger would be good for the position. To his surprise she immediately laid out all of Roger's flaws and stated that, in her opinion, his approach to journalism was old fashioned. She also explained that because of his arrogant attitude he would never be able to work with the younger writers.

This puzzled Vance, he saw Sandra and Roger together all the time. They typically ate together and took breaks together. There had been several occasions that they even carpooled. He thought they had a good relationship. He couldn't believe that she was now criticizing him like this. He knew that she only looked out for herself, but this was ridiculous.

With his curiosity piqued he inquired, "What do you think about Mark? Do you think he would make a good lead reporter?"

"Mark? Oh, he's just a kid," she replied sarcastically. She also seemed appalled he was even being considered. "No one will listen to him because he is so young and inexperienced. There is no way that he would have the fortitude to oversee the other journalists. He wasn't even responsible enough to turn in his feature article on time." Sandra replied.

Martin retorted, "Sandra, if this is how you feel about the other writers, how are going to be able to lead them…"

Before she could answer, Vance held up a finger, "Hold on for just a second." Leaning forward in his chair with his elbows on the desk he peered directly into Sandra's eye. "You just said that Mark didn't turn in his article on time. Why do you think that?"

Sandra started to squirm in her chair. She cleared her throat a couple of times. "Well, I overheard you guys talking about it the other day."

"No, we didn't discuss anything like that outside of this office," Martin rebutted.

"I don't know then, I just thought someone said that he didn't turn something in," Sandra could feel the sweat dripping down the back of her neck.

"Actually, someone had been my office the morning that Mark turned in his stuff. They went through it and stole his article and shredded it. Do you have any idea who may have done that?" Vance pushed.

"Uh, Well, you know, Roger came in and put our portfolios on your desk, I bet he was worried that Mark's article was good, and

so he stole it to keep Mark from having a chance at the promotion,"
She surmised.

"Ok, well thank you for your time," Martin opened the door
motioning for her to leave. She stood up, straightened her blouse and
walked through the office door. Mark watched he leave the office. He
could tell that she was frazzled. She scowled at him has she walked
past his desk.

After she left the office Martin turned back to Vance, "I guess
Mark was telling the truth. Someone did take his article out."

"Mark is actually a really good kid, and I know that he could
handle the workload, I just don't know if he has the leadership skills
needed," Vance replied.

"How did you know they shredded it?" Martin probed.

Vince smiled, "I didn't, but that was what I would do if I was
trying to hide something."

Shaking his head, Martin picked up Roger's portfolio and
flipped through the unorganized mess. He couldn't believe the lack of
cohesion and organization. There was no way to tell what went
together. "Have you even looked at this jumbled mess?" Martin
chuckled, "It looks like he didn't care what it looked like.

They called Roger into the office next. His interview wasn't
as long as Sandra's, and when he left the office, he appeared very
upset. He grabbed his coat and stormed out. Sandra hurriedly pursued
him. Mark knew it was none of his business, but he decided that it
might be a good time for a smoke break.

As Mark came around the end of the building, he could
already hear the yelling.

“What do you mean you thought it would be a good idea?” Roger yelled.

“They had me cornered. I panicked didn’t know what to tell them,” Sandra replied.

“You were the one that took that kid’s work. You do realize that now we’re both out of the running for this position. I told you it was a bad idea. I told you that you would get caught and now you’re trying to take me down, too.” Roger’s voice echoed against the brick wall.

Mark stood around the corner from the two. This seemed reminiscent of his parents fighting, and he felt conflicted. He had always wanted to step in and protect his mother when his parents fought. His instinct would be to protect Sandra. At the same time, he knew this wasn’t his fight, and they both deserved the consequences of their choices.

“I’m done, I have nothing left that I can do here, I can’t even show my face around here anymore after what you told them.” Roger took off towards the parking lot.

“You were the one who tried to delete the files on his computer so that he couldn’t reprint it. You’re lousy as a writer anyway. You’re lost in the 20th century, Roger. While the rest of us are caught up with the times, you’re decades behind.” Sandra called out after him.

Mark heard the car door slam and Roger leave rubber on the pavement as he drove off. Mark took the last long drag off his cigarette and dropped the butt in the can as he heard Sandra coming around the end of the building.

"What? Are you just sitting out here listening to us? Are you looking for your next scoop?" Sandra stormed passed him.

"I was just taking a smoke break," Mark could barely get the words out of his mouth before she was gone.

29

This was a crazy turn of events. He knew something weird was going on, but never knew that he would be in the middle of it. Moreover, he never thought that it would be about him getting a promotion. Mark knew that someone had taken that article out of his folder, and he also knew someone was on his computer while he was in class.

As he walked back into the newsroom Angela Wilson was coming out of Vance's office. She had a big smile on her face. It was the first time that Mark had ever seen her with makeup on and her hair styled more than just pulled back in a ponytail. She smiled at Mark as their paths crossed.

Mark noticed Martin motioning for him, so he went into the office. Martin went over the typical questions, and Mark answered everything the best he could. Martin seemed impressed that a young man who hadn't yet graduated would be as experienced as Mark was. His writing examples demonstrated a talent for journalism. Martin's compliments made Mark feel good about himself and his abilities.

Finally, Vance broke in, "Mark, we want to apologize. We found out this morning that someone took your article out of your portfolio and got rid of it. We aren't quite sure who did it, but we have two different people pointing their fingers at one another."

Mark acted surprised, "Yeah, no, it's not a problem."

"Well, you fit what we need," Vance continued, "You have the experience and the writing style. You're well-versed in new technology, and I believe that you know how to cut down your columns to fit them for internet use. However, you don't have the leadership experience for this position. You have never had to oversee other writers, and I believe that could cause a problem."

"OK, I understand, I'm glad just to have the chance to be considered," Mark's face fell. He knew that they could see the disappointment.

"Are you withdrawing your application?" Martin said.

"No, I just know that I'm young, and I shouldn't have gotten my hopes up," Mark could feel his face turning red with embarrassment.

"You give up too easily; you will never make it anywhere in this business if you give up that easily. You are your only ally. No one is going to step out for you; you must do it yourself. There are thousands of people competing for jobs in the writing industry, so if you're going to compete with them, you must be more assertive and willing to take a chance. Even if you don't get a position you were trying to get, the experience will help you next time," Martin scolded.

"Oh, well, I…I appreciate your advice," Mark responded.

"What Martin is trying to say is you have to fight for yourself in this industry. If you don't fight for what you want, you won't make it. That is why I feel, for now, you have some growing to do. But you're the only one we have with experience in internet reporting. You have a way of presenting info in a concise way perfect for the internet. I want you to take on an assistant role, focusing your efforts on the internet." Vance's words came as a surprise.

"Wow, OK," Mark didn't know what to say.

"You will be responsible for taking the work of other writers and preparing it for internet use, and then get it uploaded to the website. I'm still looking for a couple of other people to help you, but you will be responsible for making sure it gets done. Do you think that's something that you can do?" Vance asked

Mark was still in shock, "Yeah, I can do that."

"Are you sure? That response didn't sound like you were sure," Martin snapped back.

Mark smiled and cleared his throat, and then forcefully said, "Yes, sir, that is something I can do."

"That's more like it," Martin smiled at Mark as he opened the door.

Mark got back to his desk and noticed that his phone was blinking with a voice mail. While everyone was moving toward text messaging, Elizabeth was just now trying to get used to voicemail. Mark gave her a call back. The phone rang a couple of times and went to her voicemail. He would just have to wait for her to call back.

The afternoon continued, and Vance finished the final two interviews. It came time for him to make the big announcement. He called to everyone from his office door. Silence fell over the newsroom floor. People hurriedly got off phone calls, and, like prairie dogs, heads popped up from the cubicles all over the room. Everyone was waiting to hear the big announcement.

The general consensus was that Sandra would be offered the position, but Mark didn't feel she would. He looked around and saw everyone, except Roger. He wasn't back. Maybe he was serious when he said that he couldn't show his face around here anymore. Mark thought to himself, *Maybe, he is going to retire.*

"Well, everyone knows that we have been looking to hire a new lead journalist. This person would need to be energetic and able to lead the other writers and oversee news stories. After a tedious couple of weeks, we have found our new head news writer," Vance began.

Mark looked over at Sandra who had come around the end of her cubicle and was straightening her jacket so she would look presentable when he called her name. Even with everything she had done, she still believed that she would be getting the promotion. Mark couldn't believe her audacity.

"Well, without further ado," Vance continued, "We would like to welcome Angela Wilson as our new head news writer."

Sandra had already started walking to the front, when she realized her error. She turned and shook Angela's hand acting as if that was her intent all along. She returned to her desk. She got her purse and walked out the door. Mark could tell she was embarrassed.

Everyone clapped for Angela. Mark knew that she had what it takes to do the work. She was tenacious, strong-willed, and had a way of getting people to respond to her questions. He wasn't sure if it was because of her annoying nasal voice or if it was simply her unwillingness to back down when she was pursuing a story. Mark was glad to know that she would be working with him.

"Also, we would like to announce that Mark Cooper is going to be taking over the assistant news writing position that was vacated by Roger Norman this morning. Mark has a strong understanding of internet technology, and he will be working with everyone to get your work online." Vance led everyone in a round of applause.

It made him feel good that everyone was acknowledging his accomplishments. It also explained where Roger was. It was too bad for him that he had gotten mixed up with Sandra.

"Last, I would like to introduce everyone to Martin Vasquez," Vance continued, "You may have noticed the nice big truck that has been sitting in my parking spot over the past couple of weeks. It belongs to Martin. As of Monday, he will be taking over the day-to-day operations of the Chronicle. I'm going to be taking some much-needed time off. I will still be around from time to time, but you will now be answering to Martin."

Mark couldn't believe what he was hearing. He looked up to Vance and felt like he was losing a father. He was overwhelmed with sadness and couldn't believe that Vance was going to be leaving. He replayed the past couple of weeks in his head and realized that Martin had been involved in everything since he showed up. Vance had been letting him get the hang of the job before he announced his decision to the employees of the Chronicle.

As the day ended and Mark walked to his car, he felt his phone vibrate in his pocket. It was his mother. "So? Did you get the promotion?" She asked.

"No and Yes," Mark answered, "I got a promotion, but not the one that I thought I might be getting."

"That's good though, right?" She asked.

"Yes, it's very good; it's just a lot to take in right now," Mark replied. He didn't want to explain about Vance. She wouldn't have understood why he was so upset.

"Well, I'm proud of you," she reassured him.

"Thanks," that was all Mark could say.

Mark really couldn't believe the feeling of loss that he was experiencing. This was his boss, not a member of his family. Mark could barely call him a friend, but Mark was still very upset. Vance was his mentor and, in some cases, his confidant. It seemed now like Vance was dying, and Mark would never see him again.

Mark took a deep breath and let it out slowly. God knew what he was doing, and so Mark had to trust in that. That was the only option that he had, because there was nothing else that he could do.

30

It was Tuesday afternoon, and Mark had just gotten off work. He had been in class that morning before taking some time to run by the library to do some research. Now it was time for him to get ready for a very special night.

This was Mark's first date with Marie without his chaperones, Shawn and Trisha. Mark was a little nervous; they had been dating for almost two months. She was different than any other girl that he had ever dated. This was probably the longest dating relationship he had ever had. There were a few girls that he thought he was serious about, but soon figured out they weren't really into him.

Mark wanted to make tonight very special. It was Valentine's Day, and Mark didn't want to do anything that would mess things up. This relationship was different. It wasn't one of the one-night stands that he was used to. This girl could be the one to whom he would give a ring.

When he wasn't with her, he was thinking about her. When he thought of his future, she was always there. He wanted more than anything to show her how he felt.

Mark had the perfect night planned. Unlike most guys who prepared a traditional Valentine's date with an expensive restaurant and a big box of chocolates attached to a dozen roses, Mark wanted to do something a little more meaningful.

Mark washed and waxed his car. He took a cotton swab and a toothpick to clean all the nooks and crannies. He vacuumed everywhere, even the trunk, which he had never vacuumed before. It looked brand new. Well, at least as new as it had when he bought it.

Mark was crazy about Marie. The longer they dated, the more he realized that he loved her. This scared him. He had never loved a girl. This time it was different.

Throughout high school and college, he had dated like everyone else did. Kids would say they were in love with one person this week, and then with another the next week. The word "love" was thrown around so much that Mark was never willing to use the word. He felt that throwing it around flippantly would lessen its meaning. He wanted to save the word "love" for the person he really loved.

After cleaning up his car and then running to the apartment to get ready, Mark showed up at her house a quarter till 7:00. He went to the door to meet her. Trisha was already gone with Shawn, who had taken her out for dinner and a movie. Mark's plan was a little less traditional. As he waited on the steps, he held a single rose behind his back.

Marie opened the door. She was wearing a black blouse and a nice pair of blue jeans. Her boots were brown suede with fur trim on top. She had her hair neatly straightened, pulled back behind her right ear. She was beautiful. As soon as Mark saw her, she took his breath away. Slowly he pulled the rose from behind his back, extending it to her. She smiled and shyly ducked her head. Taking the rose from him, she breathed in its fragrance.

Mark felt like a schoolboy with his first crush. He was giddy, and all he could do was smile at her. He pushed his hands deep into his pockets, shrugging his shoulders, and turned towards the car. Marie locked her arm in his, and slowly they ambled towards his vehicle. As they arrived, Mark opened the car door and helped her in.

After Mark settled into the driver's seat, they sat in the car for a few moments without saying a word. Finally, she broke the silence. "Where are we going?"

"Well, I wanted to do something a little different," He replied as they pulled away from the curb. They drove through town, passing buildings with their "closed" signs up. Their lights were dim, and there was no one inside.

Mark turned the final corner and pulled in front of Dixie's Diner. Marie looked a little confused, "Dixie's?" she asked.

"Yeah, it was the first place we went to. It means a lot to me, so I wanted to bring you here to make it special. I hope you're not disappointed," he replied.

"No, I'm not disappointed," Marie reached out and took his hand, "I'm just surprised that it meant so much to you."

Mark got out of the car and raced around to the passenger side to open the door for her. She already had the door open by the time he reached it. She smiled, realizing that she had foiled his plans. He helped her out of the car and shut the door behind her.

Mark did make it in time to open the door to the diner for her when they reached it. While opening the door, he noticed a sign in the window saying, "Help Wanted: Cooks needed." He couldn't help but wonder if he knew someone who could use a job. He put the thought out of his mind.

They sat in the same location where they had been the first night they came with Shawn and Trisha. After placing their order, Mark pulled out some quarters and dropped them in the jukebox. He flipped through the songs a couple of times before he decided on one.

Mark took note of the fact that the diner was empty. Couples were most likely out at fancy restaurants, so Mark and Marie had it all to themselves. Mark crossed back to the table reaching out his hand to her and said, "Can I have this dance?"

Marie looked at him very strangely. "I can't dance," she said.

"I can't either, but that doesn't mean we can't try," he replied.

Slowly she took his hand, and he pulled her to her feet. Pulling her close, they danced between the tables. He spun her around and swung her back and forth. They laughed. It was all fun, until he didn't notice the chair behind him. As he stepped back, he toppled over it. The next thing he knew, he was lying on the floor, rubbing his back and trying to figure out what happened.

Marie tried to stifle the laugh that was bubbling up inside of her, at least until she made sure that he was alright. After she had helped him to his feet, they mutually agreed that dancing should be left to the professionals.

By the time they returned to their table the waitress came with their food on a tray. The butterflies in Mark's stomach made it difficult to eat. He was so excited to be sitting with Marie and she seemed nervous too, just picking at her fries.

"I noticed you not eating, I don't know about you, but I feel nervous, like this is the first time we've been out," he chuckled.

"I agree, we have been out several times, but we're always with Shawn and Trish. This is the first time that we have ever been alone," she shyly looked down at the table.

"I really like you a lot, and I can't help thinking about you all the time." He brushed her hair back out of her face so that he could gaze into her beautiful eyes.

She smiled, taking his hand in hers. She responded, "I also can't stop thinking about you, either."

Finally, with their mutual feelings for one another acknowledged his nerves calmed down and he was able to eat. Discussion began to flow freely, and they talked about everything. He discussed his family, and she told him about hers. They talked about their ambitions, and how they were going to achieve them. Mark had never really been open with someone like this before. While the vulnerability made him a little apprehensive, it felt good to trust her.

When the wall clock at the diner showed 9:30, he knew that he'd best take her home. While he could sit and talk with her all night, they both had early morning classes. Marie asked for a small to-go container and wrapped up the rest of her burger. Mark helped her through the door and to the car. It has been an unbelievable night, and he walked slowly not wanting it to end.

31

As they pulled up at the house, Mark took her hand. He looked deeply into her eyes. She smiled and looked down briefly, before meeting his gaze again.

He asked, "Can I come in?"

"I guess. Trisha's movie probably won't be over for a little while," Marie responded.

They walked into the townhouse. Marie led him to the couch, and she offered him something to drink. She sat beside him and he pulled her closer. As she looked into his eyes, she smiled. He moved in to kiss her. She, too, closed her eyes and leaned in as well. As their lips touched, Marie immediately pulled back and moved away from him.

"I'm so sorry, I can't," she explained.

"I'm sorry, I didn't mean to do anything," he replied.

"No, it's ok, I just, I can't do that," she said, "I really want to kiss you, but I can't."

"You can't?" he asked.

"No, I can, I just can't," she corrected. "A kiss can easily move to more intimate things, and I made a decision that I want to save that."

"I'm sorry; I wasn't trying to force you to do anything that you weren't ready to do. I wasn't trying to force you into anything physical, I just knew that we were getting closer and thought it may be time to take our relationship to the next level. I don't want to do anything that you're not ready for," Mark stumbled over his words.

"I know; I made a decision a long time ago that I wanted to maintain my purity until my wedding night. But I know that even kissing can lead to other types of intimacy, and so I decided to save that, too. It isn't that I don't want to, I just want to save that." Marie tried to smile, to make Mark feel better.

Mark had never thought about it that way. Because of his constant partying, he had given his virginity to a girl his first year in college. He had never realized that someone's purity could be so important to him or her. All his friends were having sex. Well most of them, Shawn never mentioned sex. Mark began wondering, *was this a part of being a Christian?*

Seeing the confusion in his eyes, Marie asked, "Are you alright?"

"No, yeah, I'm good," he replied. "This is just new to me. I have never felt this way before about anyone. I didn't mean to upset you."

"You didn't upset me. I don't want to upset you, but if you're serious about me, then I know you will understand and support me on this." She pulled away, "Do you think that you can do that?"

He struggled to form words, "Yeah, I can do that…I have never felt for anyone else what I feel for you. I believe I'm in love with you." The words tasted sweet as they came out of his mouth and a smile was now plastered on his face. It was the first time that he had recognized that he had fallen in love with her.

Marie smiled too, reaching out her hand to take his. "I know that this may be a different type of relationship than most, but I believe if we wait, it'll make it more special."

"Thanks, alright, I'm not in any hurry," Mark gripped her hand and pulled her close. She turned, placing her back against his chest. Holding her close to his chest, he took a deep breath and breathed in the fragrance of her hair. "I love you."

She pulled his arms around her tightly and leaned her head on his shoulder. She whispered in his ear, "I love you, too."

They sat there for a minute engrossed in the moment until they were startled by the front door opening. They could hear Trisha talking, going on and on about the movie, Shawn in tow. As they came into the living area, Marie sat up.

"What have you guys been up to?" Trisha asked.

"We went out for supper and had a really good time together. What about you guys?" Marie responded.

"Well, we went out to eat at the new seafood place across town, and then we went to see a movie at the theater. And also, we got engaged," Trisha nonchalantly spat out the words.

Marie's eyes widened, "What?"

Trisha, filled with excitement, held her hand high in the air displaying the large diamond ring on her finger.

Marie jumped up and grabbed her hand looking at the new rock on her ring, "Oh WOW it's beautiful."

"We're getting married," Trisha screamed. Trisha and Marie shared a little victory dance.

Mark gave Shawn a look; he shrugged. Trisha turned and gave Shawn a big hug and kiss. He put his arms around her and held her close for a minute before they finally broke free.

"Well, I have an early morning tomorrow, so I think we have to call it a night," Shawn said.

"Yeah, me too," Mark chimed it.

Marie put her arms around him and again whispered in his ear.

"I love you, too," he said as he kissed her on the forehead.

Shawn and Mark walked out of the townhouse together. The night air was a little brisk; Mark adjusted his collar to cover the back of his neck. He pulled out the pack of cigarettes from his pocket and lit on as he walked with Shawn to his car.

"So, you're getting married," Mark began.

"Yep, it has been a long time coming, but I decided that it was time." Shawn leaned against his car.

"I think you made a good choice. She seems like she really likes you." Mark took another drag from his smoke. "Are you a virgin?"

The question caught Shawn off guard. "Uh, well that is a loaded question…no and yes."

"What do you mean, 'no and yes'?" Mark asked.

"When I was in high school, I met this girl whom I completely adored. She was notorious for her very active sex life around the school. When she found something, or someone, that she wanted, she would do whatever it took to get it. She was having trouble in some of her classes, so her parents hired me to tutor her."

Shawn replied. "She didn't want to be tutored; she wanted someone to do her homework for her. The first day that I went to her house, she came on to me and, being a 16-year-old kid...well you know what happened. At the end of the school year she moved away, and that was that."

"Wow, you know, usually it's the guy doing that type of stuff," Mark responded. "What did you mean that you're still a virgin?"

"Right after I started college, I began really searching for something to give meaning to my life. I was asked to go to a college Bible study. They talked about getting over past mistakes, putting the past behind you. I had been feeling guilty for the things I had done. That night I talked to the team leader, and he told me that I could be free from that guilt. I accepted Jesus into my heart, but more than that, I asked him to make me a virgin again. I may not be a virgin physically, but I made a decision that I wanted to wait to have sex again until I was married."

"Whoa, that is a very big decision. I love Marie, but remaining celibate is going to be very difficult," Mark responded.

"It's very hard, and I didn't think it was something that I could do. Once you have been involved in that type of relationship, it's hard to refrain from another intimate relationship. But if you really want to make that commitment for someone you love, God will be your strength." Shawn yawned, "I've got to get going."

"See you at the apartment." Mark dropped his cigarette butt on the ground and stomped it out.

He looked back at the house. Mark really loved Marie and believed that he would spend the rest of his life with her. As he went around to the driver's seat he prayed, "God, if this is you, then please help me to do this." He sat down in the car and pulled the door to.

As he drove home, he couldn't get the thought out of his head. Marie had said that if he really loved her, then he would have to wait. But God would really have to help him, because he didn't think he could do it alone.

32

Winter was slowing turning into spring. It had been two months since Ben was first hospitalized. After time in intensive care and a couple more weeks in Oklahoma City, he was finally moved to a local rehabilitation hospital where he spent another four weeks.

This was bittersweet for the Cooper family, Benjamin was close to home, but he wasn't at home. Every day therapists worked to strengthen his legs. They would do exercises to maintain muscle mass and would test his feet for any sign of nerve or muscle reaction.

It was a very good sign that as swelling was subsiding, Ben began regaining feeling in his legs, but he still couldn't put weight on his feet. No matter how much therapy and exercise they put him through, he was unable to stand up.

Even though the MRI was didn't indicate any permanent damage, but the doctor said that it would take time for him to fully recover. For some people it took years, so Elizabeth knew that they were in for the long haul.

On Friday, March 1st, since the swelling around his spinal cord had gone down, the doctor finally released him to return home. He would still have physical therapy and multiple doctors' visits, but he was with his family again. That was what Mark had been waiting for.

Ben was also glad to be out of the hospital. It had been a long time since he had been able to sleep in his own room. His memory was still very hazy about the events on the day of his accident. He didn't want to talk about it and tried to avoid any questions that came up.

Benjamin really liked the remodel of his room. It seemed so much bigger with Mark's bed gone, and with the fresh paint on the walls, a person couldn't tell that there had been blood on them. Ben especially liked the proximity of the bed to the TV. He could now sit in bed and play video games all day long.

The day after Ben was released from the rehab center, Mark spent the entire day playing games with him. He couldn't help but feel amazed at the bond that was formed by knowing that he almost lost his brother. He had always loved his brother and would have laid down his life if that was what it took. But now there was an intense appreciation for him that Mark had never felt before. He was so glad that Benjamin was home.

The Saturday afternoon was ending, and Mark could tell Ben was getting tired. They had been playing since Mark got to the house that morning. The fragrance of meatloaf wafted down the hallway, and Mark's stomach knew that it was time for supper.

Nevertheless, there had been one question nagging at Mark all day, but he didn't want to ask. He knew that his mom would be calling them to supper soon, so if he was going to ask, he needed to ask now.

"Hey, bub, I have a question for you. Why did you shoot yourself?" Benjamin was startled by the question. Mark was just as startled by his own abrasiveness.

"I don't know what you mean," Benjamin rebutted.

Mark looked down at the floor. "I read the police report, and they believe that it was a suicide attempt. I want you to be honest with me. If there is something that you're going through, let me help you. I won't talk to anyone else about it."

Benjamin's face was turning red, and his breathing was heavy. Mark knew that sign. It was the tell-tale signal that Benjamin was becoming very angry. He tried to pull himself to the other side of his bed where his wheelchair sat. "I told you I didn't."

"Alright, stop, I have something that I want to tell you." Mark tried to grab Ben's arm, but he pulled away dumping himself onto the floor. Mark quickly made it around the bed. "Are you ok?"

Elizabeth was also making her way down the hall, "Is everything ok in there?"

"Yes, Mom, we're alright." Mark replied through the shut door.

"Ok, supper is about ready," she called back.

Ben was sitting in the floor with his arms crossed. Every attempt to get him into the wheelchair was futile at this point because when he would pull on it and it rolled away.

Again, Mark asked, "Are you ok?"

"Yes, I'm fine; I just can't get this stupid chair close enough," Benjamin replied.

"Didn't your nurse tell you to leave the brake engaged?" Mark's attempt as a joke wasn't funny for Ben.

"Just help me get in the chair, please."

"Not until you listen to what I have to say." Mark sat down beside Benjamin on the floor. Benjamin tried to ignore him. He continued to look at the floor, sitting with his arms crossed. "You were gone when I got to the hospital that night. I was very upset because the police and social workers were there trying to find out what happened. I never would have thought you would have tried to hurt yourself on purpose. I stormed out of the emergency room and got in my car to meet you in the hospital in Oklahoma City."

Ben's face was beginning to regain his normal color. Mark continued his story, but Ben didn't look up. Mark explained how he was driving and hit a patch of ice and ended up in the ditch. He described how angry he felt and how all he wanted to do was get down to the hospital. Still Benjamin sat there, seemingly uninterested.

"Suddenly, someone walked past the window of my car. It was you." Benjamin's ears perked up at Mark's words. He turned and looked at Mark, and all the color drained from his face. "I was in the middle of the snow, and you were standing right there. You were in the same clothes that you were wearing when they took you to the hospital. You had blood coming from your chest. I tried so hard to get you to come with me, but you wouldn't." Mark could feel the tears streaming down his face, and his voice had begun to crack as he talked. Ben sat there staring at him, his face still pale, almost scared to react.

Mark stopped for a moment to catch his breath. He could hardly form the words as he attempted to swallow the knot in his throat. He sniffled to keep his nose from running.

Ben opened his mouth, but his voice came out only as a whisper, "I told you to love Dad." This startled Mark. Ben continued, "While I was standing there looking at you, you asked what you could do to help, and I told you to love Dad."

Now the color had drained from Mark's face. He felt cold chills all over his body. In places he didn't know you could get cold chills. He starred at Ben with wide eyes, not knowing what to say.

Ben quickly looked down, "I'm tired of the fighting. I really thought that I might be able to get away from all of it. I…I had been looking in the encyclopedia to find exactly where my heart was. I was tired of having a broken heart. I love you, and I love dad. I hate it when you guys fight."

The waterfall was now coming from Benjamin's eyes. "I know most people try to shoot themselves in the mouth, but I knew mom would find me, and I didn't want that to be the last memory she had of me. I decided to shoot myself in the heart. I guess I didn't do that very well, did I?"

Mark was still speechless. He finally found his words, "How did you know what you said when I was out there stranded in the snow?"

"Because I was there," Ben replied, "I remember being in the ambulance. The paramedics were talking, and they were confused because there was no way I could still be alive. One of them said that the impact of the bullet should have damaged my heart. It just barely missed; I was still alive. I remember passing out. The next thing I remember was the cold. It was like my whole body was cold. I don't know how long it had been, but I saw myself outside in the snow. It was like a dream…you know when you're dreaming and you're watching yourself."

Marks chills were still moving up and down his arms. Every word that came out of Benjamin's mouth made it worse. "You mean you could see it; you were talking to me."

"Yeah, kind of, I thought I was dreaming. I was out for almost a week, but the entire time I dreamed. I dreamed of you and Jessica. I dreamed about mom and dad, and that time that we drove down to Texas. I dreamed of the past, and about school. I also dreamed about me getting older and getting married. I remember just bits and pieces, but I remember standing in the snow talking to you." Ben's tears had subsided.

Mark moved closer to him and put his arm around Benjamin's back. He pulled him up close to his chest. "I love you. I'm sorry that things have been this way. But I feel like things are changing."

Ben sat there for a minute just waiting, not knowing what else to say. Finally, he could wait no longer. "Mark, can you help me?"

"Sure, what do you need?" Mark responded. He was very concerned at what his little brother needed.

"Can you help me get in my chair? I have to go to the restroom, and this bonding is about to be called on account of rain."

Mark couldn't believe what his brother just said. "No, you can stay in the floor." Mark got up and headed to the kitchen.

"Mark, please, help me," Ben beckoned.

"Nope, you're a jerk. You figure it out," Mark continued to the kitchen, "So Mom, what's for supper."

"Fine, I will." Ben pulled the chair towards him, locked the wheels and pulled himself into the seat. "See if I ever talk to you again," he called as he shut the bathroom door.

When Ben finally made it to the kitchen, Mark was eating, and Elizabeth was making Ben's plate.

"Honey, are you feeling ok? Mark said you fell off the bed," Elizabeth questioned Ben as he entered the room.

"Yes, mom, I'm fine. I was just trying to get in the chair, and it rolled away from the bed." Ben scowled at Mark who had a smirk on his face.

"Please be careful, I don't want you to hurt your back," Elizabeth put the plate on the table where Benjamin always sat. He pulled himself toward the table.

Elizabeth made the best home-style food that Mark had ever tasted, especially her mashed potatoes. Mark couldn't help but wonder if there was a way that he could get her to find a job in a diner somewhere.

"This food is really good, Mom," Mark began, "I really think that you should give other people the privilege of tasting your home cooking."

"Son, how many times have I told you that there is no way I can do that? Especially now since Ben is home. He needs me." Elizabeth sat down at the end of the table.

"Mom, I'm ok," Ben rebutted, "I think it would be good for you to get out of the house a little bit."

Elizabeth smiled, "I don't know, I haven't been in the work force for years. No one would want my food. Even you guys complain about what we're having sometimes."

"That's different; if you worked in a restaurant, then people would actually want to eat your food," Mark teased.

Elizabeth glared at Mark, so he back-pedaled "I mean, because they would be paying to eat it. We don't always want to enjoy your food. That still didn't sound right," Mark smiled. He continued, "What I mean is, there is a little diner by the school, and they are looking for a new cook. I think you should look into it."

"Really no, your dad wouldn't want me, too." Elizabeth seemed to always use that as an excuse for why she couldn't do something.

Mark had never noticed it before, but since she has been back from Oklahoma City it became obvious. Every time she was prompted to do something that she didn't believe she could do, she used Gorman as her excuse. He knew that his father was violent and a drunk, but it seemed that most of Elizabeth's problem was her own insecurity.

However, before he could say anything about it, his cell phone went off, "Hello…Yeah, Shawn, what's going on?... Dad's in the emergency room, what happened?" Mark could feel his heart begin to race and could see the concern in his mother's eyes.

"What's wrong?" Elizabeth was filled with panic.

Mark covered the receiver, "Dad fell at work." Again, to Shawn he replied, "Ok, what room is he in?... Ok, I'm here with Mom and Ben; we're on our way."

It was crazy; everything was surreal. Benjamin had been home from the hospital for a day, and now Gorman was lying in the hospital because of an accident at work. To make matters worse Jessica was on a school trip and wasn't supposed to have her phone, so they had no way to get in touch with her until she got back that evening.

33

Before they could get very far down the road; Elizabeth was already in tears. She was praying for Gorman, but Mark could hear the fear in her voice. Mark knew that she wouldn't know what to do with herself if something happened to Gorman. Furthermore, how would she be able to take care of herself and the younger kids? Thoughts were racing through Mark's mind as he sped through town towards the hospital.

It all seemed so familiar to him, because it had been only a couple of months since the first time that he had done the same thing when Ben had been hurt. Mark was filled with apprehension; he didn't want his dad to die. He had been so angry at his father for so long, and at times he had wished that Gorman would die. But now, he was scared and felt very guilty.

Mark had learned very little about the situation, when Shawn had called. He only knew that Gorman had fallen from scaffolding at work, so Mark prepared himself for the worst. He imagined his father lying in the bed with tubes and wires attached to his body. Even worse, his father could be draped with a white sheet and a tag on his toe. He could feel the anxiety building in his chest.

Mark pulled into the circle drive by the emergency room entrance. He retrieved Ben's wheelchair from the trunk and helped Elizabeth get Ben out of the car. As she pushed Ben into the hospital,

Mark secured a parking spot close to the emergency room door. He went to open the car door but found himself unable to move. His hands wouldn't let go of the steering wheel. Breathing deeply, he tried to calm his nerves, but it wasn't helping.

He closed his eyes, "God, you know I'm new to this 'God stuff', and I really don't know what to say, but please let my dad be alright." Out of the corner of his eye, he noticed something green in the floorboard shoved up under the dashboard. "What on earth is that?"

He flipped on the overhead light and felt around on the floorboard among the paper cups and fast food wrappers. Finally, he felt the canvass under his fingers. He had forgotten all about his father's military wallet. With all the trash that he collected in his car, he hadn't been able to see it.

Suddenly the images of that night flashed before his eyes. On Christmas, he had opened the gift and when he had driven away from his parents' house, he had ended up just throwing it in the passenger seat. It must have fallen to the floor when he took off. He didn't understand how could have missed it when he cleaned out his car for the date with Marie, baffled him. It must have gotten pushed under the seat.

Running his finger along the stitching, he read his father's name on the back. As he squeezed the wallet, he could feel something stiff inside. He wondered what it could be.

He flipped it over and pulled back the Velcro clasp. Just inside the wallet was the money that Elizabeth had given him on

Christmas. Unfolding it, he discovered two crisp fifty-dollar bills, which he put in his pocket.

Exploring further in the wallet's pockets, he found a picture of his mother in front of an old-fashioned diner. He guessed it had to be the diner where she worked when she met Gorman. The diner in the picture was silver with a red diamond trim and it reminded him of Dixie's Diner. The picture had been taken with a Polaroid camera, and Mark could see that it was tattered and torn.

Hidden in another pocket was a picture of Gorman and some other guys wearing their fatigues out front of a makeshift barrack. Someone had torn the corner off the picture, eliminating one of the soldiers standing at the end of the group. Gorman never talked about the guys he served in the military with. The cryptic picture made Mark curious about who this person was and why he was torn from the picture.

Finally, Mark opened the bill pocket and found a small metal cross and a folded-up piece of paper. The paper had been ripped from a spiral and still had the small remnants of paper hanging from the edge. He flipped the cross over in his hand feeling the smooth metal between his fingers. Upon closer investigation, he noticed that there was a slight discoloration of the metal, giving it a blue tint.

Mark put the cross back in the wallet, and slowly opened the folded piece of paper. It also was discolored, but the wallet had preserved it well. Mark could see where the metal from the cross had left a blue tinge to the paper in the shape of a cross. Some of the ink had run, and there were several small tears around the edges.

Upon opening the letter, Mark realized that it had been written by Gorman. He could easily recognize the handwriting. Mark had never seen a letter written by his father before. He remembered his mother talking about the letters they had exchanged during the war, but they were put up, locked away in history.

Dear Baby,

I want to write you this letter just in case I don't make it home. Sorry, I don't know yet if you're a boy or a girl. There ain't been a day that I haven't thought of you and your mom. Since I found out that you were coming, I have been filled with different emotions. At times I'm angry because I wasn't planning on having kids. I didn't have a daddy, and so I don't know how to be a daddy. But I know what it feels like to be left and abandoned. And I don't ever want you to feel that way. I want you to know that I want to learn how to be your daddy. I'm really scared over here, but when I think about you and your mom, I can't help but smile. More than anything I want to meet you. I want you to have my last name, and if you're a boy, I want you named after me. If I get out of this alive, I will come home and be with you. I love you, even though I don't even know you yet.

Love,

Dad

Mark couldn't stop the tears that were streaming down his face. That wasn't the same father that he now knew. His dad was an abusive drunk, with anger issues that seemed to ruin everything. This letter was from someone else, a person who wanted to be a part of

Mark's life. Slowly he folded the letter and put it back in the wallet. He pulled himself together, struggled to regain his composure, and then got out of the car. He slid the wallet into his back pocket.

34

As Mark entered through the emergency room door, he walked past the waiting area where he and Elizabeth had talked to the police when Ben had been injured. He crossed to the desk where a nurse sat.

"Can I help you?" she asked in a thick, southern accent. She was a solidly built African American lady whose gold tooth gleamed every time she opened her mouth. She was wearing a pair of green hospital-issued scrubs. Her badge said, "Banks, T." under which was printed "DON".

"'D-O-N', does that mean Director of Nurses?" Mark asked.

"Yes son, it does; now is there something I can do for you?" she snapped back.

"Do you know Shawn Peterson?"

"Yes, I do, now do you want to talk to him or something, or are we going to play this game all night? I have things that I need to do," she responded impatiently.

"Sorry, I'm looking for Gorman Cooper's room," Mark responded. He now knew why Shawn sounded sarcastic when he spoke of how pleasant she was.

"Cooper, Cooper, Cooper, Gorman, room 29… around that corner, through the doors, and to the left," she replied without even looking up.

Mark pushed through the large doors that opened into the emergency area. Along the wall of the room nearest the entrance there was a large nurses' station covered with computer monitors, charts, and various supplies. Several individuals were sitting in office chairs filling out paperwork or working on a computer. On the other three walls were the patient's rooms. Several of the rooms right across from the nurses had large glass windows to make observation easier for the staff. There were nurses walking around with stethoscopes and blood pressure cuffs. A young lady with blonde hair pushed around an electronic blood pressure monitor. She smiled as she walked past.

Mark found room 29, but his father wasn't there. No one was in the room. Stepping back out into the hall, he double checked the room number to ensure that he was in the right room. After he checked it again, he went to the nurse's station.

"Do you know where Gorman Cooper is right now?" he asked the nurse behind the station.

"Are you a relation of his," the nurse asked.

"Yes, I am his son," Mark responded.

"Well I'm sorry sir but he was just taken to the morgue," she replied.

"What?"

"Wait, did you say, Gorman Cooper? He was just taken to have a CT scan," she corrected herself. "His family is waiting in the radiology waiting room. Just follow the signs around the corner."

Mark was still trying to catch his breath. He didn't know if she had the names confused or what, but that wasn't funny. Following the signs, he found the radiology waiting room and his mother and brother. Shawn was talking with them.

"So, I guess you've met my family," Mark observed when he came through the door.

"Yep, I sure did," Shawn answered.

"Something strange just happened; the nurse said that Dad was taken to the morgue. Did you put her up to that?" Mark scowled at Shawn, waiting for an answer.

Shawn smirked, "No, that would be too cruel. We had another patient earlier with a similar name; she just got the names confused."

Mark sat down beside his mom as Shawn went back to work. "Is everything alright?"

"Yes, he's in a lot of pain. They are admitting him because they think he may have severely injured himself. They are moving him to a room but haven't given us the room number yet," Elizabeth responded. She sounded very relieved. "What took you so long?"

"I don't know. I was just sitting in the car for a few minutes before I came in." Mark didn't want to talk to her about it. He wanted to wait until he could talk with this father.

It was taking a very long time for them to bring Gorman back from the CT. Mark began sitting in the chair nearest the door, but after a few minutes he felt like it was cutting off the circulation to his backside. He moved over into a chair so that he could watch television. They had the channel turned to news and the volume was turned down. For a while he read the closed captioning, but they weren't discussing anything of interest. The talking heads on the TV were arguing about the newest presidential budget deal and what it would mean for the American people.

To pass the time, Elizabeth sat reading the Gideon's Bible that she found on the table next to the chair where she was sitting, and Ben kept flipping through the magazines that had been left on the table beside him. The families of other patients came and went, but Gorman's family was left in the waiting room.

Mark kept shifting in his chair. The longer Mark sat there, the more he fidgeted. The stress of the afternoon and the waiting was really working on his nerves. He decided he would have to step outside for a smoke. Elizabeth had his cell number, so they could call him if anything changed.

He stepped outside into the smoking area. It was in a small courtyard between two of the larger buildings. He could tell by the shadows that stretched over the concrete-covered patio floor, that it was already late afternoon. It had been at least three hours since they got to the hospital, and his stomach was telling him about it. However, taking that first drag on his cigarette provided some relief, causing him to immediately feel better.

Mark stood near one of the corners where the ash cans were. There were a couple of female nurses sitting over at a picnic table in the center of the patio, one of whom was actually sitting on the table. A male nurse stood near them. Mark could tell they were talking, but he was too far away to hear their conversation. Most likely, they were discussing some doctor they didn't like, or a patient that they just saw.

Across from them stood a doctor in his white coat. He paced back and forth as he talked on the phone he held in his right hand. He waved his left hand in the air as he talked. Mark could see the lit cigarette in his left hand and watched as the ash blew away in the air. He couldn't help but think *what a waste of a good Camel.*

Mark took the last puff and dropped the butt in the can next to him. It was one of the new tall cigarette receptacles with a small hole in the top, just big enough to drop a cigarette into. His stomach was still complaining about his lack of sustenance since lunch was now long forgotten. His phone vibrated on his hip, and he quickly answered it.

Elizabeth explained that Gorman was no longer in the emergency room, but rather he had been admitted into the hospital; she and Ben were in his room with him. The doctor hadn't spoken with them yet but would be in the room in a few minutes with the results of the tests.

35

The hospital was relatively small compared to the large metropolitan hospital where Ben had stayed in Oklahoma City, so Mark easily found Gorman's room. It was dimly lit, with just a little light right at the head of the bed. Mark couldn't help but notice that it smelled like the plastic bandage strips that his mother used to use when he would fall and scratch his knee as a kid. Gorman lay in the hospital bed with his eyes closed as if he were sleeping. Ben and Elizabeth weren't there.

Mark laid his hand on his father's hand. Startled, Gorman opened his eyes. "Hey, what are you doing here?" His tone was almost accusatorial, but he sounded slightly relieved knowing that someone was there with him.

"I've been waiting up here to see how you were doing. Where is Mom?" Mark didn't want to sound too eager about his dad's welfare, but he was very concerned. This was a change for him. It had been a long time since he had been concerned about his father's condition.

"They went to go get something to eat. The nurse said that they will be bringing in my supper in a few minutes." Gorman tried to shift his position to straighten his pillows, but his movement was restricted so he couldn't quite adjust them on his own. Mark stepped in to help him. "Thanks," Gorman muttered.

"How did they leave? They rode with me," Mark inquired.

"I gave her my keys. The guys had dropped me and my truck off here at the hospital," Gorman replied.

"Alright," Mark responded. It was strange seeing Gorman like this. Mark was used to his father's drunken state, but today he hadn't had a chance to get tanked up. He seemed gentle, almost childlike, except for his crankiness.

"Dad, I wanted to again say thanks for helping me work on Ben's room. I really wanted to do something special for him," Mark didn't know how his father would react; he wasn't usually the sappy type.

"Well, it's my house, and I just wanted to make sure it was done right." Gorman responded, showing once again that he always wanted to be in control of everything. Mark just rolled his eyes at the response. "Son…thanks for doing it."

Mark was taken back; that remark was unexpected. He couldn't remember a time that his father had ever said *"Thanks."* Mark didn't even know that he knew that word.

Mark sat staring at the blue vinyl tiles on the floor. He listened to his father's breathing; it was slow and steady. He knew that this was the only time that he would have alone with his father, without his family around, but he was scared to ask him about the letter.

Finally, Gorman broke the awkward silence, "Hey, can you turn the television on?"

"Yeah, sure," Mark replied as he began flipping through the channels to let his father see what was on. There were very few channels to choose from on the television…mostly news, a couple of basketball games, and then a movie channel. Mark hesitated just a moment to see what movie was on before quickly resuming his search.

He paused again when he found another movie. Interested, they began watching it. They happened upon a chase scene where two police officers chased a subject. Everything that could go wrong did. They found themselves laughing over each little mishap. Gorman laughed so hard that he began to cough. He covered his mouth. Mark could tell he was still in a lot of pain.

Mark leaned over, "Dad, are you alright?"

Pushing him away Gorman replied, "Yeah, I'm fine."

He wiped his hand on the white sheet. Mark could see a smear of blood where he wiped his hand.

"Let me call the nurse," Mark reached for the call button.

"No, I'm fine, just let it be." Gorman scolded.

Mark sat back down, "Hey, dad, I have a question for you." Pulling the wallet from his pocket, he asked, "Dad, do you remember this wallet?"

Gorman took the wallet and looked it over, "Yeah this is my old wallet. Did your mom give you this?"

"That was my Christmas present. Do you remember what is inside?" Mark watched as Gorman opened the Velcro.

Slowly he pulled out the picture of the Elizabeth in front of the small diner where he had met her. A smile spread across Gorman's face. "I ain't seen this picture in years. I would look at it all the time when I was overseas, especially when I was lonely."

"Why did you take that particular picture?" Mark asked.

"Well I was trying to take a picture of your mom, but she didn't want me to. She was still in her pink waitress outfit and had her red hair pulled back. She had a pencil shoved behind her ear. I tried to snap the picture really quick, but she realized it and swatted at me with her apron." Gorman had a mischievous smile across his face.

Mark smiled, too.

"There should be a cross in here somewhere." Gorman dug through the wallet. "Here it is. Your mother gave me this cross the night before I left. You see the discoloration of the picture. When I was scared, I would hold the picture and the cross in my hand, squeezing it tightly. I can even see the creases where I had it folded."

Mark took the wallet and pulled out the picture of the Gorman and the other men from his squad. "What was this?"

Gorman chuckled, "Wow, it was a picture of a few guys that I met when I first got to the Persian Gulf. I haven't thought of them since I came home."

Mark pressed, "Who is the person that you tore out of the picture?"

Gorman looked back down at the picture; he unfolded the corner that had been dog-eared for two decades. "That was Tim. He saved my life." Tears were welling up in Gorman's eyes. "When I came down on that mine, he pushed me out of the way. Somehow, he saw it, and took the impact for me. I would never have done anything like that for someone else. He gave his life, to save mine." Gorman sat for a moment lost in his memories, before quickly wiping his eyes and trying to clear the lump from his throat.

"Dad, do you remember the letter?"

"What letter?" Gorman asked.

Slowly Mark pulled the handwritten letter out of the wallet. Gorman seemed to be genuinely surprised that it was still there. He took it from his son and opened it up. Slowly he perused the letter.

Mark watched his father, wondering what was going through his mind. How could a man that was usually so violent, now be so gentle? It had been years since Mark had seen his father sober.

"Dad, do you remember writing this letter?" Mark finally asked.

"Yeah, it was shortly after I found out that you were on the way. I didn't know what to do. At first, I was upset. I didn't want a baby. I never thought I would ever have children. You know my old man had been dead since I was young. I didn't know how to handle children. At that point I did what I wanted to do, and a child was gonna take my money and my time. I didn't know if I wanted that." Gorman's words were cold, but Mark understood the emotion behind it.

"Did you mean what you said?"

"You frightened me. I had lived for myself all those years. Now everything I did would be for someone else. I didn't want to give up my freedom. I talked to Tim about you, you know the guy that was tore from the picture. He was married and had kids. You know, at war you don't feel like you will ever make it home. You do things that you normally wouldn't do. While most of the guys went into town on a pass looking for a good time and find the first women that they could find. Other's found drugs and alcohol as a way to cope with the situation. Most men said that their wives wouldn't even ask about it. You know what they say about Vegas? It's even truer with war."

"Wow, I never thought about that." Mark wondered if Gorman was trying to avoid the question.

"Everyone sent into war does things that he wouldn't have normally done. But Tim was different. He had a family, and he wasn't willing to do anything that would hurt the ones he loved. We even told him, 'Your wife will never know.' And he always answered, 'She may not, but I will.' Every night he would pray and read the small Bible that we were all given before we shipped out. He prayed before he ate and was made fun of for it. I felt really sorry for him, but he didn't let it bother him.

"He would do studies with us at different times, and he talked a lot about Jesus. I never really wanted to hear about Jesus, so I tried to avoid talking to him. I would dodge him any time that I could, except when I found out about you. I knew that he had kids, so I thought he might be able to give me some advice. He prayed with me, and I felt better about the situation.

"I remember the day that I wrote you that letter. I had just received a letter from your mom. I hadn't responded to her when she said that she was pregnant. My refusal to respond scared her and made her think that I was going to abandon her. She had written me a final letter. It really got me to thinking about what it would be like to have a baby. I didn't know if you were going to be a boy or a girl, but I finally knew that I wanted you.

"While I was writing you the letter, we got the call that we were moving, and I never got to send it. Within just a few days, Tim was dead, and I was in the hospital. It's still all a blur. I actually still can't remember a large portion of the days surrounding the blast. But yes, I did mean every word."

This was the first time that Mark had ever had a heart-to-heart conversation with his father. They had talked from time to time, but never really had an emotive conversation like this. Mark couldn't help but stare at the floor. His brain was racing, and he didn't know what to say. Gorman again had his eyes closed, and Mark was unsure if he was trying to go to sleep. His mother and Ben should be back shortly.

Mark took a deep breath, "Dad, I'm really sorry for the way I have acted. I have been going to church, and I have made some decisions that have changed my attitude, especially my attitude toward you. I just want you to know, I do love you even though I haven't acted like it."

Gorman didn't answer, but Mark could see a tear forming in the corner of his eye. Since he was lying down, the tear rolled back to his ear. Gorman didn't have to say anything; Mark knew what he was thinking.

About that time Elizabeth, pushing Ben in his wheelchair, and Jessica walked in with bags from the local fast-food taco place across from the hospital. Elizabeth had stopped by the school to get Jess before returning to Gorman's side. Jess had just gotten back from her school trip. They all sat around eating.

After a few minutes the doctor stepped into Gorman's room, looking at his tablet computer. "Mr. Cooper, how are you feeling?"

"'bout as good as can be expected for falling off of a scaffold," he replied.

The doctor told Gorman, "Well, we want to keep you over night and get you up walking around. There doesn't appear to be any injury to your back, but you will be very sore for the next few days. I would, however, like you to see a gastroenterologist."

Confused, Elizabeth asked, "Did he injure his stomach or something?"

"We aren't quite sure what it is yet," the doctor continued, "but from the scans we can tell that there is a large mass in your abdomen. Have you had any tenderness?"

Gorman thought for a minute, "Not really."

"Ok, we will refer you to a gastroenterologist, and they will take a look at your records. However, you should be out of the hospital tomorrow." Due to the family's lack of questions, the doctor left as quickly as he came in.

"Honey, have you had any problems with your stomach?" Elizabeth asked Gorman.

"No, I'm fine. Don't worry about it. I should be out of here tomorrow," he responded, "It is probably better that y'all leave."

Elizabeth wanted to oppose him, but he rolled over and closed his eyes. It was no use trying to change his mind. The packed up and threw away their trash.

As they headed down to the elevator, Mark couldn't help worrying about his dad. Now, not only was Ben hurt, but Gorman had something wrong and his family couldn't find out what it was until he saw the specialist.

As Mark headed back to the apartment, he couldn't get Gorman off his mind. He stood outside his vehicle smoking a cigarette and stared up at the apartment door from his car wondering if Shawn was home. Mark was just getting used to praying, but he knew that this was as good a time as any.

Mark stood outside finishing off the last drag of his cigarette and then dropped the butt on the ground, grinding it out with his foot. He took a deep breath, "God, please help my dad."

36

Gorman was feeling better the next day when he was released from the hospital. They had kept him overnight for observation. His abdomen and lower back were very sore. They wheeled him out in a wheelchair so Elizabeth could pick him up in their car.

The hospital set up a follow-up appointment with the gastroenterologist for Tuesday. His office was in Oklahoma City, and Elizabeth couldn't go with him because Ben had an appointment that same day for a follow-up MRI. Ben seemed to be getting stronger and stronger with each therapy session, but for some reason, he still couldn't put much weight on his feet. The doctor wanted to see if there was something else wrong, so he requested another MRI. Due to the scheduling conflict, Mark agreed to take Gorman to the doctor.

As Mark pulled up to the house, he honked the horn. He watched the door, but no one came out. He honked the horn again, but still there were no signs of life. Agitated, Mark unclicked his seat belt and threw it loose. As he opened his car door, he noticed that the front door to the house had opened. Gorman was leaning against the doorframe holding his stomach, unable to move.

Mark's frustration subsided, and he felt guilty for becoming angry. Gorman couldn't get around on his own, so Mark patiently helped him limp to the car. Gorman held his distended stomach all the way to the car, groaning with every step.

Mark didn't know what to expect during their road trip to Oklahoma City. A two-and-a-half-hour drive stuck in his Mustang with his dad wasn't something Mark would have preferred to do; however, he was willing to do whatever it took to find out what was wrong with his dad. Something had to be done. He couldn't stand to see him like this.

During the ride, not much was said between the two of them. Mark didn't really know what to say. It had been years since they had travelled anywhere together.

Finally, Mark broke the silence, "So how have you been feeling?"

"Well, I've been better," Gorman responded.

Mark hesitated to say anything else. There were no comforting words. Mark didn't want his father to die. He was too young, but until they found out what was wrong there was nothing that could be done. The situation reminded him of his granddad's death. He had been merely thirty-eight when the accident had occurred.

"How old were you when your dad died?" Mark questioned Gorman.

"I was ten when he passed away," he answered, "Why do you want to know?"

"You never talk about it, and I have always wondered what happened. I have also wondered what happened to your mom," Mark responded.

"Well, after my father died, it was very hard on us. My mother worked two jobs. She also had men coming in and out of the house on a fairly regular basis. She always told me that I needed a father figure, but those men she picked were never there for me.

"My grandparents were loaded. They had all the money they ever needed, and we were struggling. Mom had those other guys because she needed someone to help out with the house and the bills.

"She set her mind on finding a husband, which turned out to be the worst thing she could do for me," he continued. "She worked as a waitress in a truck stop, and her bedroom had almost as many truck drivers in and out as the restaurant. The men were only there for a few days, some a little longer, but none wanted to deal with a kid. I couldn't understand why she kept bringing people into our lives."

"Wow, I'm sorry," Mark felt bad that he brought it up, "I didn't realize what had happened."

"Oh, you don't know the half of it. She finally found a man that she felt was going to fix everything. He was clean-cut and worked at the police station. She told me that he was in and out of the restaurant every night, that's how he caught her eye. His name was Steve, and she thought he would be the perfect man to help show 'her boy the ropes'."

"Was he your stepdad?" Mark asked.

"Actually, it never made it that far. After a few weeks the police officer moved in with us. At first it worked out well. He and mom worked the graveyard shift, so they slept most of the day while I was at school. We would eat supper together, and then they both left to go to their jobs. We actually seemed like a family. I hadn't been that happy since before my dad died. But the good times didn't last very long."

"What happened?" Mark queried.

Gorman continued, "After about a year or so, Steve was switched to first shift. This meant that they worked opposite shifts, him during the day and her overnights. One night when I was fifteen, I heard a noise coming from mom's room. I knew that mom wasn't there, but I heard a woman's voice. I sneaked down the hallway and slowly opened the door. To my horror, I discovered Steve in bed with another woman. I ran back to my room. I didn't know what to do.

"Later when the woman left, Steve came into my room. I pretended to be asleep, but Steve sat down on the side of the bed. I had my back to him, so he hit me on the back of the head and said, 'Boy I know you're not asleep. So, did you like what you saw?' I couldn't believe what he asked, I was in shock. I asked 'What?'

"He said, 'You're fifteen, and I know you look at those girlie magazines.' I was scared to have this conversation with him. I stammered with my words, barely able to get them out, 'No I don't.'"

"Seriously?" Mark couldn't believe what his father was saying.

"Yeah, I wanted to cry. What was I supposed to say? He hit me in the back of the head again. 'You gotta be looking at something, unless you're looking at other boys? You aren't a homo, are you?' I didn't want to answer him. He kept nudging me, calling me a homo. Finally, I felt tears running down my face. I yelled at him, 'No, I'm not a homo, I like girls.'"

Mark was shocked. He never knew what his father had been through. He found himself feeling sorry for his old man. "I'm really sorry."

"Well, it didn't stop there; finally, Steve asked me how I liked seeing a beautiful young woman in her prime. I didn't answer him. I was sick to my stomach. I laid there silently hoping that he would leave. Finally, I heard him sigh; he hit me in the back of the head again and went back to bed."

"What did your mom say?" Mark asked.

"I couldn't tell her. I was scared. The next morning Steve offered to give me a ride to school. As soon as I got in the car, he threatened me. He told me that if I told my mom what I'd seen, then he would have to tell her that I liked watching. I didn't know what to do. I remember I didn't eat much that night, and mom was concerned that I might be sick. She offered to call in, but Steve said that he would take care of me.

"This went on for over a year. He would come into my room when his flavor of the week would leave and taunt me about it. He even asked me if I wanted him to find me one. I would lay in my bed, scared; not knowing what to do. The longer it went on, the more depressed mom got. She would nurse her liquor bottle and sleep all day on the couch.

"Finally, the night came just after I turned sixteen. My mother got sick in the middle of her shift, and she came home early. She caught Steve and one of his girls. She pulled the shotgun on him and chased him out of the house without his clothes. As he left, I heard the words that scared me the most, 'Gorman knew, and he liked it.'"

"Did she believe him?" Mark asked

"I didn't know, she didn't say a word, she just went to bed. I thought I heard her crying in the middle of the night. When I got up the next morning, mom was strung out on the couch with several empty beer bottles and an empty vodka bottle sitting on the table. I left the house. I didn't want to go to school, so I hung out in the park all day."

The words were just flowing from his mouth. Apparently, all this had been pent up for years like a reservoir ready to breach its banks. Now it had busted loose and was flooding out.

"You know dad, it wasn't your fault," Mark comforted him.

"Yeah," Gorman scoffed, "Well, when I got home, mom was no longer laid out on the couch. Surprisingly, everything was cleaned up. The trash was out. And I could smell roast cooking in the oven. Mom was behind the stove making mashed potatoes and gravy. She had fresh greens on, and we were using the fine dishes that she kept put away for special occasions. There was even a tablecloth on the table. She talked to me about school, and later we spent time playing cards. And it felt like it did before dad died. Not one word was said about Steve and what happened. Every time I tried to say something, she would quickly change the subject.

"Finally, it was time for her to go to work and me to go to bed," Gorman continued, "I was in my bed and she came in like she used to do to tuck me in. She said, 'I put the leftovers in a box for you to take for lunch tomorrow.' Then she told me goodnight. I rolled over to go to sleep, and I heard her at the door. She asked, 'Oh, son, by the way, why didn't you tell me that Steve was bringing all of these women into my house?' I explained to her that I was scared and that he had threatened me.

"She continued, 'Son, Steve hurt me by bringing other women into my house and worse into my bed. But what has hurt me more is that you knew and did nothing about it. I thought you loved me. Since you apparently don't care about how I feel, I want you out of my house. If you don't care about me, then I don't want to see you again. Since your stupid father died, I have had to deal with you every day. I did everything around the house, worked my fingers to the bone, and you don't care anything about how I feel. I never wanted you. If it hadn't been for your father, I would have aborted you when I had the chance. When he found out I was pregnant, he begged me to marry him. I should have taken care of you then.'

Gorman was tearing up, "She told me that she thought she had the perfect man. He loved her and did everything for her, but after I was born, he changed. He forgot about her. Then she said the thing that hurt me the most, 'I wish you had been there with him the day that he died. Maybe you would have died with him. I don't ever want to see you again, so you better be gone by the time I get home in the morning.'"

"I'm very sorry, dad," Mark answered. "I hope you know now that what happened wasn't your fault. You didn't cause it to happen. It was Steve's fault." Mark couldn't believe that his father was still blaming himself.

"But I should have told her. If I had told her, she wouldn't have kicked me out. Things would have been different if I had just told her. I think she ended up drinking herself to death." By this point, Gorman was crying so heavily that he began coughing. He quickly covered his mouth. Mark noticed the blood in the phlegm on his hand.

"It's ok, Dad. Just rest, we'll be there soon,"

Mark turned the radio on. He noticed that Gorman was gazing out the window with a blank stare. Mark didn't know what to tell him, and so he just listened to the music.

Mark had never been so relieved as he was when they arrived at the doctor's office. He pulled through the circle drive and helped his father make the slow trek into the waiting room. While Gorman sat in the waiting area, Mark drove to parking spot. After parking the car, he looked in the mirror and thought to himself, *you can do this.*

The waiting room outside the doctor's office was practically empty. An elderly man sat in the corner near the stack of magazines and old newspapers. There was also a middle-aged woman and her teenage son, watching a game show on the flat screen TV at the other end of the room.

Gorman sat by the door waiting as Mark carried over the fifty-page life history that he was given at the receptionist's window to fill out. Apparently, they needed to know everything about him. Gorman's hands were shaking too badly to hold the pen, so Mark filled out the questionnaire for him.

For the next half-hour Mark grilled his dad about his health and anything he could remember about his family's history. Gorman told him everything that he could remember which was very little since he had no connection with his relatives. The longer they sat in the waiting room, the more antsy Gorman became. He had hoped that he would get home in time for a few drinks at O'Donnell's Pub.

Gorman hated doctor's offices and hospitals. He even tried to bribe Mark to take him home. Mark refused. He needed to know what was wrong and wouldn't let his dad leave without finding out.

Finally, the nurse led them back to a small examination room at the end of the hallway. In the room, there was a rack of pamphlets outlining the causes of several diseases: colon cancer, hiatal hernia, cirrhosis of the liver, etc. There was also a large poster that showed the entire gastrointestinal system.

After arriving in the exam room, they didn't have to wait much longer. The doctor was a middle-aged man with dark hair and eyes. He wore a lab coat over his button up shirt and tie. He had black slacks and pointed-toed shoes. He flipped through the file that the hospital had sent over.

He read through it for what seemed like hours, until finally he looked up and said, "It appears you're suffering from cirrhosis." His thick Arabic accent made his words sound muddled.

Then, he proceeded to ask Gorman about his family history. He talked to him in length about his alcohol intake and the effect of his use of pain relievers on his weakened liver. He also pointed out that the yellowing of Gorman's skin wasn't a tan but the jaundicing of his skin due to his damaged liver.

It ultimately came down to one thing; Gorman was drinking himself to death. No one wants to hear this kind of news, especially when his life revolves around a bottle. Mark could see the wheels turning in Gorman's head.

"What about a liver transplant?" Mark asked.

"Well, a liver transplant can be a good option, but for someone whose liver has been destroyed due to alcoholism or drug abuse, the chance of getting a new liver is very slim. The only option is a live donor, which could be a family member or a close friend. However, the donor would have to meet certain criteria," the doctor said.

He gave Gorman a lot of information to read and set up several appointments and tests for him to determine for sure the problem and course of action. The most important thing he said was that Gorman had to stay off alcohol and switch his pain medicine. The doctor was emphatic that it wouldn't fix the problem but should prevent it from worsening. The tests would show the extent of the damage, and could be set up in Gordon's hometown, so that he wouldn't have to make a lot of trips to Oklahoma City.

When the doctor's appointment was over, Mark helped his father make it back to the car. The drive home took forever. Gorman didn't say a word the entire trip. Mark kept to himself. He had texted his mother while his dad was in the restroom, and she tried to return his call, but he wouldn't answer. After they got back to town and he dropped Gorman off at the house, he drove to the apartment. He still didn't know what to say. All he could do was pray.

37

The weeks flew by. Between school and work, Mark barely had time to think. He was beginning to enjoy the internet writing, even though it was much harder than regular news writing. As a journalist, he was used to minimalistic writing. He had learned how to edit his articles down to a usable length. However, internet writing required an even greater level of minimalism. In many articles, he had to reduce the word count by several hundred words.

This required a lot of time and concentration; however, his deadlines were much shorter. As soon as news happened, he would have to get a story online in real time instead of waiting for the paper to come out. He enjoyed the fast pace of the position because it kept him busy. There was very little down time.

Ironically, a couple of more seasoned journalists, Jason Lambert and Willy Benson, were placed under him as writers. Like Mark, they had vied for the position of lead writer. Following Mark's promotion, Lambert and Benson acted like they believed themselves to be too experienced to work under someone who was just graduating college. However, after a couple of weeks, things were fell into line.

Every morning during their staff meeting, Martin met with the writers to give them daily assignments. As the news editor Martin was still getting his feel of the writers. He was learning who was the strongest and could handle the most freedom, and who needed more oversight.

Mark didn't mind the change even though he missed Vance a lot. Vance had become the dad that Mark never had. He had been there to hear Mark's stories and offer wisdom gleaned from his own experience. But now that Mark's relationship with his real dad was getting better, maybe it was good that Vance had moved on.

The whole office was quickly getting accustomed to Martin's disciplined personality, acquired from his time in the military. Everything he did was regimented, and he controlled the office like a general. It was a new experience, but a good one.

Interestingly, Sandra and Roger never showed back up for work. Mark hadn't heard anything definite about them since the day they left; however, there were some rumors going around. Some people said that Sandra moved to California and changed her name to Soma. They said that she had opened a yoga center for relaxation to teach others how to handle disappointment. Others said that she and Roger ran away together and were doing undercover investigations in China. Nevertheless, the mood of the entire team had been much more positive without the two of them.

As with all changes, it took time for people to get used to the variances. Mark knew that it wouldn't come overnight, but with each passing day people treated him with more respect than they had the day before. If he respected his coworkers, they respected him.

Ben's physical condition had also improved. He was now able to get around the house without his wheelchair, using crutches for support. If these advances in his condition continued, the physical therapist thought he might be walking independently by the summer. Since there was only a little over eight weeks left in the school year, Ben wouldn't be returning to class until the fall. To keep him on task, a tutor came by every couple of days so he would be prepared for his senior year.

After Gorman's visit with the doctor, he had several follow-up exams and tests run. It was confirmed that he had cirrhosis of the liver, and he had to begin treatment. The treatment would start with not only complete abstinence from alcohol, but Gorman would also have to follow a strict dietary regimen. His doctor also started him on several medications to help his condition until he could get in to see the specialist.

With the poor prognosis, Gorman became very aggressive and depressed, more so than normal. Since he was no longer allowed to self-medicate on alcohol, he took his frustrations out on the whole family. On one of his visits to the Veteran Affairs Clinic, he had an emotional blow up at a nurse. This led the doctor to question Gorman regarding his emotional state. It didn't take him long to discover that Gorman also suffered from a severe case of posttraumatic stress disorder.

This came as no secret to most of the family. They had known all these years that something was wrong, but Gorman hadn't been willing to go for treatment. He felt that his own method of wasting away his life at the bar was a better option than relying on pills from the "quack" doctors that the military provided. Now, since his preferred treatment option of Jack and beer had to be eliminated from his diet, he was open to other methods. The doctor began treating him for both PTSD and depression. In just a couple of weeks he had shown considerable improvement.

The day finally came for Gorman to the see the hepatologist who focused exclusively on the liver. After reviewing Gorman's case file, he told Gorman and Elizabeth that his treatment options were limited, explaining that the only thing that would help him would be a liver transplant. Knowing his history of alcohol abuse, Gorman asked him about the possibilities for obtaining a different liver.

"Well Mr. Cooper," the doctor replied, "right now you don't qualify for a liver transplant. With your history of alcoholism, we would need to be able to confirm that you have been alcohol-free for at least six months before they would even be willing to put you on a donor list."

"How long will he have to be on the donor list before he can get a new liver?" Elizabeth inquired. "Gorman has been determined to overcome his addiction and allowed me to get rid of all the alcohol in the house. He has also been coming home right after work each night instead of spending time at the bar."

The doctor nodded. "That is a great start, but it usually takes a lot more effort and commitment than just throwing away the bottles. Many people get involved in group therapy, 12-step programs, and some even find it helpful to seek spiritual guidance." The doctor then handed Gorman several pamphlets about treatment options for alcohol addiction.

Gorman was noticeably frustrated. "What about the medicines that doctor put me on? Won't that take care of it?" He thought he was doing everything that it took to fix his problem. He quit drinking alcohol and was straightening out his life, but now the doctor is telling him that there was more he had to do.

"The medicine will help you. Typically, advanced cirrhosis from severe alcohol use like you have leaves you with only about six months to two years to live. The medicines you're on now have shown to increase life expectancy to about five years. The best option, however, is still a transplant," the doctor reassured them.

"So, he is placed on the transplant list when he proves that he can remain sober for six months. So maybe he can have a new liver in seven or eight months?" Elizabeth squeezed Gorman's hand tightly and shot him a reassuring smile.

The doctor cautioned them. "There is really no way to know. While we like to think that it'll take less than a year for most patients to receive a new liver after being placed on the list, that isn't always the case. Health conditions often deteriorate, and many patients must be removed from the list. Also, the donor liver must match his blood type so it can be compatible. I really have no way to offer you an exact timeframe. I have seen individuals pass away while waiting for a suitable donor. Nevertheless, with your work to remain sober, it's a good option."

"So that is that then, I have no hope, but can expect to be dead within the next few years. I dug my own grave, and now I have to lie in it." Defeated, Gorman rose from the chair.

"Actually, there may be another option. Live donation has been around for years for certain lung and kidney transplants, because people have two kidneys and can often donate one. But over the past few years, doctors have had increasing success with live liver transplants. Basically, if someone fitting your profile is found, usually a close family member, we're able to remove a lobe from the donor liver and transplant it. The liver is made up of a left and right lobe, the right being about two-thirds of the total liver. When separated, both pieces can function independently. We will have to do some testing on your family members, but there is a chance one of them may be a match." The doctor seemed hopeful that this option might be a solution.

Elizabeth was very pleased and encouraged as they left the doctor's office. A live donor might be a viable option and offer Gorman a chance to watch his children grow into adulthood and ultimately have families of their own. On the other hand, Gorman knew that it would be very problematic. He had few close relatives other than his children. He hadn't spoken with his father's family since he was young, and his mother had explicitly stated that she never wanted to see him again. Gorman was unwilling to even consider contacting her.

To make the situation even more difficult, when Elizabeth had discovered that she had cancer, the doctors' tests had revealed that her blood type was different than Gorman's and all the children had inherited the same blood type as hers. The possibility that they could be donors was out of the question. As far as he could see, there was no hope for Gorman.

However, Elizabeth was unwilling to give up. When they returned home, she called Mark on the cell phone that he had given her and explained the situation. She knew that the only option would be to find Gorman's mother. If anyone could do it, she knew Mark would be able to.

Luckily, Mark's work at the paper gave him access to a lot of information that he wouldn't have ordinarily had, so he could research information that ordinary citizens couldn't obtain. As he began researching, he quickly located Gorman's military information and his marriage license to Elizabeth. Nevertheless, Mark couldn't find Gorman's birth certificate or even the marriage license for Gorman's parents, to ascertain Gorman's grandparents' names. Mark knew there had to be something out there; it would just take time to find it.

On an impulse, Mark searched obituaries for deaths that had occurred around the time of his grandfather's passing. Even though it takes a long time to digitize old records, some agencies had tried to keep up with the internet age by formatting their paper records into internet records. He hoped that there would be something online. It took some work, but finally he ran across a copy of an old obituary that appeared to be that of his grandfather. The paper that had printed it was no longer in operation, but the picture was listed on a genealogy site.

As Mark read the obituary, he expected to find the usual information. He found the decedent's name and age, where he was from and where his interment would be. It was a lengthy obituary, including a whole list of accomplishments that had been attributed to Mark's grandfather. It described his life and his church involvement; it also mentioned his childhood and friends.

At the very end of the article was the list of survivors. It listed his parents, James and Linda Cooper, and his brother Martin Cooper. Mark read it twice just to make sure. Not once did it mention that he was married or had a child. It was as if they had been completely erased from his life.

Mark couldn't believe that Gorman and his mother had been rejected in such a way. He had heard stories of how his grandfather's family had treated his wife and son, but he would never have guessed that they practically deleted them from the family. Either way, he had the names of Gorman's estranged grandparents, James and Linda Cooper; he could start with them.

38

Mark sat, anxiously holding the phone in his hand. The last thing he wanted to do was start trouble, but he had to find someone who would be able to give him his grandmother's name. He could feel his hands sweating as he punched in the numbers.

He dialed the number three times, hanging up before the call could be completed. On the fourth dial he allowed the call to go through. He listened to the monotone ring over and over. Mark was ready to hang up when suddenly he heard someone answer.

"Hello," answered an older female.

"Is this Mrs. James Cooper?" Mark waited anxiously for a response. He had never made a phone call like this before. He never would have believed that he would be calling anyone for this reason.

"Yes, I was Mrs. James Cooper, but James has been dead for some time. Who is calling please?" The voice on the other end of the line was very raspy like that of a long-time smoker.

"Yes, um...This is Gorman Marcus Cooper; I need to talk to you." Mark's voice cracked as he spoke.

"Who did you say this was?" She said with her fancy southern accent.

"My name is *Gorman Marcus Cooper*; my friends call me Mark," he replied with a little more emphasis on his name to ensure that she could understand.

"Is this some kind of joke? Gorman Marcus Cooper is my son's name, and he has been dead for thirty years. You should be ashamed of yourself for calling me like this." Mark could hear the frustration in her voice. He didn't want her to hang up the phone until he could ask her about his grandmother.

"Please, wait, don't hang up. My name is Gorman Marcus Cooper, and I know your son died a long time ago in a bulldozer accident. Before he died, he had a son who was named after him. His son is my dad." Mark stopped talking for a moment allowing her to process the information that he had just spit out. He could hear her breathing deeply though the phone. She seemed not to know what to say.

Finally, she answered, "I guess you're calling because you need money? I wrote your father off a long time ago when I kicked out his whore of a mother. She only wanted my Gorman because she thought he was going to be her meal ticket. You know, if it wasn't for her, I would still have my son, but she took him from me. Did your father tell you what she did?"

"No, I'm sorry; I don't know what you're talking about." Mark couldn't believe the attitude that she was showing over the phone.

"Well, my Gorman was supposed to grow up to be part of his father's firm. He was supposed to stay close and take over when his father passed away, but when Linda came into his life, she seduced him. It was her fault that he gave up the dream we had for him to become a lawyer. He ended up going into construction work…construction, of all things!

"He had scholarships to Yale and was going to follow in his father's footsteps. But she came into his life and got herself pregnant so that he would have to marry her. He was supposed to marry a good woman, a trophy wife like me. But instead she got knocked up, and so he chose to marry her. He quit school and went to work." The accusation in her voice was enough to make Mark want to hang up the phone. He could feel the tightness in his chest as she spoke, but he knew that she was probably his father's last hope.

"Yes, ma'am," Mark sheepishly responded, "I'm very sorry that you lost your son. I'm not calling for money, and I don't want anything from you; however, my dad, your grandson does need something. We recently found out that he has cirrhosis of the liver. We're trying to find a relative who might be a match and could help out with his treatment."

"Ha, I'm sorry but my son is dead, and there is no one else who could give anything like that for you. Now if you will, please, I need to go." She was about to hang up the phone.

"Wait, I know that you're upset, I would be upset, too, but this is about saving the life of your grandson. He is your flesh and blood, and all I'm trying to do is get your help locating someone in the family. I just want to know if you have any way to get in touch with your late son's wife, my grandmother. I'm just trying to track someone down, but dad doesn't remember her maiden name. I'm not asking much of you, and if you can help me, I will never ask you for anything else." The words flew from Mark's mouth before he even knew what he was saying. It reminded him of the fights he had with his dad.

"Fine, I have an old address of some of her relatives. They were from St. Louis. Her last name was Daniels. Let me find you that address." The phone went silent as she looked for the address. She came back on the line a few minutes later with an address in southern St. Louis. Then she told Mark that she expected to never hear from him again, and she hung up the phone.

Mark couldn't believe the hatefulness that she still felt even after 30 years. He had always wanted to be part of his extended family. He would dream about going to his grandparents' house for Christmas and staying there for a couple of weeks during the summer. He always imagined that they would have been fun people to be around, and if he could have just known them, maybe they would have helped him with his abusive father. Now he was glad that he hadn't known them.

Mark looked down at his desk and read over the address a few times. He knew that it was a long shot. Just because his grandmother grew up at that address didn't mean that anyone there would know who she was. Nevertheless, Mark now had a last name to go by. It wasn't much, but it was a start.

Mark would have to use his resources at the paper to find her. For now, it would have to wait, so he tucked away the sticky note into his bag until later. He had to get back to work.

39

Gorman's health began to deteriorate. During the month of March and the beginning of April he had missed more days of work than he had been there. Since Gorman worked "under the table," he had no unemployment or workman's compensation benefits so there was no extra money coming in. Periodically, Mark stopped by and gave his mother money to help. She didn't want to take it, but due to the medical expenses for both Gorman and Ben, she had to have help.

In a strange way, Mark was glad that his father had fallen at the job site. He didn't want him hurt, but Gorman wouldn't have gone to the doctor on his own. Gorman wasn't the type of person to see a doctor, not even through the VA. He would have continued to medicate with over the counter pain relievers and Jack Daniels until it killed him. Sadly, he didn't even realize that his self-medication was what was killing him.

If he hadn't fallen, he may not have discovered the cirrhosis until it was too late. Gorman was frightened by the prognosis. He didn't want to die, so something had to be done.

It was finally the middle of April, and Mark had exhausted any money that he had set aside. His family was already stressed beyond their financial limits, and Mark knew that he couldn't afford to continue paying all their bills, too. He had to have a heart-to-heart talk with his parents. That evening, he showed up at his parents' house to find his dad lying on the couch watching TV.

Gorman was already suffering from cabin fever, and his cantankerous attitude was showing through. It was hard for him to stay at home. He was used to working outside all the time, no matter the weather. If he wasn't working, he was at the bar.

Anytime he was at home, he was out in the garage. His hands were always covered in dirt and grease, from fixing a lawnmower of changing the oil in the truck. However, the forced bed rest didn't suit him well at all.

When Mark came in, he could see that Gorman was driving Elizabeth crazy. Every few minutes he was asking for something or telling her what to do. In the first five minutes of Mark's visit, Gorman had told Elizabeth that the floor needed vacuuming and the television was dusty. He complained about the blinds being open too much, causing a glare. When she adjusted them, he then complained about it being too dark. They were at each other's throats the whole time.

Mark felt that he had the solution to their problems. "I think Mom needs to get a job," Mark began. He was sitting at the end of the couch on a small stool.

Elizabeth was sitting in a chair across from him reading her Bible, and Gorman was still reclining on the couch. As soon as the words left his mouth, Elizabeth looked up from her reading. She took her drug store "cheaters" off and laid them in her lap. Gorman turned towards her and then looked back at Mark.

"I know that right now it's tight, and Mom has always been good at cooking, I think she should look at getting a job," Mark continued.

Elizabeth's face went pale; she almost looked frightened. "Well, I don't know, it has been years since I have worked in the public. I don't think I would know what to do anymore. Gorman has always wanted me to stay at home and take care of the house."

"Yeah, I did," Gorman responded, "but the kids are practically grown. Mark's out of the house, Jess is always so busy with school, music, and her friends that she is rarely here, and Ben sits in his room doing his schoolwork and playing video games. They don't need you here to wipe their noses anymore," Gorman responded.

"But what about cleaning?" she asked, "Who would do that?"

"Jess and Ben can start helping around the house. I'm too sick to do any cleaning, but I'm sure you could manage." Gorman didn't seem to be helping the situation.

Mark inserted himself into the debate. "There is a little diner downtown that we go to all the time. It reminds me of the diner in the pictures you have. It's called Dixie's Diner, and there is always a sign in the window requesting kitchen and counter help. It would be a place to start," Mark encouraged, wanting her to see the positive side of the idea.

"I just don't know," Elizabeth replied.

"I think you need to get out of this house so you ain't driving me crazy every day. It's worse than being in the hospital around here," Gorman snapped sarcastically.

"Mom, why don't you go down there with me and check it out? If you don't like what you see, then I'll bring you back home." Mark smiled a comforting smile.

"I guess I can," she said reluctantly. She looked at Gorman for a petition. He stared at the television ignoring her.

Slowly she stood up and grabbed a lite jacket. She looked back at Gorman once again just in case he changed his mind, this time he motioned for her to hurry so that she did not block the TV. Defeated, she followed Mark to the car.

The drive to Dixie's Diner was very subdued, and Elizabeth sat in the passenger seat wringing her hands. Mark knew she was nervous but having a job would help her have a life beyond taking care of her family. He turned the radio up, hoping it would calm her nerves.

As they pulled up, Elizabeth froze. She didn't want to get out of the car. She begged Mark to take her home, but he flatly refused. He knew that she would be perfect for the little diner and wanted her to at least try.

As they walked in, Elizabeth noticed the uniforms with the small white aprons. It reminded her of the old uniforms that she had worn when she was waiting tables at the little diner near the base. There were a few customers sitting around. Most of them were older gentlemen, probably coffee drinkers.

Behind the counter stood a woman in her mid-fifties taking orders and working the register. Mark approached her and explained that his mother was looking for a job. The lady smiled, "My name is Dixie, and I'm always looking for help."

Dixie had dyed-red hair, which was very short and curly as if she had a fresh perm. She also had a gruff smoker's voice. The smell of smoke lingered on her breath as she spoke. When she smiled her lips exposed her tobacco-stained teeth.

"You have any diner experience, honey," she asked with a contagious smile.

"Yes, I actually worked for several years as a waitress and kitchen help back in the late 80's. I never went back after having children." Elizabeth's voice was shaky.

"Well honey, it hasn't changed much since then, except for the prices. We still use the original cash register we had when we opened. We have added a credit card machine, but that is really it. Are you used to cooking regular diner type foods: burgers, breakfast stuff, and sandwiches and such?" She again smiled showing off her aged ivories.

To let Elizabeth and Dixie talk, Mark stepped outside for a smoke. He really liked the town he lived in. The pace wasn't like that of Oklahoma City. The people were friendly and inviting; always smiling when they passed.

When he finished, Mark dropped his cigarette butt on the ground and stamped it out. He pulled out his phone to see if he had missed any calls since he had left it on "silent". As soon as it was out of his pocket, he knew something was wrong. Ben had called several times and finally resorted to texting.

Mark called him back, "Hey, what's going on?"

"Mark, something is wrong with dad. I heard him shut the restroom door. A little bit later I got up to use the restroom and he was still in there. I knocked on the door, but he wouldn't answer. I can't get him to answer me." Ben was breathing heavily.

"OK, keep trying to get into the bathroom, but don't hurt yourself. I'll get mom, and we will be heading back to the house." Mark replied.

"Mark, I think he is dead," Ben broke into tears.

"Don't say that! Just wait! We're on the way," Mark hung up the phone.

When he walked back into the diner, he noticed that Elizabeth was no longer standing at the bar. He looked around and saw that there were only a couple of diners left in the building. He heard what sounded like hens cackling coming from the kitchen. He bent down and looked through the service window. Elizabeth was with Dixie in the kitchen. They were sharing stories and talking about their lives. Mark could hear his mother talking about how she met Gorman and how handsome he was. Mark smiled; it did his heart good to hear her talk about his dad like that.

He called out to her, and she looked through the service window at him. She waved at him, and he could see a spatula in her hand.

"We need to go. Ben needs us at the house," Mark called out.

"Ok, I'm coming," she replied and then went back to talking to Dixie. It was still a couple of minutes before she came out the swinging door from the kitchen. "Dix, I'll see you Monday morning."

As they got in the car Mark briefed her on the situation. Her attitude immediately went from excited and happy, to upset.

"I knew this was a bad idea, I should never have even thought about it. I will have to call her tomorrow and let her know that I can't take the position. If I had been there, everything would be OK," Elizabeth reasoned.

"No Mom, what would you have done if you had been at the house?" Mark couldn't believe that she was taking the blame.

"I could have opened the bathroom door. Ben doesn't know where the key is," she rebutted.

"Ok, you know where the key is," he retorted, "but whatever happened still would have happened. You aren't to blame for this. What if something happened, and he can't work ever again? Or worse because of the illness what if…"

"Don't say it," Elizabeth interrupted.

"Mom think about it. If something happens to him, you must make sure that you can take care of yourself and the kids. Just a few minutes ago you were the happiest I have seen you in years. You need to keep this job." Mark made his point, and Elizabeth remained silent.

As they pulled up to the house, they saw an ambulance sitting in the front yard. Ben was very upset, and he was afraid to wait until Mark and Elizabeth returned to get help. The fire fighters had to bust the door to the bathroom down to get in where Gorman lay.

It appeared that he had collapsed while he was using the restroom. When he fell, he landed halfway in the bathtub and halfway out. There was no obvious cause that would explain why he fell, but the fall left a large gash on his forehead.

Gorman remained unconscious when the ambulance left, transporting him once again to the hospital. Elizabeth followed behind them in her car. Mark took Ben and went to pick Jessica up from school.

They sat in the Mustang as they waited for Jessica to get to the car. Ben still had tears running down his face. He blamed himself. He worried that his video games were too loud, and he couldn't hear his dad when he fell.

The paramedics were unsure how long Gorman had been unconscious. With no obvious signs, they were very concerned about the cause of the fall. Also, they were unsure if he passed out and hit his head, or if he fell and the fall knocked him out.

"Mark, I'm scared. I don't want anything to happen to him." Ben stared out the window.

"Ben, he will be alright, they just need to find out what's going on." Mark tried to sound reassuring, but he was thinking the same thing. There had been many times in Mark's life that he had wanted his dad to leave and never show back up. There were times when he wished Gorman would get arrested and be sent to prison. He even periodically found himself wishing that Gorman were dead. Nevertheless, now the feelings of anger he once felt were being replaced by feelings of guilt.

He prayed deep down inside that Gorman would be awake when they got to the hospital.

40

ark and his two siblings arrived at the emergency room just as it began to rain. The forecast was for a chance of thunderstorms throughout most of Oklahoma.

As they walked into the emergency waiting room, Elizabeth was sitting, watching the rain roll down the window. She didn't notice her children as they sat down beside her.

Only a few people were sitting in the waiting area. There was a family with a small child asleep in her mother's arms. An elderly man was sitting in a wheelchair apparently waiting for his ride. There was a middle-aged man with his hand wrapped up in a towel. His wife wore a dark blue sundress with pink flowers on it. It reminded Mark of something that his mother would wear.

The television in the waiting room was tuned to the local news station. They were reporting on the storm that was rolling through. There had been a large outbreak of tornados, one of which did considerable damage in the area of Norman, south of Oklahoma City. Though the damage was extensive, they estimated that only about two dozen people had been injured.

The National Weather Service forecasted a high chance of tornadic activity over the next few days. Some believed that it could be one of the most active tornado seasons in several years. Mark hoped that none of that activity would make it their way. To avoid

282

anxiety over the weather, Mark turned his focus to the raindrops currently racing down the tinted window.

Time crawled by. It felt like they had waited hours instead of just a few minutes. Waiting always seemed to take forever. Mark kept checking the time on his phone. Every minute seemed to tick away more slowly than the one before. Nurses came in and out of the waiting area, but none of them came toward Mark and his family.

The little man in the wheelchair was finally picked up by his son. The family with the little girl was called back into the emergency room. Mark didn't see where the other couple had gone.

As time went on, Elizabeth's apprehension grew. Mark could feel the intensity of her anxiety but knew there was nothing that he could do to help. He stretched out his hand to take hers. She gripped it tightly. It broke his heart to see her in such pain.

Ben and Jessica were also very quiet. Mark watched them closely. Jessica sat staring at the floor. Mark could tell she wanted to cry but was holding back the tears.

Ben's eyes were red from crying. Guilt and frustration flooded his face. The longer that they waited, the redder Ben's face became. His breathing was labored, and Mark could see the flame burning in Ben's eyes.

Elizabeth and Jessica weren't paying attention to him, but Mark knew when Ben was getting upset. He had seen that look many times. Ben always had that same look when he was about to pounce on something or someone.

Mark remembered when they were kids, he knew exactly how to get Ben going. When they played video games, Mark always chose ones he knew he could win. He would do everything he could to beat Ben. This would infuriate Ben, and he would fly off the handle.

At first Mark thought it was funny, but as Ben got older and stronger, his punches hurt more. Elizabeth would step in and make them change the game or ground them from video games all together. For this reason, Mark remembered well how Ben acted when he was getting mad. Mark would push him to the breaking point but would stop just short of a Ben losing it. He could tell that Ben's temper was about to take control.

Ben stood up, and Mark followed, running interference. Ben pulled away from Mark and went straight to the glass window where the triage nurse sat. He started knocking on the window. Mark again tried to pull him away, but Ben fought him. The nurse opened the window.

"Can I help you?" she said in a long southern drawl.

"I want to know what is wrong with my dad. You have kept us out here waiting forever. He could be dead for all I know," Ben pounded his fist on the ledge where the patients sign in.

"We will get to you as soon as we can," the nurse replied, calmly. Mark was impressed that she was so composed.

"I want to know something, now!" Ben demanded. Mark went to pull him away, and he knocked over the cup of pencils that were on the counter.

"You will need to sit down, and we will be with you shortly." She smiled and slid the glass shut.

Mark grabbed Ben's arm before he could try again. He dragged Ben outside the hospital and stopped under the circle drive. In a fit of rage, Ben punched the wall as hard as he could.

"Hey, you're going to end up getting the police called on you if you down calm down." Mark attempted to intervene.

"I don't care, we need to know something." Tears had begun streaming down his face again. He went to hit the wall again, but Mark grabbed his hand.

"Calm down. You're going to break your knuckles," he told him.

"I can't do this Mark. I can't lose him. It's my fault, if I hadn't been playing that stupid game, I might have heard. He may have been calling me, and I wasn't listening." Tears were now dropping like rain from Ben's face. "I don't want to do this. I can't lose someone that I love. I would rather die."

Mark couldn't believe what he was hearing. Ben turned and hobbled as fast as he could go on his crutches, out from under the awning and into the rain. He had his head down and couldn't see where he was going. Mark raced after him. There was an ambulance pulling into the emergency drive. Ben didn't see it.

Elizabeth had been looking out the window watching the rain. She felt like she had no tears left to cry. No words could make her feel better. She stared blankly outside.

Suddenly, she saw Ben toddling across the drive. Her heart raced as she could see everything that was happening. She couldn't move. She tried to yell. She tried to do something to warn the boys of the emergency vehicle that was barreling down on them. But it was too late.

Mark, using the full force of his weight pulled Ben back onto the sidewalk and out of the way. If he had reacted a split second later, the ambulance would have hit both of them. The ambulance blew its horn as it pulled past, snapping Ben out of his trance.

The boys ended up on the ground, Ben landing with his elbow in Marks rib. The paramedic ran out from the truck to see if they were alright.

Miraculously, there were no injuries except for a little sidewalk rash from the fall. They went back into the waiting room, where their mother was waiting to discipline them for scaring her. She didn't get the chance because a nurse called her name.

Everyone held their breaths for a moment. No one wanted to move. Maybe she was calling someone else. Maybe they had misheard. As she called out Elizabeth's name once again, Elizabeth stood quickly and headed towards the window. The nurse motioned for her to go to the door.

The entire family stood near the door waiting to be buzzed in. They heard the slight click of the lock, and Elizabeth flung the heavy door open wide. The nurse saw the crowd of family members and stopped them briefly. She tried to advise them that only two people were allowed back at once, until she saw the pleading in Elizabeth's eyes. She gave them the room number and ushered them on before anyone noticed.

When they got to the room, Gorman was gone. He had been taken back for another CT scan. After a few minutes they could hear him coming down the hallway. He was yelling and cursing the entire way. He didn't want to be at the hospital and told them that he never wanted to be put in that crazy machine again.

As the attendant brought him back into the room, he was still arguing. He saw his family sitting in the room waiting for him. "I'm ready to get out of here. I want to go home. They had to cram me through that stupid machine again," Gorman complained to Elizabeth.

Mark couldn't help but think, *Yep, he is back to his old self!*

Gorman continued to rant and rave over having to wait in the room for the doctor to get there. He didn't want the IV in his arm and didn't want to lie in the bed. He sat on the side of the bed with the paper hospital gown draped over him. He was still in his shorts, but his clothes lay in a pile on the chair near the door.

There was still no word about why he was unconscious for so long. After another hour-long wait, there was a knock at the door. The ER doctor had finally arrived to brief them on the situation.

The doctor began, "Mr. Cooper, it appears that your liver is starting to back up. You're now having problems metabolizing the proteins that you eat and flushing out toxins that are in your body. We will be keeping you in the hospital for a few more days so we can begin treatment.

Disgusted Gorman asked, "What does that mean?"

The doctor began to explain, "The problem is that your liver function is so low that without some drastic changes in your lifestyle, you will become toxic. Those toxins will go to your brain and can kill you. The symptoms that you saw today were just the beginning."

He continued, "We also have to keep a watch on your fluid retention. It can lead to heart failure if we don't get it under control."

The room was silent. Gorman sat trying to take it all in. This wasn't the news that he expected to hear. No one could have imagined.

"What about the transplant?" Benjamin asked.

"That is the problem. The scar tissue that is causing the liver not to function was caused by severe alcohol abuse. You know that most people with this history won't be eligible to be put on a donor transplant list. The records show that the GI doctor is already trying other options, but there is no way that anyone will clear him to be moved up on the list. Have they talked to you about live donors?" The doctor asked.

"Yes, but the kids have my blood type. They aren't compatible," Elizabeth replied.

"Well, that's really going to be the only option. It's very expensive, and even if the VA approved the procedure, you would still be out a lot of money. Before we think about that, let's see what we can change for you." The doctor didn't say much more, instead he left the room in silence.

A nurse came in and began preparing Gorman to move to a room. Mark agreed to take the kids home because Elizabeth wanted to stay the night with Gorman. As they left no one said a word.

As they got in the car and began putting their seatbelts on, Mark paused. He looked at his brother and sister, "Guys, I would like you to pray with me."

Ben looked at him strangely, but Jessica smiled and nodded. She reached out her hand and took Mark's. Ben didn't know what to do, so he slowly stretched out his hands. They stopped and said a prayer for Gorman.

On the way back to the house, Mark stopped and got is food for his siblings. Ben loved cheap fast-food, and Jessica would eat anything. It had been a long day, and they were all hungry. After swinging through the drive-thru, he drove his siblings back to the house before he headed back to his apartment. They would be safe until Elizabeth got back home.

41

Sunday morning came early. The thunderstorm system that had hit the area two days prior was still in full force. It was 8:15 in the morning, and Mark's alarm hadn't yet gone off. His phone rang. It was his mother calling from home.

"Are you awake?" Elizabeth asked.

"I'm now, what's wrong?" His heart was in his throat. He knew that something must have happened to his dad.

"You need to get in the closet or lock yourself in the bathroom," she exclaimed.

"What?" Mark must of have missed something.

"The weatherman just said that the thunderstorm had intensified, and everyone in the path of the storm should take cover. There is possibly a tornado." Elizabeth's voice was filled with panic.

Elizabeth had always been afraid of storms. As a little girl she had been caught in a tornado in the same house where she lived now. Since then, any time a tornado warning was issued, she would grab the kids and head to the cellar. It was a metal door offset from the house about twenty feet. Gorman had it packed so full of junk that every time there had been a tornado warning, Elizabeth could be seen pushing everything to the back, making room for her family to fit in.

Every year she would threaten to throw everything in the cellar away, but never did. Mark didn't want to remind her, because she would "volunteer" him to help with it.

Mark could imagine her standing in the cellar right now trying to shove everything back away from the door. Benjamin and Jessica would probably be standing at the top of the steps complaining about being woken up early and having to stand out in the rain while she tried to make room.

"Ok, Mom, we'll go stand in the bathroom. Are you going to meet me at church this morning?" Mark asked.

"If this weather blows over, I might." Elizabeth responded.

"Ok, bring the kids," Mark said before he hung up the phone. He stood up and looked outside. The sky was filled with dark, ominous-looking clouds while rain was beating down on the ground, but Mark saw no rotation within the storm to suggest that a tornado was bearing down on them.

He scratched his head and went to the restroom. After using the restroom, he went and sat in the living room, flipping on the television. He thought to himself, I told her that I would stand in the bathroom, so I did. I didn't say I would stay. He smiled at the thought.

The local news channel had a scrolling marquee on the bottom of the screen listing all the counties under the tornado warning. The meteorologist was on-screen displaying the radar map showing the direction of the tornado and advising everyone in its path to take cover. Mark watched out the window. The clouds were moving but the wind was calm.

Just two days before, a tornado in this same system had gone through Norman, OK. It had caused considerable damage, but fortunately only one of the injured require hospitalization. The National Weather Service said that this tornado may be just as powerful.

The weatherman reported that the tornado had already touched down around Woodward, OK. It had cut through a mobile home park there, killing at least 5 people and injuring many others. Mark prayed that the same thing wouldn't happen here.

As Mark watched, the meteorologist showed the path the funnel cloud was taking. It didn't appear to be headed toward the area of town where Mark lived. Nevertheless, he continued to watch out the window hoping to see something if it headed his way.

Within a few minutes, Mark heard Shawn start moving around in his room, which meant that it was time to get ready for church. Mark grabbed his clothes and headed to the bathroom.

By the time he was done in the shower, the tornado scare passed, and the news people reported that the storm had caused only minor damage to the immediate area. For the most part, the tornado had crossed over uninhabited land. With the threat passed, Mark sent his mom a message reminding her of the time she needed to meet him at church.

Shawn and Mark rode to church together since it was more economical to carpool than waste the gas. Usually, they would take turns driving every other week. Gas prices had been going higher since 2009, and so the guys wanted to do whatever they could to save a little money.

Trisha and Marie were supposed to be waiting for them to arrive in the small coffee shop in the church foyer. It was there that Elizabeth and her two other children were supposed to be meet Mark, as well.

The girls weren't there yet, so Mark got his favorite caramel cappuccino with an extra shot of espresso. He sat at the table staring out the window. Shawn grabbed a chai tea and Trisha's mocha latte. Mark felt bad about not getting Marie a drink at the same time he bought his own, but she liked several things; so, he didn't know what she wanted this particular time.

As he waited with anticipation for Elizabeth to arrive, he doodled all over his church bulletin. He watched for Marie and Trisha to be coming out of their morning class. Today was the day he intended to introduce Marie to his mother, so he was filled with anticipation.

Over the past few weeks, he had been trying to find a time for them to meet, but because of conflicts of one sort or another it hadn't worked out. It had been at least a month since his mother had attended church with him, and Marie had been out for the past few weeks.

Mark could hear Trisha's voice as the girls came down the hall. She could never sneak up on anyone. She couldn't stay quiet long enough. It still amazed him how different Trisha and Shawn were.

"Thank you, sweetheart," Trisha said as she sat down at the table, "Sorry we're so late; the class ran long."

Looking at Marie, Mark asked, "You want something to drink?"

"Sure, um, I'll take…a cherry mocha latte, please," she replied.

Mark joined the line to the coffee counter. There were four people ahead of him. It had been that way for several minutes. There was a little blue-haired lady digging through her coin purse for three pennies that she knew were there. She found a button that she thought she had lost, several hair pins, a small ball of loose string that she pulled off her sleeve, and several old receipts. The man behind her had offered her the change, but she refused. She knew that she had just dropped the pennies into her purse the night before, and she was determined to find them.

While Mark was standing in line, his family came through the front door. Shawn waved them over. Elizabeth smiled and nodded as she walked towards him, with her two children in tow. This would be their first visit to Mark's church, and both were awestruck by the church foyer. They had attended only smaller traditional churches so this was their first time to see anything like this.

Jessica was dressed in her favorite blue dress that she had worn for her choir competition a few weeks before. Ben wore his tennis shoes and blue jeans with a button-up pearl snap shirt that he hadn't worn in a while. It fit a little snug.

He still needed his crutches to help him walk, but he preferred them to the wheelchair. At his last visit, the doctor said that he should soon be able to ditch the crutches and use a cane instead.

"Mrs. C," Shawn said, "you can come sit right here with us. Mark is in line and will be back in a few minutes." Shawn pulled over a couple of chairs.

"Thanks," she replied.

"Well, since Mark is all tied up right now, I would like to introduce you to Trisha Brown. And I don't know if Mark has mentioned her to you, but this is Marie Mills. She is Mark's girlfriend." Shawn smiled a devilish grin. He knew that Mark had wanted the honor of introducing them.

"Well, I knew Mark had a girlfriend, and I have been waiting to meet her. Honey, you're very pretty." Elizabeth smiled. This embarrassed Marie, who shyly smiled and brushed her hair back behind her ear.

Mark made his way back to the table and addressed his mom. "Well, I guess you have met my friend. I have been trying to find a time to introduce you for a while, and now since someone *else*," he shot Shawn a sour look, "did it for me, I guess I won't get to. And this is my brother Benjamin and my sister Jessica." He put an arm around each of his siblings and squeezed them. Jessica didn't mind, but Ben pushed him away.

Marie smiled, "It's nice to meet you guys."

Shawn smirked, "I thought maybe your mother had some important info to pass along to us about you. Maybe some awkward baby photos."

"No," Elizabeth responded. She rested her gaze on Marie. "Honey, I'm just glad to finally meet you. Mark wanted to keep you a secret, but I could tell in his eyes that he had found someone. All the awkward baby photos are in the photo albums at home. You will need to come by some time to see them."

"Really, Mom?" Mark exclaimed.

The auditorium doors opened just then, and the people from the first service came pouring out. The praise band was playing their call to worship, and the countdown was on the screen. Just a few more minutes and the service would be starting.

42

While his family was at church; Gorman lay resting in the hospital bed. He was put on diuretics to help flush his body of excess fluids caused by the damage done to his liver. Too much water in his system could cause heart failure. His feet and hands had shown edema when he had been admitted to the emergency room, so the doctors weren't taking any chances.

With the constant bombardment of nurses in and out of his room throughout the night, he had gotten little sleep, so he had decided to take a nap. The television had been on since Elizabeth left the night before to let Gorman rest and make sure that the kids were alright. The TV volume had been turned too low for him to hear, but the dim light helped him to see in the darkened room.

When he finally woke up, he could see an older woman sitting in the chair across from his bed. She had gray hair that was tied up in a bun on the top of her head. She was wearing a long, blue polyester skirt with a black satin blouse and a blue flowery coat. She had apparently been just sitting there, watching Gorman sleep.

"What are you doing here?" Gorman asked as he tried to sit up. He turned off the TV and set the remote beside his breakfast tray. His coffee was now cold, and his unsalted eggs and oatmeal were rubbery. The doctor had restricted his sodium intake to aid with the water shedding, but Gorman didn't like the restriction.

"Well, I came to see you. It has been a really long time," the woman responded. She looked exactly like she did when Gorman saw her the last time.

"You can leave; I don't need you here," Gorman retorted.

"I'm sorry, but when your son called me and told me that you were very sick, I thought it might be time to come for a visit," she replied. She stood and walked to his bedside. Gorman could see a little tinge of red left in her hair.

"You talked to Mark?" he asked.

"Yes, Gorman Marcus Cooper, just like his father and like his grandfather. It was good to hear his voice even though I had never heard it before. I didn't even know you had children until he called. I'm sorry that you're not happy to see me." He could see the defeated look in her eyes.

"Why would I want to see you? I thought you were dead." Gorman snarled as he spoke to her.

"I would have been, if I had continued to go down the road that I was on." She slowly sat down in the chair next to his bed. "I'm sorry for everything that happened. Not a day has gone by that I haven't regretted my actions. Since you never came back, I felt you probably found your own way."

"You should regret it; you were the one that made me leave." He pulled away as she tried to pick up his hand.

"I know, and I really am sorry," she explained, "I was hurt, and Steve was gone, so I took it out on you. I'm very sorry for doing that. That wasn't me, it was the alcohol talking. I let alcohol ruin my life, and it took everything from me that I loved. I don't want the same thing to happen to you."

"Why would that happen to me? I have a good relationship with my kids. They love me. I have never done anything to hurt them." Gorman's temper was beginning to flare.

"Yeah," she scoffed, "and when I was your age, I would have said the same thing. I would have blamed my problems on you and everyone else that hurt me. It was your dad's fault, his parent's fault, Steve's fault, or the fault of any of the other losers that I shacked up with. I drank and did whatever drugs they were doing, until it almost killed me. It was never my fault. I never did anything wrong. I was always the victim, just like you."

"Go away!" Gorman yelled angrily.

"You need to hear this. In 1995 I found myself strung out on the floor of a dirty roach motel room. I couldn't remember what had happened or why I was there. I didn't even know how long I had been there. I got up and looked in the mirror. I didn't even recognize the person looking back at me. In the mirror I saw myself as a frightened little girl who had used the world to fill the void that was deep inside of me. She was filled with rage and hatred. I had a vodka bottle lying beside me on the floor. I picked it up to take a drink and realized there was nothing left. Kind of like me... nothing left... nothing left to live for… nothing to hold on to…no value to myself or anyone else. I broke the bottle on the side of the toilet and sliced my wrists." She showed him the scars on wrists.

"I went to sleep on the dirty bathroom floor. I remember dreaming of you, and the last night that I saw you. I felt the pain that you must have felt. Then I could see a large hole in the ground. As I stood at the top of the hole, I could feel heat radiating out of it. I leaned in to look down into the hole, and I felt someone push me. I was falling towards the fire. While I was falling, I could see everything that I had ever done... everything that was wrong with my life… and it became clear to me that I was the one responsible. Not your father, not your grandparents, not Steve, and especially not you.

"There was a tree standing out in front of me with its branches stretched out. I reached out as far as I could to grab onto it, but it was always just out of reach. The third time I reached out, I felt the same hand that pushed me into the hole reach out from the tree and pull me to it. I woke up and I was in the psyche ward at the hospital. If housekeeping hadn't found me in the motel room, I would be dead."

"Mom, that is a nice story, but what does that have to do to me?" Gorman asked.

"It has a lot to do you," she replied. "You were the last picture that I could see in my head and were the reason that I didn't want to die. I ended up in a Christian rehab center, and I discovered that I was headed straight into hell. You were the reason that I wanted to change my life.

"When I got out, I did everything I could to find you, but was unable to locate you. I thought you might have died. I moved on with my life and was going to my alcoholics' support group. I also began going to church, and finally met the man of my dreams. He helped me overcome my alcoholic addiction before it killed me. I still am aware of my faults and know my limitations. Every day I know that I have the strength to overcome my temptation. I have been able to go back to school get my degree in Business Management, and now I'm the president of a bank in Virginia."

"Why do you want to come visit me?" Gorman tried to act angry, but his anger had begun to subside.

"Apparently, Mark called your father's parents and got information on me. He then began calling people with my name. One of the numbers he called was a halfway house that I lived in when I was first out of the rehab. The resident manager of the house had kept up with me through the years, and she gave him my number. My second husband passed away several years ago from cancer. He left me a lot of money in annuities. I want to help you get a liver transplant." She took Gorman's hand, he didn't resist.

"What are you talking about? Why would you want to do that for me?" He had begun to tear up. He had rehearsed for years what he would say at the moment that he saw her again. He wanted to tell her how he felt and that he wished she would be tortured for eternity for the pain she put him through. Now none of those things would come to mind.

"I'm not trying to buy your acceptance, and I want to help you even if you tell me to leave and never come back. I just feel this is the least I could do for you because of everything that I put you through. I also know what it was like for you not to have your father, so I don't want your kids knowing how that feels. Please let me help you. I know you will probably need a live donor, and since I have no other kids, I will even be tested to see if I'm a match. I just want to help you." She was crying and continued to wipe her eyes with tissues from the box that was sitting on the bedside table.

Gorman was also crying. No one had ever done anything like this for him, and he never would have imagined that she would be the one doing it. "I will have to think about it and talk to my wife. How long will you be in town?"

"I flew in last night. We landed in Dallas because of the weather in Oklahoma City. I had to drive up and then try to find a hotel. I prayed my entire way here," she replied. "I will actually be here for a few days. I would like to meet your family if I could."

"I'll let you know," Gorman replied.

His mother smiled and wrote down her telephone number on the notepad by the phone. She then walked to the door. She looked back for a moment, and then went through.

"Mom," Gorman called, she looked back in, "thanks for coming."

She smiled and then walked out.

43

Mark had waited for this day all his life. The sun was shining brightly, and there were no clouds overhead. He could hear the birds chirping, and there were a couple of squirrels chasing each other around a tall oak tree in the middle of the beautiful grassy courtyard.

The wind rustled the spring leaves as the crowd of nicely clad friends and family slowly gathered. The aroma of freshly cut roses filled the air as organ music played in the background. It was the perfect day for an outdoor ceremony.

The crowd packed in tightly attempting to find their seats; soon it would be standing room only. Mark would be walking in soon, but for now he waited inside looking out the window. Elizabeth knocked on the preparation room door. Mark stepped into the hallway to talk to his family. Everyone was there.

Gorman had been out of the hospital for a little over a week. They had finally found a good treatment to cut down on the edema, and though he didn't feel well, he was doing better. It would still be a while before any type of surgery could be done, but Gorman was going to take his mother's offer to help him.

Mark was very glad that he had been able to track down his grandmother. It was like finding a needle in a haystack, but his time and effort had paid off. They had already begun mending their broken relationship. Making it even better, Gorman was also attending church with his family. He assured his whole family that he would be there every Sunday.

There had definitely been a huge change in his attitude. Things that used to anger him no longer mattered. Since he was still unable to work, Elizabeth worked every shift at the diner that she could. To help Gorman began trying to pick up the slack in the housework at home. He had even been trying his hand in the kitchen.

He watched cooking shows for hours upon hours. His first creation was supposed to be a combination of blackened chicken and pasta Alfredo. Benjamin said it tasted more like blackened Alfredo. Elizabeth was just glad to have the Gorman back that she remembered dating so many years before.

Ben was now walking on his own two feet again. He still used a cane, but he was doing much better. He had been stuck in the house playing video games for so long that he was actually excited to be able to go outside. He even went out with his friends to shoot targets. He still had trouble keeping his balance while trying to fire his weapon, but after a couple of tries he learned how to compensate for the recoil.

Elizabeth enjoyed her job. She was happy to have a reason to get out of the house. Even though her work schedule took a little getting used to, with Jessica and Ben helping with the housework, life was slowing now into a routine. Summer was quickly approaching, and Jessica would be out of school, allowing her more time to help at home.

Since they had discovered that Gorman had cirrhosis, Jessica had already spent more time at home. Except for the time she spent away for her vocal contests and choir concerts, Jessica had been at home most of the time. Mark was unsure if it was just because of her concern for her father, or because he was staying sober. Either way, there was finally a semblance of family that had never been there before.

Trisha and Shawn had been looking at wedding dates, but nothing was set in stone. They wanted to get married around Christmas and enjoy the beautiful seasonal decorations. Mark thought it was strange that they wanted a wedding so late in the year, but it was their wedding and their choice.

Most importantly, all of Mark's family loved Marie. He couldn't have found a more perfect person. He was head over hills in love with her and wanted to spend the rest of his life with her by his side. It thrilled him that his parents liked her.

Elizabeth smiled as Mark came through the door into the hallway. "Honey, we're so proud of you. You look so nice in your black suit and tie," She said as she helped him zip up the front of his graduation gown.

Mark smiled. Everything was perfect in his life. He was happy…not because he had the perfect girl, but he did have the girl of his dreams. And not because he had made amends with his father, even though that, too, was a very important. It also wasn't just because he had the job that he had worked so hard to get.

Mark had found something that he had been looking for. He realized that things happen in life, but true happiness isn't based on those things. Real joy comes from one's attitude towards what happens. Mark's prior pessimism caused him depression and anxiety. He had let it fuel his drive for recklessness; however, he no longer had to allow it to manipulate his life. He was ready to move on.

From the hallway he could hear them announce that it was time for the ceremony to begin, and Mark had to find his place in the line. As the music started, Mark looked down the aisle and could see Marie looking back at him. She was beautiful in her white dress. He had never seen her look as she did right then.

Mark couldn't believe that this day had finally come. He was mesmerized. He was so proud. And seeing Marie now, he could feel his goofy smile stretching across his face.

As the music came to an end, Mark adjusted his hat and the tail on his gown as he sat down in the sea of square mortarboards. Mark had been the first person in his family to graduate high school; and now he was the first to graduate college.

He did not really hear what all was said during the ceremony. He only cared about hearing the dean call his name. It was the greatest honor he had ever achieved. He crossed the stage, taking his diploma from the professor's outstretched hand. It was official. He was now a college graduate. He had worked so hard for this moment. It was the culmination of years of study, work and endurance, but now it was all over, and it was most definitely worth the effort.

As they walked to their vehicles following the graduation ceremony, Mark found himself beaming from ear to ear. It was good to see everyone there… his family and his friends in support of what he had accomplished.

"So, are you going back to school after this?" Jessica asked.

"Not right now. I'm going to take some time to focus on my job before I pursue anything else," Mark responded.

"Well, let's go get something to eat," Ben blurted out.

"Where do you want to go?" Elizabeth asked.

"Let's go cheap, I know a place that has a good dollar menu," Shawn replied.

A loud, "No", rang out in chorus.

"How about checking out a little place called Dixie's Diner?" Mark proposed.

"That sounds good," Gorman replied with everyone else's agreement. "Hey Mark, hold up a second!" Gorman took his arm. While everyone else continued towards the cars, Mark stood near his father at the end of the sidewalk.

"I want to give you something," Gorman handed Mark a folded handkerchief. "Thank you for getting in touch with my mother. I didn't want to see her at first, but I'm really glad she came. Before she left town a couple of weeks ago, she gave me this. It was my father's, your grandfather's. I want you to have it."

With tears in his eyes Mark opened the handkerchief. Inside was a pair of dog tags with the name Cooper, Gorman M. They were aged, but still in good condition.

"They are from the Vietnam War. I'm sorry that you never had the chance to meet him, my father. I really think things would have been a lot different if he hadn't died when he did, but I think things are much different now than they were." Gorman had tears in his eyes, too.

"Yeah, they are different. You can't move into the future if you're still living in the past," Mark replied. He wrapped his arms tightly around his dad. He hadn't hugged him that tightly since he was a kid.

"Hey, are you two coming?" Trisha called out from the car.

"We're on our way," Mark called back.

Other Books from Scott Rasco:

Bearing Much Fruit

Growing Spiritual Fruit in
Everyday Living

ISBN: 978-1732975507

Bearing Much Fruit is a must-read for every Christian from new believers to veteran saints. It is an easy-to-read practical guide to strategically growing in the spirit every day. No matter where you are on your spiritual walk, you can learn to better understand the fruit of the spirit and effectively apply it in real life.

www.ingramcontent.com/pod-product-compliance
Lightning Source LLC
Chambersburg PA
CBHW071204100726
47908CB00002B/500